CITY
of
SCHEMES

Center Point
Large Print

Books are
produced in the
United States
using U.S.-based
materials

Books are printed
using a revolutionary
new process called
THINKtech™ that
lowers energy usage
by 70% and increases
overall quality

Books are
durable and
flexible
because of
Smyth-sewing

Paper is
sourced using
environmentally
responsible
foresting methods
and the
paper is acid-free

Also by Victoria Thompson and available from Center Point Large Print:

Murder on St. Nicholas Avenue
Murder in Morningside Heights
Murder in the Bowery
City of Lies
Murder on Union Square
City of Secrets
Murder on Trinity Place
City of Scoundrels
Murder on Pleasant Avenue

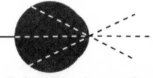

**This Large Print Book carries the
Seal of Approval of N.A.V.H.**

CITY

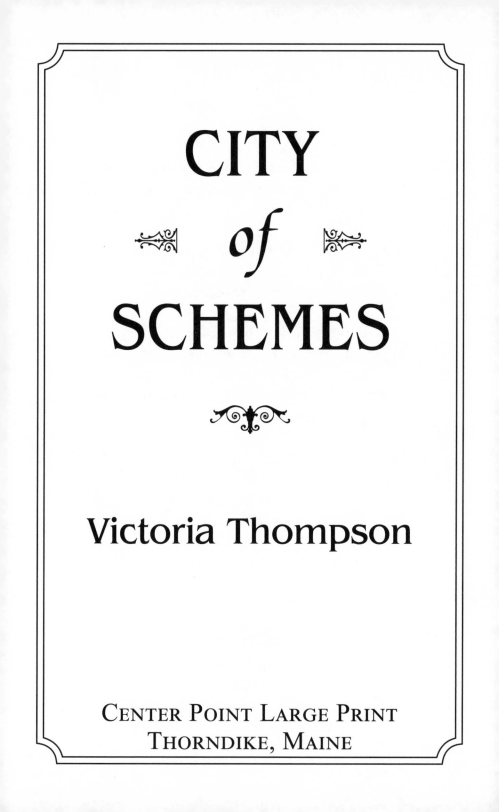

of

SCHEMES

Victoria Thompson

CENTER POINT LARGE PRINT
THORNDIKE, MAINE

I always say,
it takes a village to publish a book,
so I'd like to dedicate this book
to my "village" at Berkley.
Thanks for everything you do
to make my books better!

CHAPTER ONE

Planning a wedding was very much like planning a con, Elizabeth had noticed. With a wedding, the bride was the mark, and everyone was trying to convince her to give them her money for some ridiculous thing that sounded like the opportunity of a lifetime but which would probably turn out to be not nearly so wonderful. Even her future mother-in-law had noticed, and she'd never even heard of running a con until she met Elizabeth.

"Are you sure you want to have such a lavish meal for the wedding breakfast, my dear?" Mrs. Bates asked with a worried frown as she peered at the menu.

They were sitting in Mrs. Bates's parlor, having pulled up an extra chair to her writing desk so Elizabeth could show her all the lists she had brought along. As the mother of the groom, Mrs. Bates didn't have many responsibilities for the wedding, but she was anxious to help in any way she could. Since Elizabeth had lost her mother many years ago, her aunt Cybil was trying to fill in with the mother-of-the-bride duties, but neither

Cybil nor Elizabeth had ever even attended a society wedding. The Bates family, on the other hand, was one of the oldest society families in New York. Elizabeth didn't want to disgrace them.

"I'm not too worried about the wedding breakfast," Elizabeth said. And the wedding breakfast wasn't a breakfast at all, but rather a dinner. "The Old Man is paying for it."

Mrs. Bates smiled. She found Elizabeth's father charming in spite of his questionable occupation as a con man. "As he should, but still . . ."

"He chose the menu. He said he wants to send me off in style, but if you think it's too much . . ."

"Oh, no. I was just concerned about the cost."

Society family or not, the Bateses weren't millionaires, and her beloved Gideon had to work for a living.

Elizabeth laid the menu aside and cleared her throat in preparation for discussing a somewhat sensitive matter. "I was also wondering about the announcement, the one for the newspapers. I know Gideon and I should announce our engagement, but . . ."

Mrs. Bates frowned at Elizabeth's hesitation. "That is typically what young ladies do, but if you'd rather not for some reason, then I'm sure—"

"It's not that I'd rather not," Elizabeth hastily explained. "I want everyone to know Gideon and

I are getting married. Everyone, that is, except Oscar Thornton."

"Oh my, of course." Mrs. Bates instantly understood. Thornton had once wanted Elizabeth dead. The only reason he had abandoned this goal was because he thought she already was dead. "If he saw your name in the newspapers . . ."

"Yes, he might decide to come back for a visit."

"I see, and we certainly can't allow that. Although I seriously doubt Oscar reads the society pages, there's no use taking a chance, is there? I think a simple announcement of your wedding after it takes place that lists you simply as Mrs. Bates will be adequate. I can also send personal notes to my friends who aren't invited to the wedding. That is often done when the wedding is a small one."

Was that disappointment Elizabeth heard in her voice? "Are you sorry we've decided just to have family and a few close friends?"

"Not at all. It's your wedding, and you should do as you like. A large wedding can be something of a headache to plan, too."

"Even more of a headache than this one?" Elizabeth asked in mock despair.

"I'm afraid so, my dear," Mrs. Bates assured her.

Resigned, Elizabeth picked up her next list. "What about the flowers? I've been reading everything I could find in the etiquette books, and they say a tasteful canopy of greenery is all you need for the ceremony."

"For a simple home wedding, I'm sure that's true, although you'll probably want a few flower arrangements to set around."

Elizabeth made a note, and then she sat back and sighed. "I wish we could just elope."

"Usually it's the bride who wants a lavish wedding and the groom who wants to just run off."

Yes, Elizabeth imagined most grooms were only really interested in the honeymoon. "I don't think Gideon would mind eloping, either, but it's already bad enough that he's marrying a girl no one in society ever heard of. We can't give people more reason to gossip because we ran off somewhere."

"I'm sure Gideon appreciates your concern for his good name," Mrs. Bates said with a tiny smile.

Elizabeth returned the smile. "I'm determined not to embarrass him at least. So, what kind of flowers do you think? It won't really even be spring in March, so—"

They both looked up at the sound of the front door opening. Mrs. Bates gave Elizabeth a knowing look. "That will be Gideon coming home."

Elizabeth jumped up, all wedding plans forgotten, as she hurried out into the front hall to greet her intended. He was just unwrapping the scarf from around his neck when he saw her.

"Darling, what a delightful surprise!" A smile lit his handsome face, and Elizabeth hurried over to kiss him while Mrs. Bates couldn't see them.

When he had greeted her with the proper amount of enthusiasm, she stepped back to catch her breath and allow him to remove his coat. Only then did she notice the coat itself.

"What on earth are you wearing?"

Gideon glanced down at the beige garment he was unbuttoning. "My new trench coat. It goes with my new trench wristwatch." He held up his left arm and shot back his cuff to reveal the wristwatch she had given him last week for Christmas. It was a replica of the ones the army had issued to the doughboys because pocket watches weren't practical in battle, except Gideon's was made of real gold.

Elizabeth frowned. "I know the soldiers wore wristwatches in the trenches, but surely they didn't wear coats like that." It really was rather hideous.

"The officers did, I'm told. They're very practical. The fabric is waterproof, which must have come in handy since it rained so much in France." Gideon had been drafted too late to see any military action. "It has lots of pockets, too."

"Which you can use to hold lots of legal papers,

I'm sure," Elizabeth teased. Surely, an attorney didn't have much use for extra pockets.

Gideon grinned as he shrugged out of his trench coat. She did love his grin. "I hear they're making trench boots now, and trench hats, too. It's all the rage now that the war is over."

"I wonder if they have trench wedding gowns?"

"Waterproof ones, no doubt. Very practical if it's a long walk to the church door."

"Fortunately, I only have to walk from my bedroom to the parlor, so I don't have to worry about rain."

Gideon hung up his coat and reached for her again, but his mother's voice stopped him. She had finally come out into the hallway, probably having judged that she'd given them enough time to canoodle. "I've invited Elizabeth to join us for dinner. We've been going over plans for the wedding, and I thought you might want to hear all about them."

To Elizabeth's surprise, his good cheer vanished. "I'm sorry, I have to go to my club tonight. They're having a dinner to welcome home some of the members who were overseas."

America had wasted no time demobilizing their troops in the two months since the war's end, and thousands of them were arriving at New York City ports daily.

"Then you must attend. Logan Carstens will probably be there," Mrs. Bates said. "I saw his mother in church, and she said he was due home on Monday."

"I heard that, too. I'm glad he made it." Gideon sighed. "We're also having a memorial for the ones who didn't, but that's not for a few more weeks yet."

Elizabeth took his hand in both of hers, offering what comfort she could. He still felt guilty for having escaped the carnage. "Come into the parlor, and your mother and I will distract you with wedding plans. You can settle an argument. Do you think it's appropriate to have poison ivy in the wedding canopy?"

This brought back his smile, as she had intended. "Let me guess, the poison ivy is your brother's idea."

Gideon hadn't really enjoyed the evening at his club, but it also wasn't as painful as he'd expected it to be. Two of his old friends whom he welcomed home had actually congratulated him on missing the war, and they weren't being sarcastic. They didn't seem so much happy to be home as relieved to have the war over with. Plainly, they were glad he had been spared the ordeal, and when he saw how haggard and haunted they looked, he thought he could understand, at least a little.

His old friend Logan had spent most of the evening sitting in a dark corner and cradling a whiskey glass that other club members had kept refilling. Everyone was joking that they needed to drink up while they still legally could, with prohibition looming in the coming months.

Logan hadn't spoken much to those who made a point of personally welcoming him home, though, even cutting Gideon off when he'd started asking how Logan was doing. As the evening wore on, the crowd thinned out, and Gideon approached him again, carrying over a chair this time and sitting down beside him without being invited.

Logan's empty glass sat on the table, but he looked like he didn't need any more to drink.

"You don't seem very glad to be home," Gideon said gently. "Don't tell me Rosemary has thrown you over while you were gone."

Gideon had expected an answering grin, since he knew perfectly well Rosemary Westerly had remained steadfastly faithful to the man who had proposed to her before leaving for France. She was no doubt as deep in wedding planning as Elizabeth.

But Logan didn't grin. He ran an unsteady hand over his face and sighed. "I never should have asked her to marry me. If I'd known . . ."

This was not what Gideon had expected to hear, but his friend obviously needed his support, so he would give it. "I can't imagine what it was like over there, and I know it's probably changed you

14

in some ways, but Rosemary loves you, and I'm sure she'll—"

"You don't understand, Gideon."

"I know I don't. I wasn't there, but—"

"It's not the war. Oh, I guess it is, in a way, but it's not what you think. I'm different, yes. We all are. The things we saw . . . But it's not that. Or not only that." He picked up his glass and seemed surprised to find it empty. He set it back down and sighed again. "You see, I met someone."

"Someone?" Gideon asked, not sure he understood yet. "Over there, you mean?"

"Yes, I met a girl. A French girl."

Gideon managed not to wince. He'd heard the jokes and the crude remarks about the French girls who were supposedly so free with their favors. And the song. "Mademoiselle from Armentières." "You didn't have to know her long to know the reason men go wrong." And that was one of the tamer verses. But surely Logan wouldn't be taken in by such a woman.

"She's not like that," Logan said when Gideon didn't reply. "I can see it in your face, what you're thinking, but Noelle is . . . They made the French people take us into their homes. Did you know that?"

"I think I heard about it, yes," Gideon said.

"We got to this little town, and there was no place for our men to stay, so the army made every family in the town take a few soldiers to live in their homes. I was billeted with the mayor. Because I was a captain. They gave me the best bedroom in the house. The mayor and his wife had to share a room with their daughter, Noelle. She was a good girl. She taught in the school before the Germans blew it up and all the children left. French girls are watched just as carefully as American girls are, Gideon. They aren't like the rumors say. Oh, there are prostitutes in the cities, but most of the French women are just as respectable as women are here."

"I'm sure they are," Gideon said, although he'd never given it much thought.

"At first it was a relief to be with regular people and living what felt like a regular life, not like in the trenches. We were living in houses and sitting down to dinner with the family every night. We even went on picnics and had dances. It was just like home, only everyone spoke French."

Gideon nodded, having nothing else to offer but encouragement.

"I remembered a little French from school, and Noelle had picked up some English, so we were able to talk to each other. Then I started to have feelings for her. I told myself it was only because I was lonely and homesick."

"I'm sure that was a big part of it," Gideon tried, but Logan was already shaking his head.

"It was because she understood. She'd seen her country torn apart for years, and she knew the

16

horrors of war that we'd seen in the battles. We'd talk about what the world would be like when the war finally ended and what we would do to make things right again. I can't even imagine talking to Rosemary about things like that."

Gideon had known Rosemary as long as Logan had, and he couldn't imagine it, either. In fact, he couldn't imagine talking to Rosemary about anything important. "You said you had feelings for this girl. Did she return them?"

Gideon instantly regretted asking the question when Logan winced as if in physical pain. "She did. It happened before either of us realized it, but I was already engaged to Rosemary, so what could I do? I couldn't humiliate my fiancée by breaking our engagement. She'd done nothing wrong. In fact, she'd stood by me and written to me every week and sent me socks and scarves and all kinds of things."

Of course she had. That's what well-bred young ladies did.

"But when I realized Noelle had come to love me the way I loved her, I had to tell her the truth about my situation."

"What did she say?"

"She was very sad, of course. We both wept, but she understood. She'd been in love with a young man when the war started, but he'd died at Ypres. She thought if he were still alive, she would feel honor bound to marry him as well."

"Honor bound?" Gideon echoed. "Is that a good basis for a marriage, do you think?"

Logan gave him a look of despair. "I have no idea, but it's the only way I know to live my life."

Gideon could have explained what he had learned from Elizabeth and how his opinion of justice—the principle by which he had always lived his life—had changed in the past year, but Logan was much too distraught and drunk at the moment to comprehend. "I'm sorry," was all he could manage.

"Do you want to know the irony of it?" Logan asked with a ghastly smile. "The irony is that I was the one who had to approve the marriages for the men in my company."

"What marriages?"

"The marriages to French women. I'm not the only man who fell in love over there, you see. Thousands of other men did, too. Oh, they had all kinds of rules against fraternization, but when did that ever stop young men from seeking out the company of young women? Pershing very quickly realized that if he didn't allow our men to marry French women, they'd be leaving a lot of fatherless children behind when the war was over."

"And why did you have to approve these marriages? I don't understand."

Logan shook his head as if to clear it. "Like I said, not all the French women were respectable young ladies, so the company commanders had to personally approve any marriages to make sure our men weren't being taken advantage of by some adventuress. It was a thankless job, I can tell you. Luckily, I only had to refuse permission to a few of the men."

"And you had to refuse yourself permission, too," Gideon realized.

Logan nodded sadly. "The army is sending all the brides over here on transport ships. Those lucky girls get to leave the ruins of Europe to make a new life here, but Noelle . . ." His voice broke and Gideon pulled out a handkerchief and passed it to him.

Poor Logan. Gideon remembered only too well how devastated he'd felt when he thought he'd lost Elizabeth. He wanted to offer Logan some advice or at least some comfort, but mere words couldn't soothe this pain. "I think I should get you home," Gideon said. "I'll see if I can get us a cab."

"How sad," Elizabeth said when Gideon told her of his conversation with Logan Carstens a few days later. It was Monday evening, the night Elizabeth's aunt Cybil and her companion, Zelda, held their weekly salon for their artist and writer friends, their students and their fellow faculty members from Hunter College. Elizabeth had to attend because she still lived with Cybil and

Zelda, at least until she married Gideon. Gideon attended the salons to spend time with Elizabeth.

Elizabeth and Gideon had little interest in the literary discussions occurring in the parlor, so they had stolen away to the privacy of the butler's pantry, as they often did during these events. It was the first opportunity they'd had for a serious conversation in days.

"I felt like I should offer Logan some advice, but I realized I had no advice to give on this subject. What do you think?"

"I don't know, either," she said. They were snuggled together on the window seat, ignoring the cold air seeping through the glass. "He must have been in love with this Rosemary when he proposed to her, so he'll probably be able to love her again."

Gideon just made a noncommittal noise.

"What?" Elizabeth said, instantly recognizing his characteristic reluctance to say anything bad about anyone.

"I really can't speak for Logan, but . . ."

"Oh please! Just tell me what you're thinking."

He had to clear his throat because he really didn't like gossip. "Let's just say I was a little surprised when he chose Rosemary."

Oh my, this was growing more interesting by the moment. "Why?"

He gave this a few moments' thought. "You have to understand. I've known both of them forever. Our families attend the same church, and we went to the same schools and the same parties and the same everything. Logan and I are the same age, so we were even in the same class. I'd never seen Logan show Rosemary any particular attention, but when he was drafted—"

"How did he get drafted if you're the same age?" Gideon had missed the first rounds of the draft because he was too old.

"He's a few months younger than I am, so he made the cutoff. And Rosemary is a few years younger, but she was always there, like the children of all my family's friends."

Which meant Rosemary must be approaching her mid-twenties and might even be past them, so why hadn't she married before now? A very interesting question that she would ask someone else later because Gideon probably wouldn't want to gossip about her. "All right, so he got drafted and what? Did he suddenly realize he was madly in love with Rosemary?"

"I guess that's what I thought and what most people thought. As I said, I can't speak for Logan."

"A lot of people got engaged and even married when the war started," Elizabeth reminded him. "Not everyone is as sensible as you are."

He gave her a look. "I told you—"

"I know, you didn't want to leave me a widow and possibly with a child to raise alone," she said, using a singsong voice to remind him of how many times he'd given her his reasons and what she thought of them. "And you were right to wait. How many times do I have to agree with you?"

Gideon sighed. "I didn't realize you'd ever agreed with me."

She didn't bother to argue. "So getting back to Logan and Rosemary, you said you were surprised when they became engaged."

"A lot of people were surprised. And now Logan apparently regrets it, but he feels honor bound to marry her anyway. Besides, he's already left this Noelle behind in France."

"He could go back for her."

"Yes, he could, but did I mention that he feels honor bound to marry Rosemary?"

"Is that really so important?" Until she'd met Gideon, she'd never known anyone to whom honor meant anything at all.

"In some cases it is, and don't even think about trying to help Logan with his problem."

Elizabeth widened her eyes at him in perfect innocence. "I have no idea what you're talking about."

"This isn't something you can solve with a con."

He was probably wrong about that. Elizabeth had recently discovered several unusual problems that had been solved very nicely with a con, but she had vowed to give up her former profession, and she had every intention of doing so. "I don't even know Logan, so why would I want to help him?"

"Because you're going to meet him soon, and he's a very nice man, so you might be tempted. We're invited to a dinner party at Rosemary's house."

"How delightful. I can meet them and—"

"And nothing. You can meet them and that's all."

"But darling, if we can help your friend—"

"If he needs help, I'm sure he'll ask for it. Until then, we're going to mind our own business."

"That will be a first," Elizabeth's brother said from the doorway.

"You should be glad I minded your business a time or two," Elizabeth replied tartly.

"She's got you there, Jake," Anna Vanderslice said, having come up behind him in the doorway. "And what are the two of you doing hiding away here? According to Mrs. Ordway, engaged couples should not spend too much time together, and the young woman should not permit her fiancé to take her away in a corner from other guests for a long time."

Elizabeth gave her dearest friend a mock glare. "This isn't a corner."

"And I am convinced that Mrs. Ordway was never engaged, or she would not have made such ridiculous rules about it," Gideon added.

"Who is Mrs. Ordway?" Jake asked, thoroughly confused.

"She wrote an etiquette book that Elizabeth has been using to rule her life lately," Anna explained with a sly grin.

"I have not!" Elizabeth said.

"I'm afraid you have, darling," Gideon said gently. "But why do you know so much about it, Anna?"

"I've been reading it, too, so I'll know how to act at your wedding."

Jake rolled his eyes. "Is it etiquette to leave your brother and your best friend at a party with nobody to talk to? I don't think there's another person out there younger than sixty."

"Cybil will clock you with a poker if she finds out you said she is older than sixty," Elizabeth said. "But we're sorry if you feel neglected. Gideon has been telling me about his soldier friend who is engaged to a girl here but in love with a girl he left behind in France."

"Oh, who is it?" Anna asked with obvious delight, pushing past Jake to come all the way into the butler's pantry. It was getting crowded.

Elizabeth hadn't thought about Anna knowing all the same people Gideon knew. Even though she was much younger, she, too, had grown up in that social circle, and her brother, David, had been Gideon's best friend. Knowing how he hated gossip, Elizabeth cast Gideon an apologetic look and didn't reply. She really did need to start minding her own business.

But Gideon said, however reluctantly, "It's Logan Carstens."

"Logan? Oh dear. Did he really fall in love with a French girl?" Anna asked Gideon in wonder.

"So it seems."

"Rosemary won't be happy about that," Anna said meaningfully, although Elizabeth had no idea what the meaning was.

"Which is why you won't tell her," Gideon warned, obviously understanding the meaning very well.

"So you're just going to leave poor Logan to his fate?" Anna asked him.

"His fate?" Jake echoed with interest. "What does that mean?"

Anna turned to him. "That means Rosemary is a bit of a drip."

"Many people are," Gideon said tartly. "That doesn't mean they deserve to suffer."

"It sounds like Logan is the one who will suffer," Jake said, "but if what I've heard about those French girls is true—"

"It's not," Gideon said quickly.

"And if it were, you still wouldn't have wanted to join the army, Jake," Elizabeth said. "Admit it."

Jake shrugged, not about to admit anything of

the kind. "So if Rosemary is a drip, why is Logan going to marry her at all, even if he didn't meet a French girl?"

"That is something you will have to ask Logan," Gideon said. "Jake is right, we should rejoin the party." He rose and helped Elizabeth to her feet.

"Gideon, you and Jake go ahead," Anna said. "I need to talk to Elizabeth for a minute."

"Wedding stuff," Jake said knowingly and led Gideon out of the room.

When they were gone, Anna's expression grew solemn. "How is Gideon doing? I mean, how is he really doing?"

Elizabeth sighed. "I'm not sure. He's happy that we're getting married, I know, but every time I try to talk to him about the wedding, he remembers that he needs to ask someone to be his best man and then . . ."

David Vanderslice would have filled that role, had he lived, and now Gideon was not only grieving the loss of his best friend but also being reminded of it every time he thought about his own wedding.

"I know how he feels," Anna said. "At least once a day I think of something I need to tell David or ask him, or I look up and expect to see him. He was my brother, so naturally he could be very annoying, but I miss him terribly."

Elizabeth gave her friend a comforting hug and

offered her handkerchief when Anna needed to wipe her eyes. "I just wish the wedding didn't keep reminding Gideon that David isn't here to be his best man."

"Maybe he could ask Logan," Anna said, having regained her composure. "He was always part of their group when they were in school. I know Gideon wasn't as close with Logan as he was with David, but . . ."

"That's an idea, but I'll see how the two of them get along before I suggest it. We're invited to a dinner party at Rosemary's house on Friday."

"Oh dear. I'm sorry I said she was a drip. You should be allowed to form your own opinion."

"Gideon had already hinted that she's not his favorite person."

"So tell me about Logan and his French girl. One hears so many stories."

"This isn't that kind of story, Anna," Elizabeth warned, and she told her all she knew.

Rosemary Westerly's family lived in a new brownstone in the Upper West Side of the city. The address was far more fashionable than Gideon's family home. A lot of the older families, the ones who still had the means, had moved north as the city expanded, so obviously the Westerly family was doing well.

Elizabeth noted that the home—or at least the rooms that visitors would see—had been furnished with new pieces and not with the furniture they'd inherited from past generations that they might have brought with them from their old home. The parlor was lovely, but Elizabeth realized she preferred the warmth of furniture that had served generations of a family.

Rosemary Westerly was handsome rather than beautiful. Her pale blond hair had been artfully styled in a way that overpowered her face rather than enhanced it. She'd probably pinched her cheeks before coming downstairs, but the color had long since faded, leaving her a bit washed out. Her blue eyes were full of life however, and missed little, if Elizabeth was any judge. She offered Gideon her hands and lifted her cheek for a perfunctory peck of greeting before turning to Elizabeth.

Gideon introduced them, and Elizabeth didn't miss the way Rosemary openly studied every detail of Elizabeth's appearance, from the ornament pinned into her auburn hair to the tips of her satin pumps. Elizabeth returned the favor. Rosemary's gown was every bit as fashionable as Elizabeth's and almost as flattering. She'd chosen robin's-egg blue, probably to match her eyes and because blondes were supposed to look good in that color, but it was a bit much for one so pale.

"I'm so happy to meet you at last, Miss Miles," Rosemary said, and she seemed to mean it.

Elizabeth returned the sentiment with equal

enthusiasm. She was an accomplished liar, after all, and she had every reason to want Rosemary's good opinion. "I've been looking forward to meeting more of Gideon's old friends."

Gideon distracted her by introducing her to Logan, who had chosen to wear evening dress tonight instead of his uniform. She'd noticed that many of the returning soldiers continued to wear theirs, even after being discharged. Or maybe some of them simply didn't have any other clothes. Whatever the reason, Logan looked as if he had been born to wear formal attire. He, too, was blond, although he wasn't at all pale. His skin was weathered from his military service, and his brown eyes looked far older than the rest of him. Elizabeth felt a pang of pity for him and what he had endured.

"She's a beauty, Gideon," Logan declared cheerfully, earning a disgruntled frown from his fiancée that he didn't notice. "Wherever did you find her?"

"You wouldn't believe it if I told you," Gideon said, giving Elizabeth a knowing look. "Are your parents at home, Rosemary? I'd like to introduce them to Elizabeth."

"They went out for the evening so we 'young folks' could have the house to ourselves," she reported with a smile. "Logan, why don't you get us some drinks? Is sherry all right, Miss Miles?"

"Yes, and please, call me Elizabeth."

"Come over here with me," Rosemary said, linking arms with her. "We'll leave the men to themselves while we get to know each other."

She led Elizabeth to a grouping of chairs by the front window and at the opposite end of the room from the cabinet with the drinks. When they were seated, Rosemary said, "Where on earth did Gideon find you? You're not from New York, I know."

"How could you know that?" Elizabeth asked, genuinely curious, since she had been born and raised in the city.

"Because I've never met you before. I know everyone, you see."

Elizabeth did see. Rosemary meant she knew everyone who was important. She was hardly likely to have met the daughter of a con man.

Logan arrived with their sherry, and when he had delivered a glass to each of them, he rejoined Gideon at the far end of the room.

Elizabeth gave Rosemary her most winning smile and waited until she'd taken a sip of her sherry. "I met Gideon when I was in prison."

CHAPTER TWO

R osemary's response was a bit more than Elizabeth had expected. To his credit, Logan ran over to see if he could be of assistance when Rosemary started choking on her sherry, but she waved him away. She was made of sterner stuff than that.

"I'm terribly sorry," Elizabeth said with so much sincerity that she almost believed it herself. "I hope you're all right."

Rosemary gave one more cough before waving away Elizabeth's concern, too. "I'm fine, really. I just . . . I should have remembered. I heard about it, of course. Everyone knew Mrs. Bates had been arrested in Washington City. It was all anyone could talk about for weeks. Whatever were you doing there, though?"

Rosemary would have done far more than choke if Elizabeth had answered that question honestly. Instead, she said, "I was arrested along with all the other demonstrators, of course." If only Gideon had heard her. She hadn't really told the truth, but she also hadn't lied, either. He would be proud.

Rosemary shook her head in apparent wonder. "I can't imagine making such a spectacle of myself and all for woman suffrage. Why would a woman want to vote in the first place?"

Elizabeth should have known Rosemary would be an Anti, which was what the women who opposed woman suffrage called themselves. "Would you like me to explain all the reasons to you?"

"Certainly not. I couldn't care less about politics, but I am interested in Gideon's fiancée." She tried to sweeten her words with a smile that didn't quite reach her eyes. "Where did you say you're from?"

"South Dakota," Elizabeth lied. She'd used that one back when she'd been arrested, and it was always good to be consistent when possible. "I suppose you and Logan are planning a large wedding. Have you set a date yet?" she added to change the subject.

"I . . . Logan is still getting used to being home again, so I haven't pressed him, but I'm sure we won't wait long." Ah, so Logan was dragging his feet, probably hoping something would save him from a marriage he didn't want. "We'll have a church wedding, of course, and I imagine we'll have to invite everyone we know, so naturally, that will be a lot of people."

"Gideon and I are planning a small wedding, just family and a few close friends."

"Really?" Rosemary didn't bother to hide her disapproval. "I'm sure many of Gideon's old friends will be disappointed. I suppose that's why I haven't seen an announcement of your engagement in the newspapers, though."

Elizabeth felt a prickle of unease at the mention of such a potentially dangerous announcement, but she simply smiled and said, "Yes, we didn't think it was necessary to announce our engagement since so few people in the city know me. We'll just send out a wedding announcement."

Rosemary pursed her lips. "Perhaps that's the way it's done in South Dakota."

Elizabeth was saved from replying by the maid announcing that dinner was served.

Gideon had been alarmed when Rosemary began choking, but Elizabeth's obvious concern allayed his worst fears. How on earth could she have made Rosemary choke anyway? Elizabeth was, for some inexplicable reason, strongly on the side of the unknown French girl, but she wasn't going to do violence to Rosemary, for heaven's sake. What had made him think that, even for a moment?

No, if Elizabeth had plans, they would not involve violence, although her plans were always much more effective than anything mere brute force could achieve. And Gideon couldn't blame her in this case, either. He'd like to help Logan, too, but this was something Logan would have to handle himself.

"Are you finding it difficult to adjust to being home?" Gideon asked when he had watched Logan drain one glass of whiskey and pour himself another.

"Oddly, yes," he said, as if surprised to even hear himself admit it. "When I was in France, all I could think about was getting back home, but now that I'm here . . ."

"Have you gone back to work yet?"

Logan worked in his family's business, as was expected of a son and heir. "Father told me to take as long as I wanted before coming back, but now . . . I don't know how to explain it, Gideon, but everything here seems so . . . so unimportant."

Gideon nodded, although he knew he couldn't possibly understand. "I imagine that compared to a war, selling tinned fruit is rather tame."

Logan didn't smile. "It's not just the business. It's everything." He glanced over to where the women sat, and Gideon thought he probably meant his marriage to Rosemary as well.

"Have you talked to Rosemary about it?"

Logan laughed mirthlessly. "Have you ever tried to talk to Rosemary about anything of substance?"

Gideon remembered his admonition to Elizabeth about minding their own business, but he had to at least try. "You must have had feelings

34

for her, Logan, or you wouldn't have proposed to her in the first place. If you just—"

But Logan was shaking his head. "I don't think I actually did propose to her, Gideon. It's all kind of fuzzy now. I was drafted, and my parents had a party to see me off, and somehow Rosemary and I ended up out on the terrace alone. I'd had too much to drink, and I was feeling brave and terrified at the same time, and we talked for a bit. When we went inside, Rosemary told everyone we were engaged."

Gideon muttered a curse. "But surely—"

"Don't even suggest it. Our families have known each other forever. You must know how horrible it would be if I jilted her."

Gideon knew only too well. This was exactly how generations-long family feuds started. Logan would be vilified and Rosemary would become practically unmarriageable. The pain and anger would be immense. The families would never speak again, their friends would take sides and . . . It just didn't bear thinking about.

Gideon was saved from having to reply by the announcement that dinner was served.

Rosemary proved to be the perfect hostess, Elizabeth was pleased to note. The formal dining room table had been shortened to better accommodate four guests, and so they didn't have to shout to make themselves heard by the other members of the party. Rosemary sat at one end and Logan at the other. Gideon and Elizabeth sat across from each other on the sides. The servants came and went with each course, and Rosemary treated them kindly and showed her appreciation. To Elizabeth, this was an indicator that Rosemary might not be as bad as Elizabeth had suspected. People who were rude to servants were beneath contempt.

"Gideon," Rosemary said over the soup course, "Elizabeth tells me you are having a small wedding, with just family."

"And a few close friends," Gideon said. "I've already told Logan we'll be inviting both of you."

"We're honored," Rosemary said, "but I'm sure many of your friends will be disappointed they didn't get to see you married to your lovely bride," Rosemary said with a gracious glance in Elizabeth's direction.

"And I'm sure many of my friends will be relieved to be excluded. Not everyone enjoys attending weddings."

"Besides," Elizabeth said to stir the pot a bit, "Gideon is sparing me the embarrassment of having my side of the church empty since I don't know many people in the city."

"Won't your family come, at least?"

"Yes, they will, but I don't have much family, I'm sorry to say, and most of the women who were in prison with me are from other states as well."

"Prison?" Logan echoed in shocked surprise.

"I did say you'd be amazed if I told you how we'd met," Gideon reminded him. "She was arrested with my mother and the other suffragists at the White House."

"Which is hardly a subject to discuss at the dinner table," Rosemary hastily declared.

"But I do want to hear all about your experience," Logan said with apparent sincerity. "Perhaps after dinner?"

Elizabeth would be only too happy to oblige.

"Were you trying to make Rosemary sick?" Gideon asked as they walked over to Fifth Avenue, where they were more likely to find a cab to take them home after leaving Rosemary's house.

"I was just answering Logan's questions about what happened to me when I was in the work-house," Elizabeth said, not bothering to pretend she regretted her actions.

"I don't think I ever saw anyone actually turn green before," Gideon marveled.

"I am sorry about that. I only intended to shock her, but I suppose if you've never been force-fed before . . ."

"Just let that be a lesson to you." Gideon tried to glower at her, but it only made her smile.

"Anna is right. Rosemary is a bit of a drip, but I don't think she can help it."

"Why can't she help it?"

"Because of the way she was raised. I have a feeling a lot of society girls are just like her."

Gideon gave the matter a few moments' thought. "I suppose they are."

"Which probably explains why you were still single when I met you."

"And why I was so enchanted by you," he replied with a grin.

She didn't return his smile. "But why are they like that, do you suppose?"

Gideon didn't have to think about that. "Because they live in such a tidy little world."

"What does that mean?"

How to explain it? "New York society is very strict and very closed. The same families have known each other and married only each other for generations. The men work in the family firm or for family friends, if they need to work at all. The girls go to the same schools and are protected from every bit of unpleasantness."

"As are the boys, I imagine," Elizabeth said.

"That's true, or at least it was, until the war."

"And now the war has changed things, at least for some of them."

"I'm afraid so. Logan told me nothing here at home seems important to him anymore."

"Maybe it never was important."

Gideon looked down at her again. "You could be right."

"Do you know that Rosemary told me I couldn't be from New York because she'd never met me before?"

"Does she think she knows every woman in New York?" he asked, amazed.

"No, but she thinks she knows every woman who matters in New York, which means every woman who might be worthy enough to marry Gideon Bates."

"Good Lord."

"By the way, I told her I'm from South Dakota, because she wouldn't have believed me if I told her the truth. Did you know they haven't set a wedding date yet?"

"No, but Logan is determined to see it through. He doesn't want to hurt his family, and jilting Rosemary would cause them a lot of trouble, not to mention how much it would hurt Rosemary."

They'd reached Fifth Avenue, and Gideon turned his attention to flagging down a cab. When they were settled into one and on their way home, Elizabeth laid her head on his shoulder. "I hope I'm not going to be too much of a liability to you."

"What on earth do you mean?" he asked, genuinely surprised.

"I mean if Rosemary doesn't know me, no one

knows me. They're going to wonder who I am and who my family is and—"

"And what if they do? If it doesn't matter to me, it doesn't matter."

Strangely, she had no answer for that.

On Sunday morning, Elizabeth was running a bit late and slipped into the pew beside Gideon and Mrs. Bates just as the service was starting. Mrs. Bates gave her an odd look. At first Elizabeth thought she was simply disapproving of Elizabeth's tardiness, but then she realized Mrs. Bates's expression was more concerned than annoyed. Gideon, too, looked unhappy, but she had no opportunity to question them because the organ was blaring out the introduction to the first hymn.

By the end of the service, she was consumed with curiosity, but before she could ask her fiancé or his mother what was wrong, the lady in the pew in front of them turned around and said, "Miss Miles, I was so happy to see the news of your engagement in the newspaper this morning. I wish you both all the best. Have you set a wedding date yet?"

For once, Elizabeth found herself speechless. "I . . . thank you," she said faintly and turned to Gideon. Did he know? Did that explain his grim expression all through the church service?

Mrs. Bates, a master of all social situations,

quickly explained that they were having a small wedding at home while Gideon took her arm and tried to steer her out into the aisle to make their escape. Well-wishers had other plans, however, and they were stopped repeatedly by early risers who had seen the announcement in not just one but many newspapers that morning. Every newspaper with a society page, apparently.

"I'm so sorry, my dear," Mrs. Bates assured her when they had finally evaded the last of the congratulatory parishioners and were on their way back to the Bates house. "We had no idea this had happened, and we certainly have no idea how it happened."

"You didn't send it in then?" Elizabeth said, still slightly stunned.

"Of course not, and especially not after you told me why I shouldn't. Unfortunately, I never read the newspaper until after church is over, so I didn't see it myself."

"And I didn't see it," Gideon said, his anger obvious, if tightly controlled, "because I never read the society pages at all. The first we knew was when we arrived at the church this morning and people started congratulating me."

"Who could have sent it in, though?" Mrs. Bates said. "And to so many newspapers? Would your father have done it? Or your aunt?"

"I can't imagine my father even thinking of it, or Aunt Cybil, either, for that matter, unless she thought it was one of her duties as substitute mother of the bride," Elizabeth said. "I'll ask her, of course, but . . ."

"But who else would have even been interested enough in our business to do something like this?" Gideon said. "Your father would have known better than to put your name in the news-papers with mine."

"Would Cybil have known?" Mrs. Bates asked.

Elizabeth tried to think, but she couldn't remember ever mentioning her troubles with Oscar Thornton to Cybil. "No, I don't believe so."

"Then she might have done it in all innocence," Mrs. Bates said.

"Maybe," Elizabeth said doubtfully.

"Well, it's unfortunate, but we may be worried for nothing," Gideon said quite reasonably. "I don't think many men read the society pages, and I can't imagine why Oscar Thornton would be reading them. He doesn't even live in New York anymore."

That was one reason why she loved Gideon. He could always use logic to make things seem better, even if they weren't, because Oscar Thornton—wherever he was—would probably still very much want her dead. "You're right. We're probably worrying for nothing, but I do want to figure out who did this. We can't have people taking charge of our lives without our permission."

"You're absolutely right, dear," Mrs. Bates said. "This is a very serious matter, particularly when it could put you in danger."

"Did the announcement mention the date of the wedding?" Elizabeth asked as she realized how easy that would make it for Thornton to find her.

"I don't think so," Mrs. Bates said. "People were asking us about that, remember?"

"Oh yes." Elizabeth really was rattled by all of this.

Gideon patted her hand where it rested on his arm as they walked toward his house. "It will be all right."

Of course it would. They hadn't heard anything about Oscar Thornton for over a year. He couldn't possibly still be a threat to her, could he?

No, he couldn't. The important thing was to find out who had sent the engagement announcement to the newspapers to make sure no more mistakes like that were made.

As soon as they reached the house, Gideon dug out the two morning newspapers he had purchased that day. Elizabeth and Mrs. Bates scanned the engagement announcements in both of them, but to their surprise they didn't find any that listed Gideon and Elizabeth.

"Look," Elizabeth said after poring over the rest of the society pages, "it's in the gossip column!"

Indeed it was. Every society section had a column discussing the activities of the Four

Hundred. These reports described parties and charity events and even the occasional scandal, and buried in among this week's listings was an item about Gideon and Elizabeth's "unannounced" engagement and speculation on when the wedding would take place.

"So it wasn't sent in as a formal announcement at all," Mrs. Bates said.

"This is infuriating," Elizabeth said, suitably infuriated. "How do these gossip columnists get their information?"

"By listening to gossip, I imagine," Gideon said, also infuriated.

"They also have sources among the members of society," Mrs. Bates said somewhat apologetically, "although I never dreamed our family was interesting enough to merit this kind of attention."

"Which means someone must have purposely notified them of our engagement and probably even hinted that there was something interesting about it," Elizabeth said. "That eliminates Cybil and the rest of my family. They'd never even think of doing such a thing."

"And we know we didn't do it," Gideon said.

"But who else would even care about your engagement?" Mrs. Bates said.

When she put it like that, Elizabeth realized she knew. "It was Rosemary!"

"What?" Gideon asked in surprise.

"Rosemary Westerly?" Mrs. Bates asked, equally surprised. "Why would you think she did it?"

"Because she's the only one outside of family with whom I have even discussed my engagement announcement. She actually mentioned that she hadn't seen one and she obviously disapproved of my decision not to do one."

"And you think she took it upon herself to notify these gossip columnists?" Gideon asked, obviously not wanting to believe it.

"But that would be very presumptuous of her," Mrs. Bates said, probably not wanting to believe it, either.

"Do you have any reason to think she isn't capable of being presumptuous?" Elizabeth asked.

"She is perfectly capable of it," Gideon said, bless him.

"Oh dear. If it really was Rosemary, it was inexcusable," Mrs. Bates said, "even though she certainly couldn't have known she was putting you in danger."

Which was her only saving grace. "That's exactly what I was thinking," Elizabeth said, wondering how on earth she was going to put Rosemary securely back in her place without causing a rift between Gideon and Logan.

Unfortunately, she couldn't remember seeing a chapter on this subject in Mrs. Ordway's book.

• • •

Gideon looked up in gratitude when his law clerk tapped on his office door. He'd been lost in thought, the legal papers before him forgotten after an odd phrase had triggered a memory of his dear friend David Vanderslice chiding him for working too hard. David had never worked too hard in his life, and Gideon had always thought it a fault. If only he could see David one more time to admit how wrong he had been. "Yes, Smith?"

"A gentleman is here to see you, a Mr. Logan Carstens. He says you are acquainted. He did not have an appointment, but . . ." Smith was a great believer in appointments.

"Yes, Mr. Carstens is an old friend. I'd be happy to see him."

Gideon shoved the documents back into their folder and stood up to greet Logan. He knew a moment of unease, remembering Elizabeth's theory that Rosemary was the one responsible for sending their engagement announcement to the newspapers. In the past four days, just to make certain, Elizabeth had dutifully questioned and eliminated everyone else who might have done it, as she had informed him last night when he'd dined with her at Cybil's house. But if Rosemary was responsible, Logan certainly would have known nothing about it.

Gideon came around his desk to shake Logan's hand, but his welcoming smile faded when he

46

saw Logan's expression. If he had been less than happy the past few times Gideon had seen him, he was positively miserable today.

"What's happened?" Gideon asked.

Logan just shook his head and sat down abruptly in one of the overstuffed chairs designated for visitors. "I . . . I got a letter from Noelle."

Gideon didn't need much imagination to guess what the letter must say. Noelle had allowed her American soldier to get away, and now she was most likely making one last effort to get herself to America by telling him she was carrying his child. "I gather it wasn't good news."

Logan reached into his suitcoat and pulled out a tattered envelope. He handed it to Gideon, who took it reluctantly, having no real choice. He held it gingerly and went to sit back down behind his desk. He stared at the envelope for a long moment before making any move to remove the letter inside.

That was when he noticed something strange. "This letter isn't addressed to you."

"No, it's not. I . . . Oh, Gideon, it's going to sound so craven when you hear it, but I . . . I didn't really trust myself. I love Noelle with all my heart. I never felt that way about any other woman. So when I knew I had to leave her behind and never see her again, I didn't leave her with any way to contact me. I was afraid if

47

she did, I . . . I wouldn't be able to resist her. I was only strong enough to leave her once, you see, and I would probably throw away everything just to be with her if I were tempted again. She knew I lived in New York, of course, but that was all."

"Then who is this Sergeant Kellogg?" Gideon asked, reading the name on the envelope.

"He was one of the sergeants in my company. I . . . He must have given her his address, or maybe she asked for it when I . . . I don't know. At any rate, she wrote to him and asked him to see that I got her letter. He brought it to me yesterday."

"Do you want me to read the letter?" Gideon asked, although he had no desire to read another man's love letter.

"Oh no. It's in French anyway, so . . ."

That was a relief. "Then maybe you can just tell me what she said that upset you so much." Even though Gideon was pretty sure he already knew.

Logan sighed and rubbed a hand over his face. "She said . . . Did I tell you how honorable she is, Gideon? She didn't even ask me to reconsider and marry her after all. She understands that I'm committed to another woman, and she would never ask me to break that commitment."

"Yes, that's very honorable," Gideon said carefully. "But what does she want?"

"She . . . Things are very bad in France now."

"I know. I read the newspapers."

"People are going hungry, and parts of the country—the part where she lives—were practically destroyed. Most of the young men are dead or maimed, and there's no work and no real future for her. She . . . she'd like to come to America."

So no mention of a child. That was interesting. "I thought you said she didn't ask you to marry her."

"That's just it, she doesn't expect me to marry her. She doesn't expect anything at all. She's only asking me to send her money for . . . for her passage," he said, but for some reason he looked away when he said it, as if he could no longer meet Gideon's eye.

Elizabeth, who had much more experience at this than Gideon, had explained to him that breaking eye contact was an indication that someone was lying. What was Logan lying about? "She just wants money for her passage?" Gideon repeated with the barest hint of skepticism.

"Things are very bad in France," Logan repeated, still not meeting Gideon's eye.

"So she needs money for more than just her passage," Gideon guessed.

Logan swallowed. "She needs papers to travel. The government is being very careful about who can immigrate now. They don't want any Bolsheviks sneaking in."

"So she needs to bribe someone to get these papers," Gideon guessed.

"If she was an army bride, there would be no problem. When a woman marries an American, she automatically becomes a citizen and can come here with no questions asked, but I didn't marry her, Gideon." The anguish in his voice told Gideon just how much he now regretted that.

Still, Gideon couldn't help suspecting that something was not quite right with Noelle's request. "How much did she ask you for?"

Logan shifted in his chair in obvious discomfort. "She has to bribe a lot of people."

"How much?"

Logan sighed again. "A thousand dollars."

Gideon frowned. Passage from France to America would only cost about a hundred dollars. "That is a lot of money." A good half-year's salary for an ordinary workingman.

"She promises she will repay me," Logan said hastily. "She'll get a job and work very hard."

But they both knew a woman could never hope to repay such an amount no matter how many years she worked. She was really asking for a gift. "Do you have that kind of money readily available?"

Logan smiled mirthlessly. "Not in cash, no, and I can't ask my father for it for obvious reasons, which is why I'm here. I have that trust that my grandmother left me, though. There's more than enough in that, but I don't remember the conditions of the trust. It never mattered before, did it? But now . . . Can I use some of that money to—?"

Gideon raised a hand to stop him. "I don't know the terms of the trust offhand. I think Mr. Van Aken handled it. He was your grandmother's attorney. I'll have to look up the documents to see what's involved, and that will take some time. Why don't you make an appointment with Smith to come back tomorrow. I should be able to answer your questions by then."

"And we'll have to figure out the best way to get the funds to Noelle in France. I'm sure that won't be easy."

"What does she say about that in the letter?"

"Something about entrusting them to Sergeant Kellogg, but I'm sure that's just because she doesn't understand how funds are transferred between different countries."

Gideon felt the hairs on the back of his neck prickle. Nothing about this had felt right from the very beginning, and this was the biggest warning of all. "Yes, well, we'll figure it all out. Just leave it in my hands for now."

"I can't just abandon her in France if things are as bad as she says," Logan said.

Gideon nodded his understanding, if not his agreement. "Could you possibly translate the letter into English for me? Not the personal parts, of course, but the pertinent parts? So I can under-stand exactly what she's asking for?"

"Of course. It will give me something to do while I'm waiting. I can't thank you enough, Gideon. I've been frantic trying to figure out how to help her."

Gideon was careful to promise nothing as he escorted Logan out of the office and turned him over to Smith. When Smith returned after scheduling Logan's appointment and showing him out, Gideon said, "Would you get Miss Miles on the telephone for me?"

Elizabeth couldn't imagine what Gideon wanted to "consult" with her about. He had actually used that word, too. It sounded very legal, and since she wasn't an attorney, she was doubly mystified. He hadn't even waited until the end of his work day to come to see her, either, which meant the matter was of some urgency and really did have to do with business.

She jumped up from where she'd been waiting in the parlor the moment she saw the cab stop outside of the house, and she'd thrown open the front door before he even reached the porch steps. He came in on a burst of frigid air and greeted her with such a perfunctory kiss, she knew something was seriously wrong.

"I'm sorry to bother you like this," he said, shrugging out of his trench coat, which didn't look nearly as warm as a wool coat would have been, but he seemed determined to be fashionable.

"Don't be silly. How often do you ask me to help you with a client?" she teased.

"More often than I would ever have guessed," he replied, rubbing some warmth back into his hands.

"Come along to the kitchen. It's nice and warm there, and I made some coffee."

He followed her obediently and sat down at the kitchen table while she poured coffee for both of them.

"Now tell me why you've come. I'm dying of curiosity," she said when he'd had a chance to take a few warming sips.

"It's Logan Carstens."

"Oh my, don't tell me he strangled Rosemary," she teased.

Gideon couldn't help smiling at that. "Even if he did, he wouldn't come to me. I'm not a criminal defense attorney. He got a letter from Noelle."

"The French girl? How delightful! Is he going to marry her after all?"

"That's the strange part. Or at least one of the strange parts. She didn't ask him to marry her."

"She didn't tell him there's a baby and he must make an honest woman out of her?" she asked in genuine surprise.

"Oddly . . . or perhaps not so oddly . . . that was my first thought, too, but no, she doesn't ask him to marry her, or so Logan claims. And he didn't mention a child at all."

"What on earth does she want then?"

"Money."

Now he had her interest as well as her attention. "Money? For what?"

"To pay her passage to America."

She frowned, trying to make sense of this. "So he can marry her?"

"No, so she can escape France, where things are very hard."

"I don't suppose I can blame her for that."

"No one could, except that the amount of money she is asking for seems . . . exorbitant."

"How exorbitant?"

"She wants a thousand dollars."

Elizabeth blinked in surprised. "How many people is she bringing along with her?"

"Apparently, she will need travel documents. The American government is going to be very particular about who they allow in the country now that the war is over, and she isn't an army bride, so she will have to bribe some officials to get these documents."

"Even still, that's an awful lot of money."

"Indeed it is, which is why I wanted to tell you this amazing story and see what you thought about it."

"Obviously, this Noelle doesn't have enough money to pay these supposed bribes and buy a ticket herself."

"Obviously, or she wouldn't be asking Logan."

Elizabeth gave the matter a few moments of consideration. "Does she expect Logan to just give her this money?"

"She is asking for a loan and promises to pay it back when she gets to America."

"How will she pay it back if she doesn't have any money to start with?"

"She will work very hard once she gets here."

"That's ridiculous. She could never earn enough money to do that."

"I agree."

Elizabeth stared at her beloved across the kitchen table and realized she had just fallen in love with him all over again. "You came to tell me about this because you knew I could figure it out."

"I was very confident that you could, yes. Was I right?"

"Oh yes, my darling. I have it all figured out."

CHAPTER THREE

A re you sure you won't feel awkward seeing Logan, knowing what Rosemary did?" Gideon asked Elizabeth one last time. They were in his office, waiting for Logan to arrive for his appointment.

"I'm sure Logan had nothing to do with it and probably knows nothing about it. Besides, by helping Logan, I just might figure out a way to free him from Rosemary," Elizabeth said, managing not to rub her hands together in glee at the very thought.

But Gideon was shaking his head. "Rosemary will never let him go now."

Elizabeth sat up straighter in her chair at that. "What do you mean?"

"I mean now that she's got him hooked . . . Did I mention that Rosemary is at least twenty-five?"

"That isn't so very old."

"For a debutante it is. And she had several false alarms that probably left her feeling a little desperate."

"What do you mean, false alarms?"

"I mean young men who paid her particular attention but who vanished when the rumors started that they had proposed. Apparently, Rosemary has a history of assuming too much and frightening off her suitors."

"How desperate would a woman have to be to lie about being engaged?" Elizabeth marveled.

Gideon smiled knowingly. "I would expect you to know the answer to that."

Elizabeth didn't have to feign her outrage. "I didn't lie about it. I really was engaged to David."

At the mention of his name, though, they both sobered, and Elizabeth instantly regretted reminding Gideon of his lost friend.

"Poor David," she said.

Before Gideon could reply, Smith knocked on the office door and announced that Logan had arrived.

He came in looking anxious and stopped dead when he saw Elizabeth seated in one of the client chairs. "Elizabeth, how nice to see you," he said with forced cheer. He was a well-brought-up young man who remembered his manners even when he was distressed. "I'm sorry, I'll wait until you're finished with your visit."

"Elizabeth is here for our meeting, Logan," Gideon said. "I have explained your situation to her, and I think she can be helpful."

Plainly, Logan could not imagine how Elizabeth

might be helpful to his situation, but he did feel the need to excuse himself. "You must think very badly of me for the way I treated Rosemary, Elizabeth. I know I never should have allowed this to happen, but——"

"Nonsense, Logan," she said, raising her hand to stop his needless explanation. "Things like this happen all the time, and if you give us a chance, I think we can work everything out."

Logan did not appear convinced, but he took the seat Gideon offered and declined any refreshments, although he looked like he could use a good stiff drink.

"Did you translate the letter for me?" Gideon asked, taking his own seat behind his desk.

"Oh yes, I did." Logan pulled an envelope out of his suit coat and offered it to Gideon, who then passed it to Elizabeth. She started to take the sheets of stationery out of the envelope but stopped when she'd seen what was written on the front.

"Who is this Sergeant Phillip Kellogg? You didn't mention him to me, Gideon."

"He was one of the sergeants in my company," Logan said.

Elizabeth frowned. "What does that mean?"

Logan glanced at Gideon, who gestured for him to explain. "You see, the army is divided up into units of increasing size. A company is made up of four platoons——"

"Groups of soldiers," Gideon added, which was all Elizabeth really needed to know.

She nodded for Logan to continue.

"A company has around two hundred and fifty men, with a captain in charge."

"And you were the captain?" she guessed.

"That's right. I had a first lieutenant as my executive officer and two more first lieutenants and two second lieutenants under me as platoon leaders. Then I had a first sergeant, a supply sergeant and a mess sergeant. Under them were a lot more sergeants and corporals, but Kellogg was my first sergeant and my good right hand. He was a godsend because he was career army and the only one of us who had any military experience at all."

"I would have thought the lieutenants would be your good right hands," Elizabeth said. "Aren't they higher up?"

Logan gave her a smile that she was very much afraid was condescending. "Lieutenants do outrank sergeants, but they are merely boys with no useful experience whatever."

"Good heavens. So how old a man is this Sergeant Kellogg?" Elizabeth asked.

"I don't know exactly. Mid-thirties, perhaps."

Elizabeth nodded, as she formed a mental image of him. "Why is the letter from Noelle addressed to him?"

Logan looked away, and he actually blushed,

which intrigued Elizabeth all the more, but she waited patiently for him to explain.

After a painful minute, Logan said, "I thought Gideon might have told you. I deliberately did not give Noelle an address since I knew it was important to cut off all contact with her. I think she must be desperate indeed to have tried to contact me through Kellogg."

"How would she have known his address?"

"Sadly, I didn't think to ask him when he gave me the letter, but I . . . I've given this some thought since Gideon asked me the same thing yesterday. I'm afraid she may have gotten it from Kellogg's, uh, sweetheart."

"Kellogg had a French sweetheart, too?" This was getting more and more interesting by the minute.

"He was . . . involved with a French woman, but it came to nothing. He must have given her his address, however. How else would Noelle have gotten it?"

Elizabeth had no idea, but she decided she'd learned what she needed to know about Sergeant Kellogg and pulled the letter out of the envelope. Logan had also translated the part addressed to Kellogg, asking him to pass the rest of the letter along to Captain Carstens. Noelle was very trusting to expect Kellogg to perform such an important duty and very ignorant of American geography if she didn't understand that Logan and

Kellogg might have been discharged to homes on opposite sides of the continent. That would have made her request nearly impossible. But by some miracle, Kellogg was also apparently living in New York. How convenient.

The letter contained surprisingly little to indicate Noelle and Logan were formerly lovers. She simply says how much she misses him and how she hopes he is doing well. Then she complains about how difficult things are in France and how she would like his help in immigrating to the United States. She mentions how everyone must be bribed and then promises to repay him if it takes the rest of her life. It was all very heartrending.

"Does Noelle know your family is well-to-do?" Elizabeth asked.

Logan squirmed at the question, as she had expected him to. The old society families never admitted to being rich. Of course not all of them were, which made it doubly awkward, but she supposed any of them could be expected to come up with a thousand dollars in a pinch.

"We never discussed such things," Logan finally said.

"Let me phrase that another way. Did the French girls have the idea that all Americans are rich?"

Logan frowned as he considered this. "I suppose we must have seemed rich to them. We had food and chocolate bars and money to spend, while they had been destitute for years because of the war."

Elizabeth folded up the letter and the translation and put the pages back into the envelope.

"What do you think?" Gideon asked her.

"It's the Spanish Prisoner."

Logan and Gideon both frowned at this.

"But Noelle is French," Logan protested, "and she's not a prisoner."

"No, she's not, but that's the name of the con, the Spanish Prisoner."

"Con?" Logan echoed.

God bless him, he was truly innocent.

"It's a confidence game," Gideon said. "Is that right, Elizabeth?"

"Yes. The way it works is a victim is identified, in this case you. Someone informs you that an important person is in a dangerous situation and must escape. That person is the Spanish Prisoner, or in this case, the abandoned French girl."

"But what does Spain have to do with it?" Logan asked, still confused.

"Nothing at all. It's an old con, and when it started, Spain was often used as the place the prisoner was trying to escape from. They were probably at war or something."

"Spain often was," Gideon remarked.

"So a go-between, in this case your Sergeant Kellogg, tells you that the prisoner, Noelle, needs your help to escape. In most versions of this con, the prisoner is wealthy, too, and promises to repay you with generous interest once he or she is free. That version plays on greed, while this version plays on your love for Noelle. You wouldn't even expect to be repaid, would you?"

"No, of course not," Logan said indignantly, "but you're wrong about this, Elizabeth. Noelle would never . . . I mean, I know she must be desperate if she went to so much trouble to contact me."

"Perhaps she is," Elizabeth said, "but why is she asking you for so much money?"

"For bribes, like she says in the letter," Logan said, but Elizabeth could hear the doubt in his voice.

"I notice she instructs you to give the money to Sergeant Kellogg. How do you suppose he intends to get the money to France?"

"I . . . I guess the same way I would," Logan said. "By wiring it to Noelle."

"Then why doesn't she ask you to send her the money directly?"

Logan opened his mouth but nothing came out. She gave him a few minutes to consider what she'd told him. "How do you know all this? About the Spanish Prisoner business, I mean?"

"Elizabeth has an interesting background," Gideon said before Elizabeth could speak. "We're not at liberty to disclose her . . . well, the services she has performed for the government, so I'll have to ask you to keep her part in this confidential, Logan."

Logan's eyes were enormous as he looked at Elizabeth in a whole new light. "Was this . . . because of the war?"

Elizabeth didn't trust herself to speak, so she simply turned to Gideon to see how he was going to answer. So far he'd managed to explain her unique knowledge of the grift without divulging that she herself had been a con artist, but also without even telling a small white lie. Could he keep that up?

Gideon simply said, "Let's just say that a group of German saboteurs is in prison because of her efforts."

Which was—remarkably—absolutely true.

Logan needed a few moments to absorb all this, and when he did, his doubts returned. "So you're saying you think someone is trying to convince me that Noelle is in danger so they can cheat me out of a thousand dollars."

"I'm very much afraid that is the case, yes," Elizabeth said.

"But that's impossible. Noelle would never be involved in anything the least bit underhanded. Besides, she really is stuck in France, where things really are very difficult. She might even be starving right this moment."

"Let me ask you this," Elizabeth said. "Did

your Sergeant Kellogg know about your romance with Noelle?"

Logan blushed again. "I . . . I'm sure many people knew about it."

"And he obviously knew you didn't marry her and bring her back with you."

"Of course he did."

"So maybe he simply used this information to try to cheat you out of some money, and Noelle knows nothing at all about it."

But Logan frowned. "That does make more sense than anything else, although I can't believe Kellogg would do something like that. He was such a good soldier."

"Many soldiers are bitter about the war, though," Gideon said. "And they're having a difficult time finding jobs now that they're home."

But Logan wasn't listening. He was apparently still thinking about Noelle. "But things really are very bad in France. Suppose Noelle truly does need my help. I can't just ignore her if she did write that letter."

Elizabeth glanced at the letter. "Are you sure this is her handwriting?"

"I . . ." Logan's faith faltered, but only for a moment. "I've never actually seen Noelle's handwriting before, but it's obviously written by a woman."

Elizabeth had to agree the handwriting did look very feminine. "Then let's put Noelle to the test,

66

shall we? Do you have an address to which you can reply to her?"

"Yes. I lived in her family's house."

"Then write back directly to her."

"But her letter specifically says not to do that," Logan protested.

"Can you think of any reason why you shouldn't?" Elizabeth argued.

Logan frowned. "Well, no, now that you mention it, I can't."

"Then reply to her. Tell her you received her letter and you want to make sure she receives the money she needs and that if she will confirm she is still with her family, you will wire her the money there."

"That's sounds like a perfect solution," Gideon said. "If she really does want to come to America, you can help her. If not, you will save yourself a lot of money."

"But what will I tell Kellogg? He'll want to know why I'm not responding."

"Blame it on me," Gideon said. "Tell him there are problems with the trust and you can't get the money. I can stall him for a few weeks while Noelle has time to receive your letter and reply. If you still want to send the money to her then, I'll make sure she gets it."

"And Mr. Kellogg should be glad to be relieved of this burden," Elizabeth added.

After a bit more persuasion, Logan agreed

to this plan, but as he was preparing to take his leave, he thought of another problem. "I don't have any idea what to say to Noelle. How do I offer to send her money to come to America if she never requested it in the first place? Won't she misunderstand and think I've changed my mind about marrying her?"

"I can see how that might be a problem," Elizabeth said before Gideon could offer his services, because he would probably be just as ham-handed at this as Logan. At least Logan knew he couldn't handle such a sensitive issue. "I would be happy to assist you, Logan."

Gideon, to his credit, looked relieved. "Perhaps the two of you would like to use one of our meeting rooms to compose a draft."

"That sounds perfect," Elizabeth said.

Smith escorted them to an empty room and provided the necessary paper, pen and ink.

"I can't tell you how much I appreciate your help, Elizabeth," Logan said when they were seated at the table.

"I'm just glad I can be of assistance." Elizabeth was sure that's exactly how Mrs. Bates would have responded, although she would have had no idea what the Spanish Prisoner was or how to keep poor Logan from being taken. "I hope you can translate this into French, because I certainly can't."

"Yes, I can, but I'm afraid I don't have any

idea even how to start a letter like this," Logan admitted when Elizabeth had arranged the writing materials to her satisfaction.

"Would you like her to know that you've been thinking about her?"

Logan's handsome face twisted in pain. "I've been thinking about her constantly, but I don't want to give her the impression that I . . . that my situation has changed."

"I understand. How about if you just say you were surprised to receive the letter she sent to you via Sergeant Kellogg and happy to know that she is well?"

"Yes, that's good."

"I think we should proceed as if you believe the letter is really from her, in case it really is."

"Yes, I see. I certainly wouldn't want to insult her by making her think I doubted her."

"Exactly. If she really did write it, she'll be pleased to hear back from you. If she didn't, she'll be confused but also pleased that you were so willing to come to her rescue."

Plainly, Logan understood the benefits to him. Either way, he would look like a hero. He nodded vigorously. "Yes, I like that."

"And we won't mention the amount of money. We'll simply say you are willing to wire the sum she requested to pay her fare."

Logan had lost any trace of condescension he might have harbored. The look he gave her was pure admiration. "Those German spies never had a chance against you, did they?"

"No," Elizabeth graciously agreed, "they did not."

By Sunday morning, Elizabeth was still feeling very virtuous for having used her extensive knowledge of grifting to help Logan. She hadn't even had to run a con herself, either! Was it possible she had reformed completely?

No one she had ever known had, but miracles did happen, didn't they?

She was still feeling virtuous after a sermon on turning the other cheek. The new minister was a lovely man who gave a good sermon and finished on time and what more could anyone ask of a man of God? Considering how far short his predecessor, a depraved man more concerned with monetary gain than tending his flock, had fallen, Elizabeth couldn't imagine.

While Gideon and his mother chatted with some friends, Elizabeth glanced around to see if there was anyone lingering in the sanctuary she would like to speak to. Before she could find anyone, Rosemary Westerly hove into view.

"Elizabeth, how are you?" she asked with a rather smug smile. Did she expect Elizabeth to be prostrate with apoplexy after reading the announcement of her engagement in the gossip columns last Sunday?

"I'm doing very well." Elizabeth gave Rosemary the dazzling smile of a rich woman without a care in the world. She had practiced that one many times.

Rosemary waited a few seconds for Elizabeth to ask after her health in return, but she waited in vain. She didn't let that distract her from her mission, however. "I do hope that we can be friends, Elizabeth. I know Logan and Gideon would like that."

Elizabeth knew that Rosemary would like that, although Rosemary's idea of friendship was probably much different from Elizabeth's. "I don't know any reason why we shouldn't be," Elizabeth said guilelessly. She'd practiced that, too. "Do you?"

Rosemary blinked a few times, but her smile never wavered. "Of course not. I was hoping we might have lunch tomorrow." She mentioned the name of a quaint little tearoom where respectable ladies could go unescorted and enjoy crustless sandwiches and Earl Grey.

"I do happen to be free," Elizabeth admitted, wondering what on earth Rosemary might be up to. Surely, Logan hadn't told her about the letter from Noelle or the help Elizabeth had given him in replying. Still, she didn't think Rosemary really just wanted to be friends, either.

"How lovely. Can we meet there? Let's say one o'clock?"

"That would be fine."

"And afterward, I'll take you to meet my modiste."

Her eyes took on a crafty expression, as if she expected that Elizabeth wouldn't know what that word meant. "Are you suggesting my wardrobe needs improvement?"

"Oh no, not at all," she insisted, although she looked a little disappointed. "But this woman does marvelous work. She's French, you know."

"The French do have such a sense of style," Elizabeth agreed.

"And you'll be adding to your trousseau, I'm sure."

"Very likely."

"Then I shall see you tomorrow."

"I'll look forward to it."

Elizabeth decided not to mention her luncheon with Rosemary to Gideon. She didn't want him to worry.

The following morning, Gideon had just summoned Smith to show a client out and was finishing up his notes on their meeting when Smith returned wearing a disapproving frown. Gideon had learned to recognize the expression.

"Did someone ask to see me without an appointment?" he asked as sympathetically as he could. Smith was far more jealous of Gideon's time than Gideon was.

"He's been waiting almost an hour while you finished with your last client. I encouraged him to schedule a time tomorrow when you would be free, but he said he preferred to wait."

So it wasn't someone Smith knew. "Did he give his name?"

"Oscar Thornton."

Gideon was glad he was sitting down. Hearing the name was like a punch in the gut. The last time he had seen Oscar Thornton, Gideon had unwittingly helped cheat the man out of a fortune and Elizabeth lay dying at his feet. Thornton had fled that day, and Gideon had never expected to see or hear from the man again. Until the debacle with their engagement announcement, Gideon hadn't even thought of Thornton in almost a year.

So much for his theory that Thornton didn't read the gossip columns. Rosemary Westerly had a lot to answer for.

"Show Mr. Thornton in," Gideon said, pleased to hear his voice sounded perfectly normal even though his heart was hammering in his chest.

Plainly, Smith sensed Gideon's unease, but he nodded and hurried out to do his bidding. A few moments later, Smith escorted Thornton into his office.

He looked older than Gideon remembered. He'd lost some weight, though, so perhaps that was it. His cheeks were hollow and his eyes a bit sunken. His hair might have been thinner as well. His clothes were as good as ever, though. He wasn't destitute if he could still afford a good tailor.

Gideon didn't rise to greet him, nor did he invite Thornton to sit down. The two men stared at each other across the width of Gideon's large desk until Smith discreetly closed the door behind himself.

"Thornton," Gideon said at last.

Thornton smiled at that, a grin that bared his teeth but otherwise changed his sour expression not at all. "Bates. I hear congratulations are in order."

Gideon refused to react. "Are they?"

"You're engaged, I hear. Or rather I see in the newspapers. To Miss Elizabeth Miles."

Gideon said nothing.

"Elizabeth Miles, who I thought was dead." He waited, and when Gideon still did not reply, he added, "She must've recovered."

"Is that all you came for, Thornton?" Gideon said, not having to feign his annoyance. "Because I'm very busy and—"

"No, that's not all I came for, Bates," Thornton said, ostentatiously taking a seat on one of the client chairs, much to Gideon's dismay. "I want my money back."

Of course he did. "As you very well know, I do not have your money."

"But you know who does."

"No, I do not." Gideon took great pride in never telling a lie, and this was technically the truth. He could guess, but that wasn't the same as really knowing.

"Maybe not, but you can find out. Elizabeth Miles knows."

"How could she? She wasn't even there."

"But she was behind it, her and that no good brother of hers."

"Mr. Thornton," Gideon said, using the tone of voice he had perfected for getting unreasonable clients to understand their true situations, "you were there and saw the same thing I did. The army arrested General Sterling and confiscated everything. Have you taken up the matter with them?"

"Of course I did. They never heard of General Sterling, and they didn't know anything about my money, and when I went to reclaim my property, I couldn't prove I owned it because the army or whoever it was had taken all the papers. By the time I got things straightened out, the warehouses were empty."

"That's . . . unfortunate." Which was perfectly true.

"Do you know how much I lost on that deal?"

"No, I do not." He had made it a point to know as little as possible about it.

"Oh, I thought maybe you got a cut."

Gideon saw no reason to reply to that, but he did

75

give Thornton a glare that didn't seem to faze him.

"I lost a lot," Thornton continued, "and that doesn't even count what Elizabeth and her brother took from me the first time."

"I don't know anything about that, either, and I don't have any idea where your money is, Mr. Thornton. I'm afraid I can't help you at all."

"Maybe not, but Elizabeth can, and she will. You tell her I want it all back, every penny."

"Miss Miles does not have that kind of money." At least not that Gideon knew about.

"If you don't know how much it is, how do you know she doesn't?" Thornton taunted.

"All right. How much is it?"

"If you will recall, the government was going to pay me three-quarters of a million dollars, but I'm willing to settle for two hundred and fifty thousand."

Gideon almost laughed out loud. "Are you insane?"

"Not at all. She took that money from me, and I want it back."

Gideon wondered if Thornton had really lost that much, and thought perhaps he had. "As I already reminded you, Miss Miles was not involved in your dealings with the army, and even if she was, she could never lay her hands on that much money."

"Then you'd better figure out who can, because if you don't, you'll be very sorry."

"Are you threatening me, Mr. Thornton?" Gideon asked, wishing he didn't already know the answer.

"I most certainly am." He glanced around Gideon's well-appointed office. "You've got a pretty nice life here, Bates. You've got your old family name and your society friends and your good reputation, but this girl you're going to marry, she doesn't have any of that, does she? And what's more, she's a common thief."

Gideon was halfway out of his chair when Thornton raised both hands as if to ward him off.

"Don't get excited. You know it's true. Oh, she's pretty enough, and I guess she can pass for a lady, but if people ever found out the truth about her, all those society friends of yours wouldn't be so friendly anymore, would they? In fact, none of them would ever speak to you again. And your job here? Would people want to do business with a man married to a grifter? Would anybody ever trust you again?"

Gideon had never believed the old saw about your blood turning to ice, but he believed it now. He had also never hated anyone quite as much as he hated Thornton at that moment. "No one will believe you."

"Oh, I think they will. I've still got a few friends in this town. All it would really take is a word to a reporter at one of the big newspapers, and they would do the rest. They'd find out all about her and put it right on the front page. You know it's true."

He did, too. "If you ruin Elizabeth, you'll never get your money back," Gideon pointed out logically, "but we can't stop you because we don't have that much money to give you. I believe we have reached an impasse."

But Thornton wasn't convinced. "You might not have that kind of money, but she can get it, even if she has to con it out of somebody else. I don't particularly care. I just want what's mine."

"I can't give you an answer today, Thornton. I'll need some time to . . . to figure this out."

Thornton smiled, and this time it actually reached his eyes. "Of course you will. And Elizabeth will need time to raise the money. I'll give you a month, but never doubt that I'll do what I say, Bates. Ruining you and your lovely bride won't cost me anything and will bring me a lot of pleasure."

"And how do I know you won't do it even if we give you the money?" Gideon asked, furious.

"You don't," Thornton said with satisfaction. "You'll have to worry about me for the rest of your lives."

Elizabeth arrived very early for her luncheon with Rosemary because she figured Rosemary would try to be the first to arrive. Indeed, Rosemary seemed a bit disconcerted when she was escorted to the table Elizabeth had claimed for them. A generous tip to the maître d' had secured them the best spot, right beside the fountain that bubbled deliciously.

"What a lovely dress," Elizabeth said quite sincerely as Rosemary arranged herself in her seat. The plum color was a bit dark for Rosemary but would have looked wonderful with Elizabeth's coloring.

"Thank you," Rosemary said absently. "I hope I'm not late."

"Not at all. I was finished with my morning errands and decided to wait here where it's so pleasant."

Rosemary smiled bravely, determined to get the upper hand again. "I'm so glad you were free today. But I suppose you don't know many people in the city yet."

"Gideon and his mother have been very helpful. I've made a lot of new friends, although so many of Gideon's associates were in the army that I'm just now getting to know them."

"Like Logan," Rosemary said.

"Yes." Elizabeth fell silent as the waitress came to offer them menus that were handwritten on embossed vellum cards.

Rosemary had several questions that the waitress patiently answered, and then they placed their orders.

As soon as she was gone, Elizabeth leaned

forward and said, "Now you must tell me all of your wedding plans. I know my wedding won't be nearly as grand as yours, but I want to make sure I haven't forgotten anything really important."

Rosemary didn't exactly blanch, but she did look faintly alarmed. "I . . . Well, I think I told you that we haven't set a date yet. Logan has just gotten back and is still adjusting to civilian life, as he calls it."

"But you must have some plans, even if they're just daydreams at the moment," Elizabeth said. "Will it be a morning wedding or afternoon? Evenings are becoming more popular, I understand. And have you sent your engagement announcement to the newspapers yet?"

"Well, of course," Rosemary said, a little offended. "I did that even before Logan left for the army."

"As you know," Elizabeth confided, "we had decided not to send one out because our wedding is going to be so small, but . . . Well, perhaps you saw the mention we received in the various newspapers."

"I . . . Yes, I do think I saw that," Rosemary said uneasily. She really wasn't a good liar. So few people were.

"We were so surprised to see it mentioned," Elizabeth marveled. "Oddly, it happened right after you had asked me about it, too. I was actually wondering if I should take your advice and put the announcement in anyway when our names were mentioned in the gossip columns, of all places. I didn't think Gideon and I were interesting enough to be mentioned in the gossip columns."

"I'm sure you are being too modest," Rosemary said in a tone she probably meant to be kind.

"I don't think so. After all, nobody in New York even knows me, do they? You told me so yourself," Elizabeth reminded her with elegant brutality. "Why would our marriage be considered gossip? And who would have taken it upon themselves to notify the newspapers— almost all the newspapers in fact—about our engagement?"

Rosemary was almost squirming. "I'm sure it was done with the best of intentions."

"Really?" Elizabeth didn't have to pretend to be skeptical. "And what would those intentions have been?"

"I . . ."

"And who would even think that providing those awful columnists with information was a good idea? Those people are always trying to ruin someone's reputation or create some sort of scandal. I know Gideon did not at all appreciate seeing our names mentioned in the same place where others are accused of adultery and even worse."

Rosemary sighed and folded her hands in what might have been surrender. "You are so right. It was an awful thing to do."

Elizabeth smiled sweetly. "Then why did you do it, Rosemary?"

CHAPTER FOUR

ortunately for Rosemary, the tea arrived at that moment. Elizabeth's smile lasted through the entire little ceremony, as the waitress set out the teapot and the sugar and cream and filled the cups. Meanwhile, Rosemary simply stared at Elizabeth in disbelief, her face almost devoid of color.

When the waitress had gone, Elizabeth daintily dropped two sugar cubes into her teacup and gave it a stir with the small silver spoon.

"I . . . I don't know what you mean," Rosemary finally managed.

"I think you do. Forgive me for being so forthright. I can see I've shocked you, but I'm afraid I was taught to be honest," she lied. "That's the way they do things in South Dakota."

Plainly, it wasn't the way they did things in Rosemary's New York, however. She couldn't even summon a response.

"Sugar?" Elizabeth asked, dropping a cube into Rosemary's cup without waiting for an answer. "It's good for shock, I'm told."

Rosemary picked up her cup and took a sip.

Somehow she managed not to spill any, even though her hand was shaking a bit. When she'd gotten the cup safely back on the saucer again, she said, "I really don't know what to tell you, Elizabeth."

"Then just tell me why would you do such a thing when you knew I didn't want it done?"

"I . . . People will want to know," she said faintly.

"I'm sure they will. People love knowing other people's business, but what I really want to know is how you managed to put it into all the newspapers at once. That was quite a feat."

"It wasn't difficult at all," Rosemary said, regaining a bit of her old confidence. "I know all the gossip columnists. They come to every event I attend, and they always have. They are always desperate for news, so I simply wrote them each a note."

"Which you must have done the morning after our dinner or perhaps you stayed up late into the night, scratching out your missives, and had them hand delivered to arrive in time," Elizabeth guessed, pleased to see the color rising in Rosemary's cheeks was a blotchy red.

"I was only trying to help," she protested. "You were going to defy convention, and I couldn't let you do that. Think how it would embarrass Gideon."

"Neither Gideon nor his mother thought we

were defying anything, and they weren't the least bit embarrassed."

"Then they should have been," Rosemary said stiffly.

Elizabeth considered her companion, watching as Rosemary added another sugar cube to her cup and stirred it vigorously. "And what did you get in return?"

Rosemary looked up in surprise and ill-concealed alarm. "What do you mean?"

"I mean people usually have good reasons for doing what they do. I don't believe for a moment that you were really trying to keep me from making a serious social blunder. I think you may have been doing this for reasons of your own, and I'd like to know what they are."

She tried very hard to look astonished. "What possible reason could I have?"

Elizabeth sat back to consider the question just as the waitress delivered the tray of tiny sandwiches and tea cakes that passed for lunch. When she had gone, Elizabeth devoted herself to the business of choosing her sandwiches before replying, and then she waited until Rosemary reached for one.

"I'm thinking that you have a secret you wouldn't like to see in the gossip columns, so you feed the columnists tidbits about other people in exchange."

Rosemary had obviously never needed to

85

disguise her true feelings because her dismay was almost comical. "What secret could I possibly have that gossip columnists would care about?"

"Do you really want me to guess?"

Rosemary's cheeks were flaming now. "Elizabeth, this is a very inappropriate topic for us to be discussing."

"And why is that?" Elizabeth asked with genuine interest.

"Because women in our position are expected to exercise a certain amount of discretion."

"You mean like not sending gossip about each other to the newspapers?"

Was Rosemary actually grinding her teeth? "No, like not upsetting each other in a public place."

Elizabeth was not a bit upset. She took a bite of one of her sandwiches and chewed thoughtfully. When she'd swallowed, she said, "I appreciate your efforts to instruct me in the finer points of life in New York society, Rosemary. I obviously have a lot to learn."

Amazingly, Rosemary seemed to think Elizabeth was sincere. "That's only to be expected, and I'm only too happy to assist in any way I can. I'm sure South Dakota is very different from New York."

Since Elizabeth had never even been to South Dakota, she couldn't judge, but she now knew Rosemary's New York operated under a very different set of rules from the rest of the world. Rosemary's rules suited Rosemary and no one else. "I'm very glad to know I can call on you for whatever I might need."

Rosemary smiled graciously, somehow believing she had won their little battle of wills. "As I told you, I want us to be good friends, Elizabeth. I know that's what Logan and Gideon would want, too."

Elizabeth thought she knew what Logan and Gideon really wanted, though, and if they got it, she and Rosemary would never be friends.

That evening was the salon at Cybil and Zelda's house, and Elizabeth was hoping she could get Gideon alone for a few minutes to speak with him about her encounter with Rosemary that day. Being the kind man that he was, he hadn't wanted to believe Rosemary was the one who had given the news of their engagement to the newspapers, so he needed to know that she had actually admitted it. Gideon probably wouldn't approve of getting revenge for such an outrageous act, either, so Elizabeth would have to temper her instinctive response, at least for now.

When the doorbell rang a good hour before their salon guests were expected, Elizabeth went to answer it, since Cybil and Zelda were still upstairs. Gideon and Anna were waiting on the porch. He always escorted Anna to the salon because her mother would never let her attend alone. But Elizabeth's delight at seeing them lasted only a moment before she noticed their grim expressions.

"What's happened?" Elizabeth asked, ushering them into the house.

Gideon and Anna exchanged a look. "Oscar Thornton came to my office today," he said after a tense moment.

Elizabeth gasped as her stomach clenched with dread. "Your office? What did he want?"

"Oh, Elizabeth, I'm so sorry," Anna said, her lovely face drawn with worry. "He saw the engagement announcement in one of the newspapers."

"I'm going to murder Rosemary Westerly," Elizabeth said.

Gideon took her hands in his cold ones. "Now, darling, you don't know—"

"But I do know. I had lunch with her today, and she admitted it. She thought she was doing us a favor."

Gideon's frown deepened as he considered all the implications of this admission. "She really did it?"

"Yes, she did. Now, what did Thornton say when he saw you?" Elizabeth asked again.

"Let's go inside and sit down and I'll tell you. That's why we came early," Gideon said.

He helped Anna off with her coat, and when

he'd removed his trench coat as well, they all went into the parlor, an over furnished room stuffed with as many chairs and sofas as would fit and banked with heavily laden bookcases on every wall. A cheerful fire crackled in the hearth, and Elizabeth threw another log onto it before taking a seat beside Gideon on the sofa. Anna sat on a chair at right angles to them.

Gideon cleared his throat. "Thornton saw the announcement, like I said. He immediately figured out that you hadn't died, as he'd been led to believe."

"How astute of him," Elizabeth said bitterly. Their plans had been so carefully laid. "Does he expect an invitation to the wedding?"

Gideon sighed wearily. "He wants his money back."

"Of course he does. I hope you told him you don't have it."

"I did, and I also told him you don't have it, but he doesn't care. He still wants it back. He said . . ." Gideon looked away.

Elizabeth rubbed her forehead where a head-ache was trying to form. "Just tell me."

"He expects you to run a con on someone else if you can't get it any other way," Anna explained when Gideon couldn't bring himself to. Plainly, Gideon had told her everything on their trip over.

Elizabeth was impressed in spite of herself.

Thornton had clearly thought this through. "And what will he do if he doesn't get his money back?"

Gideon and Anna exchanged another look, but Anna silently refused to speak for him again. "He will tell everyone about your . . . background." Her background as a con artist, of course.

"Everyone?" Elizabeth asked to make sure she understood.

"He'll tell the newspapers," Anna said. "He'll publicly humiliate you."

"And Gideon, too, of course," Elizabeth said, furious now. How ironic that she was now being blackmailed when she and Gideon had so recently foiled a blackmail scheme. Blackmail was such a perfect crime. The victim couldn't possibly report it to the police because doing so would produce the exact effect that paying the blackmail was supposed to stop.

But perhaps it wasn't as bad as she thought. She didn't have Thornton's money, at least not all of it, but she did have a tidy sum saved up. As much as it galled her to do it, paying off Thornton might be the easiest way to be rid of him. "How much does he want?"

Gideon actually winced. "Two hundred and fifty thousand."

The nerve of that man!

"Could he really have lost that much?" Anna asked with what appeared to be admiration.

Elizabeth had never known the exact total, since she hadn't been involved in every aspect. "It's possible," she admitted. And she didn't have nearly that much saved up, so paying him off wasn't really an option.

"The army was supposedly going to pay him three-quarters of a million dollars in the end," Gideon said. "I guess we should be thankful he didn't demand that much."

Elizabeth wasn't thankful about any of this. "When does he expect to be paid?"

Gideon sighed wearily. "He gave me a month."

"What are you going to do?" Anna asked.

"I'm going to consult with the Old Man," Elizabeth said.

"Do you think that's a good idea?" Gideon asked uneasily.

Elizabeth smiled sweetly. "If I have to run a con to get the money, it's a very good idea."

Now Gideon was furious. "You aren't going to do that. We'll go to the police and—"

"Nonsense," Elizabeth said. "The police can't help us, and going to them will only ensure that the whole story is reported in every newspaper in the city."

"But you can't con someone else out of two hundred and fifty thousand dollars," he argued.

She could, of course, but she said, "Probably not, which is why I need to discuss this with the Old Man."

"Rosemary Westerly has a lot to answer for," Anna said darkly.

"She couldn't have known that she'd be putting Elizabeth in such a dangerous situation," Gideon said, trying to be fair as usual.

She did love him for that, but it could also be annoying, because she had no desire to be fair to Rosemary. "You're right, she was simply trying to manage our affairs for us, which is also inexcusable but usually not fatal."

"At least Thornton didn't threaten your life," Gideon was quick to assure her.

"Of course not. He won't get his money if he murders me," Elizabeth pointed out, making him wince again.

"But surely you don't intend to pay him," Anna said.

"Heavens no." Elizabeth thought Gideon looked surprised, but he shouldn't have been. "Paying a blackmailer just encourages him to keep asking for more and more."

"What else can you do, though?" Anna asked.

Elizabeth smiled with a confidence she did not feel. "Don't worry. We'll think of something." Before anyone could challenge her, she turned to Anna. "I've been trying to figure out how Rosemary got on such friendly terms with a bunch of gossip columnists. Do you have any ideas?"

"Heavens no! No one even wants to speak

to those people for fear of having their words twisted and reported in the Sunday edition."

"But Rosemary said she knows them very well because they come to all the events she attends."

Anna frowned. "That's true, at least the part about them coming to everything. Hostesses make sure they're invited, and they report on who attended and what everyone wore and if anyone behaved inappropriately."

"But you're not friendly with them?"

"Not at all! And neither is anyone I know. Reporters are viewed more like spies than anything else."

"And yet Rosemary Westerly claims she knows all of them well, and she certainly is on good enough terms with them to send them information about our engagement and expect it to show up in their columns."

Anna turned to Gideon, who raised his hands defensively. "Don't look at me. I don't read the society pages."

Elizabeth gave Anna as much time as she needed to consider the situation. At last Anna said, "I've always suspected that some people in society give bits of gossip to those columns. It's a perfect way to embarrass or get revenge on an enemy, and how else would these columnists know some of the things they report? I mean, people don't have love affairs in the middle of a ball where reporters can see them, do they?"

"No, and reporters aren't likely to witness what goes on in the privacy of a hotel room or wherever an affair does take place," Elizabeth said. "But Rosemary wasn't trying to get revenge on Gideon and me or even to embarrass us, so why did she report our engagement?"

"Because she's a meddling harpy," Gideon said with uncharacteristic vehemence.

"Goodness, Gideon," Elizabeth said in feigned amazement.

"Well, she is. If it wasn't for her, Thornton would never have even known you were still alive."

"You are so right, and I hope you remember that later when she has reason to regret her decision."

"What does that mean?" Gideon asked with a touch of alarm.

"Not a thing. Anna, I have a theory about Rosemary and why she's so friendly with the gossip columnists."

"Do tell," Anna said with great interest.

"I suspect that Rosemary may have a past indiscretion that she does not want reported, and so she passes along whatever gossip she hears to keep the columnists from reporting her own."

"That is a very interesting theory," Anna said.

"But even if it's true, what difference would it make to us?" Gideon asked.

"A lot of difference if I could find out what it

is," Elizabeth said. "It might even give Logan a reason to break their engagement."

Gideon sighed. "And what if the ensuing scandal just made Logan feel a greater obligation to protect Rosemary by marrying her?"

Elizabeth sighed, too. May heaven protect her from honorable men.

Later that evening, after the regular guests—including her brother, Jake—had arrived and Anna was engaged in a very serious discussion with two of her college classmates on one of the finer points of philosophy and Gideon was politely listening to a professor expound on his theory about mankind's propensity for war, Jake approached Elizabeth. She'd sought out the quiet of the kitchen, where she could think about the situation with Thornton.

Her half brother would never inquire about her well-being, but he did look oddly concerned. "Anna told me Thornton showed up at Gideon's office today."

"Did she tell you how much money he wants to keep quiet?"

"He's a greedy son of a gun all right. What are you going to do?"

"Well, I'm not going to try to raise that much money."

"That's too bad, because I was going to offer to help you," he said with a grin.

"The last time you helped me with Thornton, we both ended up running for our lives," she reminded him.

His grin vanished. "I'd do better this time."

She felt a stab of pity for him, but Jake wouldn't want her pity. "I know, but that's not the answer. You can't go near him, and we've got to beat him once and for all this time."

"Just let me know how I can help. I've got a score to settle with him, too, don't forget."

She hadn't forgotten. She considered Jake for a long moment. "Did Anna tell you how he found out that I'm still alive?"

"Yeah, something about your engagement being in the newspaper."

"Yes, someone found out about our engagement and sent the news to all the gossip columnists when she found out I wasn't going to put in a formal announcement."

"Who would do a thing like that?"

"Do you remember the story we told you about Gideon's friend who fell in love with a French girl?"

"Yeah," he said uncertainly.

"Well, it was the woman that fellow is engaged to who decided to announce our engagement."

Jake let out a low whistle. "No wonder Anna said she was a drip."

"Exactly. So now I'm more determined than ever to save him from her so he can marry his

French girl. Oh, by the way, I've discovered that somebody is also trying to run the Spanish Prisoner on Logan."

"Logan? Is that the guy who's in love with the French girl?"

"Yes. The French girl is supposedly the Spanish Prisoner." She briefly explained the situation.

Jake got a dreamy look in his eyes. "I've never run the Spanish Prisoner before."

Elizabeth smiled. "Neither have I."

The next afternoon, Gideon was in his office when Smith announced, "Your next client is here, Mr. Bates. His name is Sergeant Phillip Kellogg."

Gideon wasn't sure which part of this was most surprising: that Kellogg had presented himself at Gideon's office or that he apparently had an appointment. "Was this visit scheduled?"

Smith straightened importantly. "Sergeant Kellogg came this morning, but I convinced him that he would be much better served if he returned at a more convenient time."

"I see." Gideon really did see. Kellogg had bent to Smith's will, which was very interesting. "Please show the good sergeant in."

Sergeant Phillip Kellogg was a man of medium height and compact build who carried himself with the erect posture of a military man. He was also still wearing his uniform, and Gideon remembered that Logan had called him a career army man. Perhaps he had not actually been discharged.

"Sergeant Kellogg, pleased to meet you."

For all his military bearing, he stepped forward hesitantly to shake Gideon's offered hand. He was a rather ordinary looking man, not someone who would make an impression if you just met him once. His dark eyes darted around, taking in every detail of the room before he sat down in one of the client chairs at Gideon's invitation. Even then he did not relax.

"What can I do for you, Sergeant Kellogg?" Gideon asked, still smiling in an effort to put the man at ease.

"I . . . My captain, Mr. Carstens, he said you knew the situation with Miss Fortier."

"The French lady, yes. He explained it all to me."

Kellogg glanced around again, as if looking for an escape, but he made no move to leave. Finally, his gaze settled on Gideon once more. "She needs to get out of France. You don't know how bad things are there. Or maybe you do. Were you in the army?"

"No," Gideon said with honest regret. "I was on the train, ready to head to training camp, when the Armistice came. I understand that you are career army."

"What?" he said in surprise. "Oh no. Who told you I was?"

"Mr. Carstens."

Kellogg smiled at that, a quick quirk of his mouth that vanished almost instantly. "I was in the army years before the war. I joined up when I was a kid, but it wasn't for me. Too many rules, I thought back then. I got out when my enlistment was over."

"I suppose they were glad to get you this time, though," Gideon guessed.

Kellogg's strange smile flickered again. "Yeah, that's why they made me a sergeant. I already knew how to march and follow orders, but those boys they sent to France . . ." He shook his head at the memory. "They'd trained carrying sticks, most of them, because we didn't have enough rifles. Never even loaded a gun before. Babies, all of them."

"Even Logan, I suppose," Gideon said.

Kellogg's head jerked up at that, as if he thought Gideon were trying to trick him somehow. "Captain Carstens did his best."

"I'm sure he did, but he mentioned how much he relied on you. He called you his good right hand."

"He did?" Kellogg seemed pleased by that. "Well, I guess he knew he could depend on me."

"I'm sure he did. The men who were in France don't talk about the things that happened there, or at least not the ones I've encountered, but I know you saw some terrible fighting."

Kellogg's ordinary face darkened at the memories. "We lost a lot of good men over there."

Gideon let that comment lie in respectful silence for a long moment. That gave Kellogg time to remember why he was really there.

"Anyway, about Miss Fortier," he said abruptly. "The captain said there was a problem with the money."

Gideon gave Kellogg his most professional apologetic smile. "I'm sure you'll forgive me, Sergeant, but I'm not allowed to discuss my clients' private business with other people."

"But I'm not other people. Didn't he tell you? She asked me to help her. Me, not him."

"Yes, he did explain that, but I must admit, I'm still a bit confused. Why wouldn't Miss Fortier write to the captain herself?"

"Well, you see . . ." He shifted uneasily in his chair. "Didn't the captain explain? He's already engaged to another lady."

"I did know that, yes."

"And he didn't give Miss Fortier his address."

"Then how did she know yours, Sergeant? You weren't involved with her, too, were you?"

"Me? No, why would you think that?" He seemed outraged at the very thought.

"It just seemed odd to me that she would contact you about such a sensitive matter in the first place, but also that she happened to know exactly how to contact you."

"How should I know? Maybe the army gave her my address. There's a lot of mademoiselles over there trying to find their doughboys because the boys left them with a little surprise, if you know what I mean."

"Is that Miss Fortier's reason for contacting you?"

"What? No! I never had nothing to do with her. Not that way, at least."

"Then you did know her."

"Of course. The captain was staying in her house. Well, her father's house. We all knew who she was. Her father was the mayor after all."

"I see. So that's probably how she knew you as well."

"What do you mean?" He seemed very confused now.

"I mean if the captain was staying in her father's house and you were his right hand—"

"I was his first sergeant."

"So she would have met you."

"She would have seen me around, sure."

Gideon nodded sagely. "So naturally when she wanted to contact Captain Carstens, she wrote to you."

"I don't know if it was natural or not, but that's what she did."

"And you can read French?"

He shifted in his seat again. "My parents were French."

"Really? They emigrated from France?" Gideon asked with interest. Although many thousands of immigrants had settled in New York City through the years, not many were French.

"French Canadian," he admitted reluctantly. "They live up north, in New York near the Canadian border, with a lot of other French Canadians."

"I guess that explains how you speak French. I suppose you spoke French to the people you met in France."

He winced a little at that. Perhaps his French wasn't as good as he made it out to be. "I could talk to them, yes."

"And that would explain why Miss Fortier would feel comfortable writing to you, knowing you could read her letter."

Plainly, he hadn't given this much thought. "I suppose, but what does it matter? The fact is that she wrote to me and asked me to find the captain. She wants to come to America, and he owes her."

"Does he?" Gideon asked with interest.

Kellogg seemed a little taken aback. "Well, yes, he does."

"Why?"

"Because . . . Well, because he led her on. He had no business doing that when he was already engaged, did he?"

"I thought he'd been completely honest with

her. Her letter clearly says she doesn't expect him to break his engagement and marry her."

"I . . . Uh, yes, but . . . She still fell in love with him."

"I agree that's unfortunate, but things like that happen all the time without obligating the man in question to pay the woman an enormous sum of money."

"Are you saying he's not going to help her?" Kellogg demanded, suddenly angry. Or was he simply alarmed? It was difficult to tell.

"I'm afraid I can't speak for Mr. Carstens. Did he indicate to you that he intends to help her?"

Now Kellogg was thoroughly annoyed with Gideon. "He told me he was going to do what she asked, but that he had to get the money from something he trusted and that would take some time."

"He may have said he needed to get the money from a trust," Gideon suggested.

"Yeah, that's it. That's what he said. So what's taking so long?"

"Perhaps Mr. Carstens didn't explain himself clearly," Gideon said patiently. "A trust is a financial instrument that allows a third party, a trustee if you will, to hold assets on behalf of a beneficiary."

"I don't know what any of that means," Kellogg admitted grudgingly.

"Then let me explain it this way. Suppose I'm

wealthy and I have a son who is still young. I don't want to leave him my fortune outright because he might squander it, so I leave it to him in a trust. I name a trustee, who is literally a person whom I trust, to manage the money and take care of my son. I can also make rules about when my son can take money out of the trust and why and how much, and I can designate how much authority the trustee has over distributing the money. I can set it up in any number of ways, but the purpose is to provide money to support my son while not allowing him to spend all the money on riotous living."

"And somebody left the captain one of these trusts?"

"So it would appear, if he told you he has one, but as I said, I cannot discuss my client's business with you."

"All right, all right. So who is this trustee who decides if the captain gets his money or not?"

"You will have to ask Mr. Carstens that."

"Don't you know?"

"Of course I do but—"

"—but you can't discuss it with me," Kellogg said, completely exasperated. "What I don't understand is why it's taking so long to get the money."

"I'm not sure what you consider a long time, but it has only been a few days since Mr. Carstens first consulted me. And a trust is not a bank

104

account, with money just sitting there waiting to be spent. It is invested, and turning those investments into cash can take some time."

"How much time?"

Gideon managed a nonchalant shrug. "I really don't know. You'll have to—"

"—ask Mr. Carstens. I understand. You're not going to answer any of my questions or tell me anything."

"I think I've answered as many of your questions as I can, Sergeant Kellogg. I only wish I could be more helpful."

"I wish you could, too," Kellogg said, standing up with all the dignity he could muster. He stormed out without another word.

Poor Smith. He'd be very upset if Kellogg didn't at least allow him to show him to the door.

Elizabeth took a cab up to Twenty-eighth Street to Dan the Dude's Saloon. She didn't even bother wearing a veil or trying to disguise herself. If Thornton was going to ruin her, what did it matter if she was seen going into a saloon? Well, going down the alley beside the saloon, at least, where a nondescript side door led to a room only a handful of people even knew existed.

Elizabeth rapped out the correct series of knocks and was admitted after someone had given her a cursory glance through the sliding panel.

"Contessa," the doorkeeper greeted her happily,

using the honorary title she had earned. "What brings you to our little den of iniquity?"

"How are you doing, Spuds?" she asked the man whose face was as wrinkled as the last potato in the bushel.

"I'm right as rain. I guess you're here to see the Old Man."

"If he's in."

"He is at the moment."

"Good. I'll find him, then."

She set off down the narrow hallway that ended in a large room furnished with several tables. A few men had gathered around one to play cards, and they all looked up and greeted her enthusiastically. She had known every one of them since she was a young girl, and she returned the greetings.

"I hear you're getting married," one said slyly.

"Yeah, to a Mr. Bates." They all laughed at that, even Elizabeth, because "Mr. Bates" was what con men called a mark.

"I'm afraid so, but you'll never con him, I promise you."

"Lizzie," the Old Man said, having come out of his office to see what the laughter was about. He looked as elegant as ever with his silver mane of hair and his impeccably tailored suit. "What a nice surprise."

"It won't be so nice when you find out why I'm here."

The Old Man frowned, but he never revealed his true feelings, so he didn't appear to be too worried as he escorted her into his utilitarian office and closed the door. When she was seated in the wooden chair beside his desk, he said, "Now tell me what has you all worried."

"Oscar Thornton saw my engagement announcement, and he showed up at Gideon's office."

He frowned again, his blue eyes narrowing. "I'm going to assume he wants his money."

"Yes, and if he doesn't get it, he's going to tell the newspapers that Gideon is marrying a con artist."

"That's troublesome," he said with characteristic understatement.

"That's blackmail, but I spent most of last night thinking about this, and I realized that I can simply blackmail him right back."

"And how can you do that?"

Elizabeth paused a moment for effect, certain he was going to be impressed by her reasoning. "By threatening to tell the newspapers how he tried to cheat the government during the war."

But the Old Man leaned back in his chair and shook his head. "That will never work, Lizzie, and it will only come back on you."

CHAPTER FIVE

When Gideon arrived home that evening, he was delighted to find Elizabeth in the parlor with his mother. At least he was delighted until he realized Elizabeth had been crying.

She smiled when she saw him and hurried over to greet him, but he could see her eyes were still wet and a little red. They were also very sad.

"What is it? Is it Thornton? Has he—"

"No, nothing like that," she hastily assured him. "I just . . . I was just asking your mother's advice about something and . . ."

"And my advice was a bit upsetting, I'm afraid," his mother said apologetically.

"Advice about what? And why would it be upsetting?"

"Come in and sit down and we'll tell you, dear," his mother said.

Elizabeth took his hand, led him to the sofa nearest the fire and sat down beside him. His mother sat in a chair nearby, her sewing forgotten in her lap.

"Now tell me what this is all about," he said.

"I went to see the Old Man today," Elizabeth said.

Gideon tried not to let his voice reflect his dismay over this necessity. "I hope he was helpful."

"He was. You see, I've been thinking about how we can handle Thornton. We can't give him any money, of course, because then he'll just keep wanting more and more."

"And you certainly aren't going to start running cons on other people in order to raise that money," Gideon said, which was what he'd feared Mr. Miles would suggest.

"Of course not," she agreed, to his relief. "But I thought that if turnabout is fair play, then why shouldn't we threaten to ruin Thornton's reputation in return? We know an awful lot about him that would create quite a scandal."

Blackmailing a blackmailer didn't sound like a very promising strategy, but before he could point this out, his mother said, "Elizabeth suggested this idea to her father, but he did not think it would work, so she came to me. She thought perhaps Mr. Miles simply didn't understand how people in society think and how the slightest hint of scandal can ruin a person's reputation."

Which was true enough, but . . . "Only if you're a female," he said.

"Which is so unfair!" Elizabeth said, color darkening her cheeks. "The things we know about Thornton should ruin him!"

"You're right, my darling," Gideon said, taking her hand in both of his. "Or at least you should be. He tried to sell defective rifles to the army."

"And he killed his wife," Elizabeth reminded him.

"For which he should be imprisoned," his mother said. Thornton's wife had been his mother's beloved cousin. "Unfortunately, we have no proof of it."

"Except that he confessed it to me," Elizabeth said bitterly.

"Which he would deny, if you accused him," Gideon said.

"Even the rifles wouldn't cause that much of a scandal," his mother said. "Far too many men made fortunes selling shoddy equipment to the government during the war."

"And a lot of men would even admire his initiative," Gideon said.

"So you're saying that society would overlook all of Thornton's sins," Elizabeth said angrily.

"Sadly, yes," Gideon said.

She sighed. "But not mine."

"It isn't fair, I know," his mother said. "But women are held to a much higher standard. The slightest whiff of scandal and—"

"And they are ruined." She fumed for a moment. "It's too bad Gideon isn't a middle-aged millionaire. Then he could marry anyone he liked and society would end up accepting her."

"I suppose middle-aged millionaires do occasionally marry unsuitable young ladies," his mother said, "but you're wrong if you think they are accepted by society."

"They aren't?" Elizabeth asked in surprise.

His mother shook her head. "They are invited places and are seen everywhere with their wealthy husbands, but society women have a thousand ways to make those poor girls feel uncomfortable and unwelcome. You're too young to remember, but when William Vanderbilt married Alva, no one wanted to know her at all. She was from Alabama, of all places. Mrs. Astor completely refused to acknowledge her."

"Mrs. Astor?" Elizabeth asked.

"Caroline Astor, the woman who invented the Four Hundred," Gideon explained.

"He means she was the one who came up with the idea that there were only four hundred people in New York society who were worth knowing and therefore important enough to invite to her parties," his mother added.

Elizabeth was clearly astonished. "Why was she influential enough to do something like that?"

"Because of her social position. She was the leading hostess in New York at the time," his mother said.

"And what happened to this Alva after Mrs. Astor snubbed her?"

His mother smiled. She loved telling these

old stories. "Alva Vanderbilt held the biggest masquerade ball New York had ever seen. They say she invited a thousand people."

"That's a lot more than four hundred," Elizabeth pointed out.

"She wasn't as strict as Mrs. Astor," Gideon said.

"No, she wasn't," his mother agreed. "Everyone who was anyone was invited except Caroline Astor's daughter, Carrie."

"But Mrs. Astor wouldn't care, would she? Not if she was so important," Elizabeth asked.

"Maybe not, but Carrie cared very much. All her friends were going, after all, and she already had a costume. When asked why Carrie was not invited, Alva Vanderbilt said she couldn't possibly invite Carrie because she didn't know her mother. You see, Caroline Astor had never called on Alva socially. This gave Alva the perfect excuse not to invite Carrie. So to save her daughter the pain of missing the party, Mrs. Astor had to call on Alva. Alva then invited Caroline and Carrie both to the party. They attended, thereby granting Alva the ultimate social acceptance."

"So I guess I'll have to throw a party for a thousand people if I want people to forget I'm a con artist," Elizabeth said with a sigh.

"You'd also have to be married to a millionaire who can afford a party like that," Gideon said.

"Since neither of those things is going to happen," his mother said sternly, "you need to make sure no one finds out you're a . . . You're anything other than what you appear to be."

"That Mrs. Vanderbilt was a clever woman, though," Elizabeth said. "Whatever happened to her?"

His mother smiled again, because this part of the story was even better. "She eventually divorced William Vanderbilt and married Oliver Belmont. She's our own Mrs. Belmont."

"The lady who gives all that money to support woman suffrage?" Elizabeth asked in awe.

"The very same."

Elizabeth sat back on the sofa and got a dreamy look on her face. Gideon had seen that look before, and it terrified him. "What are you thinking?"

"I'm thinking Alva Belmont is a pretty good con artist."

Gideon frowned, but his mother chuckled appreciatively.

Elizabeth didn't even notice. "I'm also thinking that there's a way around this business with Thornton. We just haven't thought of it yet."

"Elizabeth, dear," his mother said in her gentlest voice, "you do have to be careful."

Elizabeth's beautiful blue eyes sparked at the reminder. "Oh, I understand. The slightest breath of scandal will ruin me. Gideon will still marry me, because he's too honorable to desert me, but his friends will snub him and he'll lose clients and our lives will be miserable."

"Elizabeth," Gideon tried, but to his horror he couldn't think of a single comforting thing to say because she was absolutely right. Certainly, he would never desert her, no matter what happened. He loved her too much. But he couldn't bear the thought of her being so unhappy. "None of that would matter to me, darling."

She squeezed the hand still holding hers. "Don't worry. I'm not going to do anything foolish. I may not understand the world you live in, but I'm not going to break the rules if I can help it, because I want to live in it with you."

"And Elizabeth is probably right," his mother said with forced enthusiasm. "There must be a way to beat Oscar Thornton. We just haven't thought of it yet."

Gideon was finding it difficult to concentrate on his work the next morning. He'd spent most of the previous night trying to think of a way to deal with Thornton's extortion demands and had come to the conclusion that he and Elizabeth would need to move to Europe and just hope Thornton didn't find them there. The fact that he had no desire to move to Europe and no reason to think Elizabeth did, either, told him this was a ridiculous solution to their problem, but so far it was all he could come up with.

A rap on the door distracted him, and grateful for the interruption, he looked up as Smith stepped into his office.

"Mr. Miles is here," he said, not bothering to hide his disapproval. Obviously, Mr. Miles did not have an appointment.

"Show him in." Gideon rose to greet Elizabeth's father, not sure whether he should feel dread or anticipation at this visit. Perhaps he should feel both.

"Gideon, thank you for seeing me on such short notice," Mr. Miles said for Smith's benefit.

Gideon came around his desk to shake the hand Mr. Miles offered. "You know you're always welcome, sir. Thank you, Smith."

Smith managed one more disapproving frown before slipping quietly from the room.

"I hate to upset your man like that," Mr. Miles said with a small smile, "but this really couldn't wait."

Gideon invited him to sit down in one of the client chairs while he returned to his own, safely behind his large and imposing desk. His future father-in-law would not be here with good news. "I guess this is about Thornton."

"Of course it is. I can't believe he's making a nuisance of himself again."

"I can't believe it, either, but here we are."

"Lizzie came to see me yesterday."

"I know. She told me. She went to see my mother after she left you. She thought you were wrong about blackmailing Thornton and wanted my mother to confirm it."

"I hope Mrs. Bates told her I was right."

Gideon had to smile at his worried frown. Mr. Miles was not ordinarily overly concerned about his children. "She did. She told Elizabeth in no uncertain terms that she can't possibly ruin Thornton's reputation no matter what she reveals about him."

"Good, then perhaps we can persuade Lizzie to leave this to me."

That was the part Gideon had been both hoping for and dreading. "To you?"

"Yes. We should have made certain Thornton couldn't come back, so this time we need to take care of him once and for all."

"Once and for all?" Gideon echoed in alarm. "You're not going to kill him, are you?"

Mr. Miles stared at him in amazement. "What on earth gave you that idea? Murder is a very messy crime and draws far too much of the wrong kind of attention."

"Then how can you be sure Thornton won't just come back again and again?"

"By making sure he can't ever show his face in New York City, and if he does, he will be laughed out of town."

"Can you do that?"

"I'm going to try."

"But how—?" Gideon began but caught himself. "No, don't tell me."

"I wasn't going to."

Gideon wasn't sure whether to be insulted or not.

"Just be sure you don't forbid Lizzie from participating," Mr. Miles said.

Now Gideon was really confused. "Are you going to use her somehow?"

"No, but if you forbid her from it, she'll insist on helping. We can't have that. It's too dangerous."

"Oh yes, I see."

"I'm glad. Now Jake tells me somebody is trying to run the Spanish Prisoner on one of your friends."

Gideon blinked at the abrupt change of subject but he said, "That's what Elizabeth thinks."

"She's probably right. Your friend is lucky that you recognized it."

"I didn't recognize it. I've never heard of the Spanish Prisoner before."

"But you knew something was up and asked Lizzie to help."

"Then I'm the lucky one, because I had Elizabeth to consult."

"I'm glad you realize that. You fascinate me, Gideon. I've never known a man like you before."

Once again, Gideon didn't know whether to

be flattered or insulted. "I don't think I'm that unusual."

"Oh, but you are. Grifters have a saying, 'You can't cheat an honest man.' "

"I'm sure that's true."

"It is, but you see, it's also a joke, because no men are truly honest."

"But that isn't true," Gideon said, sure he was right.

Mr. Miles smiled sadly. "No, I suppose there are a few. I seldom meet them, though. Lizzie was lucky to find you. No one will ever take advantage of her as long as she has you to protect her."

Now it was Gideon's turn to smile, this time with true amusement. "If you think Elizabeth needs me to protect her, you don't know your daughter as well as you think."

"Well, I'm sure of one thing. The two of you make a formidable team."

Gideon hoped he was right. "I've changed my mind. I'd like to know what you have planned for Thornton."

"Nothing yet, but no blood will be shed, I assure you."

Only later, after Mr. Miles had gone, did Gideon realize the Old Man hadn't agreed to tell him anything at all.

"What is this all about?" Anna asked, eyeing Elizabeth with good-humored suspicion. They were seated in the parlor of Cybil's house in the dying sunlight of the winter afternoon. Anna had come by after her Thursday classes at Hunter College were over, at Elizabeth's invitation.

"I need your help with something."

Anna didn't actually rub her hands together in glee, but she did sit up straighter in her chair and her blue eyes sparkled with delight. How had Elizabeth ever thought her plain? In the year since they'd met, Anna had grown positively beautiful. Confidence could do that for a woman. "Do you want me to shoot you again?"

Elizabeth couldn't help musing that if Anna had liked boys, she would have been a good match for Jake. Maybe she'd have been able to keep him honest. But then again, maybe not. Jake was probably a hopeless case. Also, Anna didn't like boys, so he and Anna would always just be good friends. "Sadly, no, I don't need you to shoot me again."

"But please say you want me to help you with a con," Anna said.

"Actually, I do."

"Does it involve Thornton? Have you figured out a way to get rid of him?" she asked eagerly.

"No, I'm going to leave that up to the Old Man."

"You are?" Anna looked disappointed.

"I know, I'm furious about it, too, but he came over last night and we talked it over. He thinks it's too dangerous for me to be involved, and he's probably right, although I'd never tell him that."

"Then is your father the one who needs my help?"

"No, I do. I'm going to run a con of my own."

"Not on Thornton, though."

"No."

"So what do you need me to do?"

"I need you to be the roper."

"Like a cowboy?" Anna asked, highly amused.

That made Elizabeth laugh. "Not exactly. Your job is to rope in the mark and help me tell the tale."

"I remember what the tale is. That's the story you tell the mark to get him interested."

"That's right. Your part is easy but very important. You'll be helping me, and we just need to make sure the mark meets the inside man and knows who he is."

"Don't you mean the mark needs to know who the inside man is supposed to be? Because the tale is all made up, isn't it?"

"Oh, Anna, I fear we have completely corrupted you," Elizabeth said.

"And thank heaven you did. You have no idea how dull my life was before I met you, Elizabeth."

Actually, Elizabeth did know, but since they'd met, Anna had spent time in prison and started attending college and committed a murder, albeit a phony one. Not bad for the first year. "Are you sure you want to do this?"

"Of course I'm sure. Just tell me who the mark is."

"Rosemary Westerly."

Oscar Thornton pushed away his empty plate, glanced around the crowded restaurant, and pulled out his pocket watch to check the time. The days moved so slowly now. Why had he thought returning to New York City was a good idea? He'd left here, nearly bankrupt, over a year ago. What had made him think his luck would be different this time?

But it was already different, he reminded himself. If he hadn't returned to New York, he never would have seen the newspaper, and he wouldn't have known that Elizabeth Miles was still alive. So that had been a good thing.

If only he hadn't given Bates an entire month to come up with the money. He just might die of boredom in the meantime if he didn't find something useful to do with his time.

Thornton looked up in annoyance as a man passing behind him bumped his chair.

"Excuse me," the fellow muttered. "It's so crowded in here." Then he stopped and frowned. "Thornton? Oscar Thornton?"

Thornton frowned back at the man who did look familiar. "How do I know you?"

The man smiled, obviously pleased to have his suspicion confirmed. "I'm Leo Vo—" He caught himself and glanced around guiltily, as if worried someone might have heard. Then he lowered his voice and leaned in close to Thornton's ear. "I was Leo Volker, but I've changed my name. I'm Vane now."

Thornton nodded. Lots of people with German names had changed them during the war. Too many "good Americans" were reporting everyone with German ancestry to the American Protective League as spies, even though virtually none of them were.

"I sold you some rifles last year," Volker-Vane recalled. His grin widened. "I realized later that I should've waited, though. I'll bet you made a fortune on them."

Thornton hadn't made a dime on them, but he wasn't about to admit that to Vane. "I remember you now. I hope you did as well in the war as I did."

Vane's smile vanished. "Not as well as some, I'm afraid, but I did all right. Actually, I wonder if you might have something going that I could get in on."

He did all right, eh? "I might. Are you heading to an appointment now?"

"I was going to run some errands, but they can wait if you have time. I'd rather talk about making money."

"I've got a suite upstairs," Thornton said, throwing his napkin onto the table. "We can talk there."

Thornton had chosen the hotel because it was cheap, but his suite was at least presentable. The maid had cleaned it that morning and stacked all his newspapers neatly. He and Vane settled down in the two upholstered chairs, smoked some cigars that Thornton had produced and drank a few shots of the whiskey he kept for visitors. Thornton felt obligated to make a remark about enjoying the liquor while they could, but he really didn't find the prospect of prohibition very funny.

Thornton outlined several deals he was working on. He'd struggled for a while after the debacle with the phony army contract, but only a fool could have failed to make money during the war. He'd managed to scrape together enough cash to buy up a few odds and ends that the army really had bought—unlike the deal that Vanderslice and Bates had arranged where his rifles and his money had completely vanished—and for far more than they were worth. He'd then used that money to buy more matériel and had managed to earn back at least a small part of the fortune he had lost. Now he was looking for more opportunities in the peacetime markets, and Vane could have some valuable connections.

But after half an hour, Thornton came to an unfortunate conclusion. "So you don't actually have any cash to invest right now."

"Not at this moment, but I will soon," Vane said with apparent confidence. "I have a . . . a project I'm working on, and when it's over, I'll have plenty of money."

"What kind of a project is it?" Thornton asked with genuine interest. "Maybe I'd be interested in it, too."

"It's not really a business deal," Vane said apologetically. "It's something personal."

"Something personal that will earn a lot of money?" Thornton didn't bother to hide his skepticism. "Do you have a rich uncle on his deathbed?"

Vane laughed at that. "Not exactly, but something like that."

"Then come back to see me when he's dead," Thornton said.

They talked for a few more minutes without making any more progress. Then Vane pulled out his overstuffed wallet and located a business card. "How long will you be in town?" he asked, handing the card to Thornton.

"A month or so," Thornton said, managing not to sigh.

"I'll have the money before then," Vane assured him, stuffing his wallet back into his coat pocket. "I'll let you know when I'm ready." He took his leave, pumping Thornton's hand vigorously before stepping out the door.

Thornton shook his head when the man was gone. Vane or Volker or whatever he called himself was probably never going to see a penny of his rich uncle's money.

Later, when he had finished reading all the newspapers he'd purchased that morning and was thinking about going out for the afternoon editions, Thornton noticed an envelope on the floor beside the chair where Vane had been sitting.

It was postmarked from Mexico. Vane had obviously dropped it, probably when he pulled out his wallet. Since the envelope had already been opened, Thornton didn't hesitate to pull out the letter inside.

"Dear Cousin," it began. "I have arrived safely in Mexico. I will always be grateful for the great risks you took helping me to escape from the Fatherland. I know it will be difficult for you to get me into America, so I am prepared to wait. Perhaps you can come to me and dispose of some of my holdings in American corporations. Would you be able to raise enough money to help me by doing that? I will be anxiously awaiting your reply. Please advise me. Your loving cousin, Berta."

How interesting. Was Cousin Berta the relative he expected to get money from? It seemed unlikely that anyone had escaped from Germany with any money at all, but who knew? If her holdings were in American securities, then maybe she hadn't been able to negotiate them during the war. In any event, Vane would have the devil's own time of it getting her into the United States. Nobody wanted any foreigners coming in just now, with the threat of communists and anarchists looming all over Europe, and Germans had been the first ones barred. Berta's securities were another story, however. Maybe that was Vane's plan, to meet her in Mexico and relieve her of them. If he succeeded in that, Thornton would happily advise him about what he should do next.

Anna and Elizabeth had arrived early at Delmonico's Restaurant on Fifth Avenue and Forty-fourth Street. Elizabeth wanted to make sure everything was arranged, although she should have known it would be. The landmark restaurant, known to locals as "the Citadel," was doing a brisk business with Saturday shoppers and businessmen enjoying their time off from their offices, so she and Anna easily got lost in the crowd.

The two of them were sitting in chairs off in a corner of the restaurant's ornate lobby where they wouldn't be immediately noticed when they saw Rosemary enter. She wore a stylish gown of emerald green that Elizabeth envied. Perhaps she should have accepted Rosemary's offer to introduce her to her modiste.

Anna rose and waved to catch Rosemary's attention.

"I feel so strange coming into a restaurant unescorted," Rosemary marveled when she had made her way over. Until the war, few respectable eateries would seat women who did not have a male escort, and the few who did restricted them to ladies-only dining areas.

"But isn't it nice to be able to dine out with a friend without dragging along a man who doesn't want to be there?" Anna said.

"I suppose." Rosemary didn't look convinced. Perhaps she thought a male escort was an essential accessory, like a hat and gloves.

"I'm so glad you were able to meet me today," Anna said, and Elizabeth knew she wasn't lying. Planning this luncheon engagement had thrilled her. "I haven't seen you in ages, and we have so much to catch up on."

Elizabeth stood up then. Rosemary noticed her for the first time and stiffened with what might have been alarm. Or maybe Elizabeth was just hoping she was alarmed.

"You know Elizabeth, don't you?" Anna was saying as if oblivious to Rosemary's reaction. "She asked if she could join us, and I thought it would be more fun with three of us, don't you?"

Rosemary's smile was slightly strained, but Elizabeth hastened to reassure her. "I know we got off to an awkward start, Rosemary, but I thought about what you said, and I agree. Logan and Gideon would want us to be friends."

"I'm so glad you feel that way," Rosemary said, apparently relieved. "I would hate for there to be any tension in our relationship."

"Elizabeth?" a male voice asked.

All three women looked up in surprise. A handsome young man in a well-tailored suit had approached them. His dark curls were artfully arranged to appear tousled, and his dark eyes danced with pleasure. A neat mustache and goatee gave him a continental appearance. He stood staring at Elizabeth with a questioning smile.

"Elizabeth Miles?" he asked again.

"Percy, is that you?" Elizabeth said in wonder.

"Indeed it is. I wasn't sure it was really you, though. You're all grown up, and I never expected to see you in New York in any case."

"I would never have expected to see you here, either," she said. "What on earth are you doing in America?"

He glanced around nervously and put his finger to his lips in a signal for her to be quiet. "No one knows I'm here. It's all very hush-hush, I'm afraid." His British accent was delightful, and Rosemary and Anna were obviously impressed.

"Then is it all right if I introduce you to my friends or is your true identity a state secret or something?" she teased.

"Not a state secret, certainly," he assured her with good humor, nodding politely to the other ladies.

"Miss Westerly and Miss Vanderslice, may I present an old friend of our family, Mr. Percy Hyde-Langdon? Or should I say Earl Hyde-Langdon, now that your dear father is gone. I'm very sorry, Percy. We were all so sad to hear of his passing."

"Thank you. We miss him terribly, as you can imagine."

"He was such a dear man," Elizabeth said, lost in her memories for a moment.

"Did you say Earl Hyde-Langdon?" Rosemary asked, breaking the spell.

He managed a polite smile. "Actually, I'm more correctly the Earl of Hartwood, but just Percy to my friends, and I hope we shall be great friends, Miss Westerly."

Obviously, she did, too. She offered him her hand, which he raised to his lips instead of shaking it. That brought the color to her pale cheeks and the light of calculation to her pale eyes.

Not to be outdone, Anna gave him her hand as well, and he obligingly kissed it, too.

"I suppose you ladies are meeting someone here for luncheon," Percy said.

"Oh no," Rosemary said before anyone else could speak. "We were going to enjoy a little hen party, just the three of us, but if you aren't otherwise engaged, Sir Percy, perhaps you'd join us."

"I'd hate to ruin your little tête-à-tête," Percy said with just the proper amount of insincere regret, making it clear he would like nothing better than to do just that.

"We'd love to have you join us," Anna said. "We can talk to each other any time, but how often do we get to lunch with an earl?"

"I am forever in your debt. I do hate eating alone. One receives the oddest stares, or even worse, offers of company from people one would never wish to dine with. You ladies have saved me."

Percy took care of getting the maître d's attention and then having them seated. The waiter was very attentive, getting them something to drink and then explaining the menu to them. At long last, their orders placed, he left them to themselves.

"How do you and Elizabeth know each other?" Anna asked as soon as the waiter was gone.

He glanced at Elizabeth, who said, "We lived in England for . . . oh, I guess it was almost two years, back before the war. My father had business interests there, and he thought it would be good for me to live abroad for a while."

"And you met the earl in England?" Anna asked.

Elizabeth and Percy exchanged an amused glance. "Percy's family sort of took us under their wing," she said.

"Mama is an American, you see," Percy said.

"She and my mother were old friends," Elizabeth added. "So she treated us like family. All those house parties at Hartwood . . ." Elizabeth sighed at the nonexistent memories.

"It was a very different time," Percy said.

"Please tell me the war didn't reach Hartwood," Elizabeth said.

"No, fortunately, although all the horses are gone," he added sadly.

"Oh no, all those beautiful horses from your stables?" Elizabeth said.

"Yes, the army took them for the war. There's hardly a horse left in England now, I'm afraid. That's one reason I'm here, to buy some breeding stock."

"Now you must tell us, Sir Percy, why your visit here is a secret," Rosemary said. "And it can't be because you're buying horses."

"It's Lord Percy," Anna informed her. "That's right, isn't it, Lord Percy?"

"Yes, but you may simply call me Percy," he assured them both. "I do not wish to call undue attention to myself."

"But why?" Rosemary asked, plainly not willing to be distracted.

Percy glanced around, as if checking for eaves-droppers. Finding none, he leaned in a little closer and lowered his voice. "I'm here on behalf of the British government. I'll be negotiating some . . . Well, some business arrangements. I don't want to bore you ladies with the details."

"Does that have to be a secret?" Anna asked.

Percy shrugged one shoulder. "Not particularly, but if word got out that I am in the city, I'm afraid all the hostesses would insist on inviting me to parties and balls, and I won't have time for anything else."

"But can't you meet businessmen at parties and balls?" Rosemary asked.

"Perhaps I could," Percy said dismissively. He turned to Elizabeth. "How are your dear parents?"

"They're very well, thank you."

"Still in South Dakota or are they here with you?"

"Still in South Dakota and thankful they left England when they did."

"They got out just in time," Percy said with a sigh. "The German U-boats torpedoed the very next ship."

"Were you in the army, Lord Percy?" Rosemary asked.

Percy gave her a small smile. "Sadly, no. My health would not allow, but I was able to work as a diplomat, traveling back and forth to

America to ask our friends here for assistance."

"What does your wife think of all this travel, Lord Percy?" Plainly, Rosemary loved saying Lord Percy.

"Unfortunately, I am not married as yet. I haven't had time to even think of such a thing because of the war and my duties abroad." He actually looked sad, as if not having found a wife was somewhat of a tragedy. He turned to Elizabeth. "I should have followed my father's example and chosen an American bride."

"Not Elizabeth," Rosemary said with undisguised satisfaction. "She's already engaged."

Percy feigned disappointment. "I see I have missed my chance. I should have proposed to you before you left England. I was at least half in love with you back then, you know."

"Nonsense!" Elizabeth scoffed good-naturedly. "We were children, and you barely tolerated me. Don't think I didn't see those faces you pulled whenever your mother told you to take me riding."

"What does one call the wife of an earl?" Rosemary said in an obvious effort to get Percy's attention back. "I know a duke's wife is a duchess, but . . ."

"She's a countess," Elizabeth reported with a measure of satisfaction.

"A countess," Rosemary echoed in obvious delight. It really was a lovely title, one guaranteed to charm any American girl. Rosemary was appropriately charmed. "What sort of place is Hartwood, Lord Percy?"

"It's absolutely lovely," he said with affection. "The manor house dates back to the sixteenth century, but every earl has added on to it, so now it has about seventy rooms."

"Seventy!" Rosemary nearly yelped.

"So I'm told. I've never actually counted them. The grounds are what I love most about it, though. Acres and acres of rolling hills. Before the war, we kept a stable of Thoroughbreds, and the hunting was superb."

"But you said the horses are gone," Anna recalled sadly.

"Yes." Percy shook his head. "As I said, I hope to replenish our stables during my sojourn here. We can use motorcars for so many things nowadays, but one can't hunt in a motorcar, can one?"

"Hartwood sounds heavenly," Rosemary said.

"It truly is, but enough about me," Percy said. "Tell me about yourselves. Rosemary, do you live here in the city?"

"Yes, I've been here all my life, although we do go to Newport in the summers."

"Newport?"

"It's a town in Rhode Island," Anna explained.

Percy apparently didn't know whether to be impressed or not.

"Do you ever get to London, Lord Percy?" Rosemary asked.

"Oh yes. We have a house there that we use during the season and when I'm in Parliament."

"Parliament?" Rosemary echoed again, this time almost comically interested. "Isn't that like our Congress?"

"Similar, yes. I serve in the House of Lords. It's all rather boring, but one must do one's part, mustn't one?"

"Indeed," Rosemary murmured.

"Tell me, Rosemary, are you married?"

"Rosemary is engaged," Anna said before she could speak for herself. "Her fiancé was in the war, and he's just gotten home."

"How wonderful for you."

"Yes, it is." But for some reason, Rosemary did not seem as full of wonder as she should have been. "Tell me, Lord Percy, would you really be upset to be invited to a party or two? My mother has been wanting to have a small gathering to welcome my fiancé home, and I would love it if you could attend."

"I suppose something like that wouldn't be too much of a distraction, and I should very much like to meet the man who is lucky enough to have captured your heart, Miss Westerly."

Rosemary's pale cheeks pinkened at that. "You are too kind, Lord Percy. I'm sure Logan would love to meet you as well." Then she seemed to remember that the two of them were not alone. "And of course both of you will be invited, and Gideon, too. Anna, is there someone you would like to bring as an escort?" Did her question seem a bit barbed? Elizabeth thought so.

"No one I can think of," Anna said, unfazed. She smiled at Percy. "I'm the only lady at this table who isn't engaged."

"Then perhaps you'd allow me to escort you, Miss Vanderslice," Percy said gallantly.

"I can't think of anything that would please me more," Anna said, pretending not to notice how Rosemary's face had flushed unbecomingly.

Their food arrived at that moment, so they were spared whatever remark Rosemary would have made.

When they had been served and begun to eat, Anna said, "How long do you plan to stay in the city, Lord Percy?"

"As long as my business takes me. A month or two, most likely, perhaps even longer."

"You'll have to stay longer if you want to find an American bride," Anna said sweetly.

"I don't know about that," Rosemary said with an odd smile. "You might be surprised how many American girls would like to be a countess."

CHAPTER SIX

Oscar Thornton was trying to decide whether to read another newspaper, go for a walk or take a nap when someone knocked on his hotel room door on Saturday afternoon. He opened it to find Leo Vane looking harried. "Thornton, I'm so glad I caught you in. I was wondering if you found a letter that belongs to me. I've been looking everywhere for it, and I finally realized I might have dropped it when I was here the other day."

"From Mexico?" Thornton asked with a knowing smile.

"Yes, that's the one. Then you did find it," Vane said, obviously relieved.

Thornton stood back, silently inviting Vane inside. "I've been wondering if I should try to return it to you, but then I figured if it was important, you'd come for it."

"It's not really important, but it's private and . . ."

"And you wouldn't want it to fall into the wrong hands," Thornton guessed.

As he'd expected, Vane's eyes widened in

alarm. "I don't know what you're talking about," he said with very little conviction.

"If I'm not mistaken, you're considering smuggling a German national into the United States without the proper papers. I can't imagine you'd want that generally known."

"You read the letter," Vane accused in an effort to regain the high ground.

"I looked at it, yes. I thought it might be a letter I dropped myself, so naturally I checked to see what it was."

"And now you know it does not belong to you. May I have it back, please?" he asked stiffly.

Thornton went over to the desk in the corner of his suite and retrieved the letter. Vane snatched it from his fingers and stuffed it into his coat pocket without even looking at it. "What are you planning to do? Report me to the League?"

"The American Protective League?" Thornton asked tauntingly. "Are they still active now that the war is over?"

Vane merely glared back at him.

"Calm down, Volker," Thornton said, pleased to see him wince at the name. "I have no intention of turning you over to the League or anyone else. What I am interested in is what you intend to do about your cousin and her American holdings."

Vane rubbed a hand over his face. "I . . . I honestly don't know."

"Then sit down and we'll have a drink, and you

140

can tell me more about this Berta. Maybe I can help you."

"You'd help me?" Vane asked in astonishment.

"If we can work out a suitable arrangement, yes, I would be happy to help you. Now sit down before you collapse."

Indeed, Vane did look more than a bit unsteady. He took the offered seat and the glass of whiskey Thornton poured for him.

"Now tell me about dear Berta."

"She's my cousin, as I'm sure you know now. I had a lot of relatives in Germany, but most of them died in the war. Some of them, most of the men that is, were in the army, of course, but the civilians didn't fare too well, either. Things were very bad there at the end. No one had enough food, and no one had any money."

"And yet Berta apparently has a lot of money."

"Not money. Her father had invested heavily in American industries and railroads, but when the war started, he was unable to escape Germany or to do anything with his holdings. He couldn't even admit he owned them for fear they would be confiscated by the German government."

That seemed likely to Thornton, so he nodded for Vane to continue.

"After the war ended, Berta was the only one left of her family. I was able to arrange for her to escape to Mexico, but it took every penny I had. She was able to smuggle out her valuables

141

in a trunk with a false bottom. She brought the securities and a lot of jewelry that had been in her family. She has promised me half of her fortune if I can get her to America."

"How much does she have?"

"I believe the securities she is holding would be worth over half a million dollars, but it may be even more than that."

Thornton managed not to react to that amazing sum. "Why doesn't she just cash them in herself in Mexico?"

"She'd only get about thirty percent of what they're worth there, which is why I had planned to advance her the money to get her into the United States. Then she'll more than repay me when she gets here."

"But," Thornton remembered, "you spent all your money just getting her as far as Mexico."

"Yes," Vane said sadly. "I was hoping to get in on a deal with you and make some more money, but . . ."

"But you'd need some money to invest first," Thornton said impatiently. The man was an idiot. "What are you planning to do now?"

Vane shrugged. "I was going to go down to Mexico and get some of her securities so I can bring them to New York and cash them in here. We'll get their true value that way. Then I'll use that money to hire a boat or even buy one if I have to in order to smuggle her into New York."

"That sounds like a good plan," Thornton said.

Vane sighed. "Except that I don't even have enough money to get myself to Mexico in the first place."

"How much would you need?" Thornton asked.

"About five hundred dollars, but I'll repay you with interest as soon as I get back from Mexico," Vane said.

"I don't care about the interest on five hundred dollars. I can finance the whole deal, but I want a cut."

"A cut of what?" Vane asked nervously.

"Of your half. How much will you give me?"

"I . . . I'd be willing to give you, uh, thirty percent."

"I want half."

"Half!" Vane croaked.

"How will you get her out of Mexico without my help?"

Vane swallowed. "I don't know."

"Exactly. You need me, and you'll still get a lot of money out of this, at least a hundred twenty-five thousand, by my reckoning. After we're done, I'll help you invest your share so you can make even more. I'd even be willing to advise Berta." More than willing.

"I . . . I suppose I don't really have any choice. I can't just leave Berta all alone down there for heaven knows how long, while I try to raise the money myself."

Thornton pulled out his wallet and counted out five hundred dollars.

Vane didn't bother to pretend he wasn't impressed. "How can I ever thank you, Thornton?"

"The expenses are coming out of your half," Thornton said. "How soon can you leave for Mexico?"

"Did you see it?" Anna whispered to Elizabeth as Gideon helped her off with her coat. He and Anna had just arrived at Cybil's house for the salon on Monday evening, and Gideon had known since the moment Elizabeth had stepped out of her front door to meet him that something was going on.

Something he knew absolutely nothing about.

"See what?" Gideon demanded as he hung Anna's coat on the rack. "And don't bother saying nothing, because I will simply keep asking until you tell me."

"Are you asking if I saw the gossip columns?" Elizabeth asked Anna, as if she really wasn't sure. She was a much better liar than this, so she wasn't really trying to fool him. Somehow that eased his mind a bit.

But only a bit.

"Yes. They were all very mysterious, weren't they?" Anna said.

"Don't tell me Rosemary put something else about us in the newspapers," Gideon said in dismay.

"Not about us," Elizabeth assured him.

Anna's eyes were fairly sparkling with her suppressed glee. "No, not you. The Earl of Hartwood, although they called him the Earl of H. You know how the gossip columns try to be so discreet."

"Who is the Earl of Hartwood?" Gideon asked, although he was sure he would regret it.

"He's the Earl of Hartwood," Elizabeth said quite reasonably. "Who else would he be?"

Knowing Elizabeth, he might be anyone at all, but Gideon said, "All right, why should you care that he's mentioned in the newspapers?"

The two of them exchanged a knowing glance that worried him.

"We just think it curious that Rosemary met him on Saturday and on Sunday he's mentioned in the gossip columns," Elizabeth said.

This was getting more disturbing by the minute. "How do you know she met him on Saturday?"

"Because we were with her," Anna said. "Didn't Elizabeth tell you? We all had luncheon at the Citadel."

"Yes, alone and unescorted," Elizabeth said, as if she were recounting some scandalous deed, "until the earl rescued us. He was quite charming."

145

"Rosemary thought so, anyway," Anna said.

"Anna thought so, too," Elizabeth said. "According to the gossip columns, he's escorting her to Rosemary's party."

"What party?" Gideon asked, thoroughly confused.

"The one she is having to welcome Logan home. We haven't received an invitation to it yet."

"Oh." Which would explain why he knew nothing about it.

"Is Jake here?" Anna asked, peering into the parlor at the guests already gathered.

"Not yet," Elizabeth said. They exchanged another look, and this one made him positively uneasy. "And speaking of Logan, Gideon, have you heard from him?"

"No, I haven't."

"Shouldn't he have received an answer from his French lady friend by now?"

"That depends on how long it takes a letter to go from here to somewhere in France. It takes at least a week to cross the Atlantic each way, and then who knows how long to go from the port to the town where she lives and back again. I imagine mail service is rather unreliable in France just now."

"Yes, I can see that might take a while. Has Sergeant Kellogg been nagging you?"

"Not at all."

"He probably will."

"I'm sure of it. Now tell me more about this earl fellow."

"Well, according to the gossip columns, he's here on some secret mission for the British government," Anna said.

"Did they actually say that in the newspapers?" Gideon asked, shocked.

"Of course not," Elizabeth said. "The earl told us that, which is how Anna knows, but he swore us to secrecy. The gossip columns just said he was hoping to make the acquaintance of some influential Americans while he is here."

"And buy some horses," Anna added.

"Horses?" Gideon echoed in confusion.

"The government took all the horses from his estate for the war effort," Anna told him solemnly. "Do we know anyone who breeds horses?"

"Probably," Gideon said.

"We should introduce them to the earl then," Anna said.

"When is this party going to happen?" Gideon asked. He really needed to meet this earl fellow.

"Soon, I would imagine," Elizabeth said. "Rosemary is very interested in announcing to everyone that she knows an earl."

Poor Logan. "How does Rosemary happen to know this earl?"

"Elizabeth introduced them," Anna said innocently, still peering into the parlor. "Ah, my friend Barbara is here." She wandered off before Gideon could even react.

He turned to Elizabeth. "You introduced them?"

"I had to or appear rude," Elizabeth said sweetly.

"And how do you know an earl?"

"Through the Old Man, of course."

Of course. He saw it all now. Or at least some of it. Or maybe only a tiny little piece of it. But he did see. Which didn't mean he liked it, especially when he thought they'd already agreed that Logan's problems were his own to deal with.

"Elizabeth . . ." he began, not really certain what he could say, but she silenced him with a look.

"Logan is still free to do whatever he likes with his future. I wouldn't dream of interfering with that."

She was, he could easily see, telling the truth. But this was Elizabeth, and she had a knack for using even the truth in ways he had never dreamed it could be used. He would just have to wait until the party to figure out what was going on.

Gideon had just arrived at his office the next morning when Smith announced that Logan Carstens would like to see him if he had a moment.

"Normally, I wouldn't dream of bothering you, Mr. Bates," Smith explained, "but Mr. Carstens seems rather upset, and I thought perhaps it was an emergency."

Thinking Logan might well have heard from Noelle by now, he told Smith to show Logan in.

Logan did look upset, but not in the way Gideon had expected. When Logan had slumped down into one of the client chairs, Gideon said, "Have you heard from Noelle?"

"I . . . I'm not really certain," he said with a sad smile.

"What does that mean?"

He pulled an envelope out of his coat pocket. "Kellogg came to see me yesterday. He's had another letter from Noelle."

"Why didn't she write directly to you this time?"

"Apparently, she hadn't yet received my letter when she wrote this one."

"What does she say?"

"I wrote out a translation for you, but what she says is that she's desperate to escape France because she is carrying my child. Her family has discovered her shame and has thrown her out, and she's begging me to send for her."

Just what he had originally feared. Gideon managed not to wince at this news. "She wants you to marry her, I assume."

"Oddly, she doesn't seem to think I'll even

consider that. She just wants me to bring her to America and provide for her and the child."

This wasn't an unreasonable request, although Gideon could understand why it would upset Logan. Bringing one's pregnant mistress to town was certain to create all kinds of ugly gossip, no matter how quietly it was done. Then he would have to support both her and his child, who would be forever tainted by his or her illegitimate birth. Logan would also be worried about the embarrassment to his fiancée and her family. Even if Rosemary broke it off with him, she would be humiliated.

"You wouldn't have to keep her in the city, you know," Gideon said, his mind racing as he tried to figure out how Logan could handle the very sensitive situation. "You could find a place in a small town, and—"

"Gideon, you don't understand."

But he did. "I know you care very much for Miss Fortier, and you'll want to do the best you can for your child, but—"

"Gideon, stop," Logan said, shaking his head and smiling.

Smiling? Why would he be smiling? "But—"

Logan raised both hands to silence him. "Gideon, there is no child."

"What do you mean?" And how could he know that?

"Because Noelle and I never . . . I never

took advantage of her. I told you, she was a respectable young woman from a good family. I treated her with the same consideration I would have shown any young woman I fell in love with, and we were never even alone for more than a few minutes. So there couldn't be a child."

Gideon sat back in his chair and considered this very interesting piece of information. "And she clearly says that she's expecting in that letter?" He nodded toward the envelope Logan still held.

"Yes."

Gideon didn't want to suggest it, but Logan did need to consider the possibility. "Maybe there is a child and it belongs to some other man."

Logan nodded. "I did think of that. In fact, I'm ashamed of how quickly I thought of it, but I only thought of it for a moment, because even if she were pregnant, Noelle would know the child couldn't be mine, and so would I."

"And she would know that you would know," Gideon realized a little sheepishly, "which means she'd never bother trying to trick you."

"Exactly, so why did she write me this letter?"

Wasn't it obvious? "Because she's the Spanish Prisoner."

"Noelle?" Logan asked in confusion.

"No, the person who wrote the letter, who obviously isn't Noelle."

"But why would the person make up a baby that couldn't exist?"

At least Gideon could figure that part out. "Because you and Noelle are the only ones who are sure it couldn't exist. From what you told me about the French war brides, not all the American soldiers were as honorable as you were, Logan, and it would be reasonable to assume that you did take advantage of Noelle, so it would also be reasonable to assume there could be a child."

Logan sat straight up in his chair. "You're right. I know because I was charged with approving marriages for the men in my company."

"Yes, you told me."

Logan frowned. "I did? When did I do that?"

"At the club, the night of the welcoming party. You were rather drunk, I'm afraid."

Logan winced a little at the memory. "So you know I had to sign off on every marriage request for the men in my company. Most of the marriages were of necessity, I'm sorry to say."

"Which proves my theory about American soldiers."

"But it doesn't help me know how to deal with this." He held up the envelope.

"My instinct is to advise you to simply ignore this latest request, since it is obviously not from Noelle, but I'm not sure that would be the most prudent response. I think we also need to figure out who is behind this and put an end to it once and for all."

"Do you think you can do that?" Logan asked.

"No, I don't," Gideon had to admit. "Not by myself, but would you mind if I consulted an expert in this matter?"

"Elizabeth?" Logan asked with another smile.

"Yes, Elizabeth."

Elizabeth could hardly wait for Gideon and Logan to arrive. The telephone call from Smith had been formal and businesslike as he asked if it would be convenient for her to receive Mr. Bates and Mr. Carstens this morning. This morning! Which meant they were in a hurry to speak with her. Surely, Logan had heard back from Noelle. But what did they need to discuss with her?

By the time the doorbell rang, Elizabeth was fairly bursting with curiosity.

Gideon greeted her with a chaste kiss on the cheek, and Logan greeted her with a respectful nod. When she'd taken their hats and coats— Elizabeth couldn't help noticing that Gideon had finally abandoned his trench coat for something warmer—and offered them coffee to chase away the chill, she seated them in the parlor and looked at Gideon expectantly.

"Logan got another letter." He nodded at Logan who produced it and handed it to her.

"This one was sent to Sergeant Kellogg, too," she noted with a frown. Neither man replied, so she proceeded to read the English translation that Logan had obviously prepared.

"Oh dear," she said when she had finished reading. "She could be lying, you know. About the baby, I mean."

"She's definitely lying about the baby," Gideon said. "Logan assures me that his romance with Miss Fortier could not possibly have produced a child."

"Not possibly?" Elizabeth asked Logan, who appeared to be blushing.

"Not possibly," Logan said quite confidently.

Elizabeth sighed with relief. "Then we know for sure that Noelle did not write this letter."

"That's what Logan and I had decided, so I'm glad you agree. The question is, what do we do now?"

Elizabeth gazed adoringly at Gideon, thinking how very much more she loved him now than she had even five minutes ago. "You are asking for my advice?"

"Indeed we are," Gideon said.

"Because you know all about the Spanish Prisoner," Logan added, in case she was in any doubt.

"This does appear to be a classic example of that, especially because this letter asks for far more money than the first."

"It does?" Gideon asked.

"Yes. Didn't Logan mention it? She now wants five thousand dollars, because she has introduced a new complication—the child—which will mean more difficulty."

"I see, so she would need even more money to support herself and the child," Gideon said.

"That would definitely raise the stakes," Logan said. "A baby should make me more anxious to help her, too. But could it also mean Noelle is really asking for my help?" Logan said with a frown.

"Not unless she's a complete fool," Elizabeth said, "which she would have to be to lie about having your baby. No, this is definitely someone just trying to get you to send them money."

"But how can I be sure the woman writing these letters isn't Noelle?" Logan asked in obvious despair. "Now you've got me doubting again. What if Noelle is totally naïve and doesn't actually know how women"—he gestured helplessly for a moment—"how women get babies? What if she simply observed that many of the French women marrying American soldiers were with child as a result of having an American suitor and in all innocence decided that was a good way to get me to help her?"

"That's possible, I suppose," Elizabeth said without much confidence.

"Or suppose she's in truly desperate straits," he continued, obviously warming to his subject, "and someone is forcing her to write these letters, someone who might assume our relationship could have produced a child?"

Neither Elizabeth nor Gideon had an answer to that.

"You see, you can't be sure," Logan said when they didn't argue. "If this really is Noelle, I can't refuse to help her, even though I know there can't be a child to consider."

"What would you like to do?" Elizabeth asked, earning a scowl from Gideon, who most likely had intended to advise Logan to forget he'd ever received these letters.

Logan stared back at her in surprise, probably having given no thought at all to what he might like in this situation. "I . . . I would like to bring Noelle to America."

"But we decided the woman writing these letters is not Noelle," Gideon reminded him.

"And what if we're wrong?" Logan asked, his face twisted in anguish. "I can't just leave her there, not when it's in my power to help her."

And, as Elizabeth could clearly see even if Gideon could not, Logan dearly wanted Noelle in this country, in his city, whatever that might mean for the future. He wanted it so much, he was willing to cling to even this slender thread of hope.

"Can you afford to lose a few hundred dollars if this person turns out not to be Noelle?" Elizabeth asked.

"But she asked for five thousand," Logan reminded her.

"This time she did, but she only wanted a thousand the first time, and she probably only really needs her passage paid, so a few hundred would probably be enough to get her here, and maybe another hundred for bribes. Once she's here, you can decide what to do from there."

"That's still a lot of money to lose," Gideon reminded him.

"But worth every penny to know for certain," Logan said. "I wouldn't even have to ask my father for the money or wait to get funds from my trust."

"Bear in mind that I'm not advising you to do this," Gideon said, earning a scowl from Elizabeth to repay him for the one he'd given her. "But if you send the money and it turns out not to be Noelle, at least we may be able to find out who is behind this."

Elizabeth forgave him everything. "You're absolutely right, darling, but if that is your other goal, we need to be smart about how we lay the trap."

Gideon gave her an adoring smile. "Which is why we came to consult you in the first place."

Oscar Thornton found Leo Vane waiting anxiously for him in the lobby of his hotel at midmorning on Wednesday. He'd just returned from a walk along Fifth Avenue. He'd found the mansions inspirational, and the sight of Vane was comforting after nearly a week of uncertainty. He'd half expected the man to abscond with his five hundred dollars, never to be seen again. The way his luck had been running since he'd met Elizabeth Miles, nothing would have surprised him.

"How was your trip?" Thornton asked when he'd shaken Vane's hand.

"Grueling. I can never sleep on a train, but I wanted to get back as quickly as possible." He did look tired.

"Let's go up to my suite and you can tell me all about it."

When they were ensconced in his suite with whiskey and cigars, Vane complained some more about the accommodations on trains. He'd apparently had an upper berth on the way home, which had annoyed him. "Oh, I almost forgot," he said at one point. "I only spent about four hundred dollars on the trip, so here is the rest of your money."

Thornton took the offered bills, mentally condemning Vane as a fool to return money that Thornton had no intention of asking him to account for, but also impressed by the man's honesty. At least he wouldn't have to worry about Vane cheating him.

Finally, Thornton asked, "Did you at least find your cousin?"

"Oh yes, of course. She's staying in a rather

shabby hotel just across the border in Matamoros. I hated seeing her there, but she assured me it was much better than what she would be enduring in Germany. At least she can eat regularly in Mexico." He set down his drink and placed his cigar in the ashtray, then reached for the briefcase he had brought with him. "Berta gave me some of her securities, so when I've sold them, I'll have enough money to go back and arrange to have her smuggled into New York."

He opened the case and pulled out some elaborately printed papers, which Thornton instantly recognized as stock certificates. They didn't call them gilt-edged securities for nothing. "How much are they worth?"

"Face value, about fifteen thousand."

Impressive. "Where were you planning to take them?"

"To a bank. I hadn't really decided which one," Vane said with a worried frown. "I should probably cash them in quickly. It isn't safe carrying them around like this. I've been scared to death ever since I got them."

"I do business with a bank that's nearby. I'm sure they'll be glad to help you." And Thornton would be able to trust what the banker told them about the securities.

Vane agreed eagerly, so they finished their drinks and then set out for the bank. The doorman greeted him by name, Thornton was gratified to note. Vane seemed impressed at least. Thornton asked to speak to the president, and the two men were soon escorted into the man's imposing office.

Thornton introduced Vane to William Diller, who invited them to sit down. He was a distinguished looking man with iron-gray hair and a full beard. His slight paunch gave him a prosperous air.

"What can I do for you gentlemen today?" Diller asked, peering at them from across his shiny desk.

"My friend here has some securities he would like to cash in," Thornton said.

Vane opened the briefcase and produced the documents, which he passed across the desk to Diller. Diller examined them. Thornton watched his expression and saw no indication that he doubted their authenticity, which was Thornton's last remaining concern.

"Where did you get these?" Diller asked.

"From my cousin," Vane said. "She recently emigrated from Europe and asked me to take care of them for her. She needs the money to get a good start in this country."

"Is there a problem?" Thornton asked uneasily.

"Not with the certificates," Diller said, "but I can't cash them for you because they are not endorsed."

"Endorsed?" Vane echoed uncertainly.

"Yes, your cousin will have to sign them to authenticate them. Once she does that, I'll be happy to cash them for you."

"And I can't do anything with them until she signs them?" Vane asked in dismay.

"I'm afraid not, but if she's in the city, that shouldn't be a problem."

"No, not a problem at all," Vane said with forced cheer. "I guess we've just wasted your time."

"Not at all," Diller assured him. "I hope your cousin will choose to deposit her funds with us when she does get these cashed. We would be happy to serve her."

Thornton and Vane thanked Diller for his help and left the bank.

When they were out on the sidewalk again, Thornton was ready to berate Vane for his stupidity, but Vane muttered a curse, forestalling him. "Now I have to make that trip to Mexico and back again to get Berta's signature so I can cash the securities, and then I'll have to return to Mexico a third time to arrange for her transportation to New York."

That would take weeks, and Thornton didn't want to stay in New York a moment longer than it took to get his money from Elizabeth Miles. With that payoff and his share of Berta's fortune, he would be a rich man once more.

And now that he knew Berta's fortune was real, he didn't have to wait.

"I already told you that I'll advance you the money to get your cousin out of Mexico," Thornton reminded him.

Vane didn't look as excited as Thornton had expected. "I think . . ." He glanced around. No one seemed to be paying attention to them, but they were on a public street. "Maybe we should go back to your hotel to discuss this."

He was right. Even if Berta hadn't been trying to get into the United States illegally, talking about that kind of money on the sidewalk wasn't a good idea. Thornton nodded and they set off back to the hotel. When they were safely back in the suite, Thornton said, "What's the matter? I thought you'd be happy that I'm still willing to finance your little adventure."

"I am, but . . . I didn't tell you what I found out when I met Berta in Matamoros."

"What did you find out?"

Vane went over and sank down wearily into one of the chairs. Then he sighed and ran a hand over his face. "I was originally planning to bribe a captain to take her aboard a regularly scheduled steamer. That would have been expensive, but also fairly easy. She would have to arrange for false papers, but that's easily done in Mexico, too."

"That sounds like a good plan."

"Except it won't work, because I found out no one will take her onto their ship for any price.

The authorities are stopping every commercial vessel and searching them. Apparently, Berta isn't the only German refugee trying to sneak into the United States, and no one wants to get caught carrying one."

"So the whole plan is off then?" Thornton asked, outraged.

"Not off, but it's going to be a lot more expensive. The only way to get her out now is to buy a small cruiser that can sneak by the patrols. Then I'll have to equip it and hire a crew. Finally, I'll have to bribe a few officials to get the licenses and documents I'll need."

So, not impossible, but Vane was right, a lot more expensive. "How much will all that cost?"

"I think around fifteen thousand, which is how much those securities are worth, or so I thought. I know you probably don't have that kind of money, so—"

"What makes you think I don't have that kind of money?" Thornton asked, stung.

"Well, not many people do," Vane said sheepishly. "I didn't mean to insult you, but it's not often I need to go begging for that much money."

"And yet you're begging for it now." Thornton took a moment to enjoy Vane's helpless fury. "I told you I'll give you the money, but for this much you'll need to sign a promissory note. And of course you'll repay me out of your share."

"Why should it all come out of my share?" Vane demanded. "I thought we would split the expenses."

"Because I have the money and you don't. I'm taking all the risk here, so I should get the greater reward. Now do you want my help or not?"

Vane fumed for another minute or two, but finally, he said, "I do."

CHAPTER SEVEN

E lizabeth was eagerly watching out the front
window Wednesday morning when she saw
her visitors arrive in a motorcar she'd never seen
before. Percy had obviously decided to fetch her
last, since Anna and Rosemary were already in
the vehicle when he escorted her out.

"I'm so glad you were able to join us, Elizabeth," Rosemary said when Elizabeth had taken
her place in the back seat with Anna. Rosemary,
she noticed, had managed to claim the seat up
front beside the earl. "I apologize for arranging
this outing by telephone, but the earl only
suggested it yesterday when he came to call, and
there wasn't time to send you a note and get a
reply."

"I don't mind," Elizabeth said, giving Anna a
knowing glance. Rosemary had neatly let them
know that Lord Percy had singled her out with
a personal visit. "I wouldn't have missed this.
Percy, where on earth did you get this motor?"

"I borrowed it from a friend. One can't take
three ladies out in a cab, can one? I hope you will
all be warm enough."

"I'm sure we will be. These lap robes are quite impressive," Anna said, running her hand over the fur rug she had spread over her lap.

They were indeed impressive. Elizabeth had a lot of questions, but she wasn't going to ask any of them right now. "Where are we going?"

"Out to Brooklyn. Someone told me about a breeder with horses for sale there. I thought I would look them over, but I didn't see any reason to go alone. We can have a lovely ride and find a place to stop for some refreshment on our way back."

The lovely ride would be gloomy and pretty cold, even though Percy had found a motor with side windows, but Elizabeth wouldn't point that out. "Did Percy meet your parents when he called on you, Rosemary?"

"He met my mother. He wanted to thank us in person for inviting him to our party, which was so thoughtful. Mother was quite taken with him."

Elizabeth was sure she had been. "Gideon and I will be at the party, of course."

"And I'll be escorting Miss Vanderslice," Percy said, glancing over his shoulder at her, "so we know she will be there."

"Has Lord Percy called on you yet, Anna?" Rosemary asked a little too condescendingly.

"Of course he has," Anna said sweetly. "You don't think my mother would allow me to go driving with a complete stranger, do you?"

"I'm sure your mother was quite taken with him as well, wasn't she?" Elizabeth asked.

"Oh yes. I'm afraid all Americans will be completely charmed by your accent, Lord Percy," Anna said.

"Is that why everyone has been so friendly?" Percy asked with a laugh.

They chatted happily as they crossed the Brooklyn Bridge and proceeded through the ever more rural countryside until they reached a gated entrance. A sign above it read, HAPPY HILLS, even though Elizabeth couldn't see any hills to speak of. The gates stood open, and Percy turned in. Large fenced fields stretched out on either side of the drive. The grass was winter brown now, but a few horses nibbled at the shriveled tufts. They looked up with mild interest as the motor roared past them, then resumed their snacking.

A lovely farmhouse sat at the end of the drive, but the shutters were closed up tightly, as if the inhabitants had left for the season.

"Are you sure this is the right place?" Rosemary asked with a worried frown.

"I followed the directions my friend gave me," Percy said, refusing to be discouraged. "He did say the owner was away, but the farm manager should be about somewhere."

At that moment, a man emerged from a door on the side of an enormous barn nearby. He waved as he made his way across the lawn. Percy hopped

167

out of the motor, and although he'd closed the door, they could easily hear the conversation.

"You must be that English fellow who telephoned," the man said.

"Yes, Percy Hyde-Langdon, at your service." Percy sketched the man a little bow, even though the fellow wore a ratty old coat over a pair of dirty overalls.

The man shook his head. "I never did see why English people needed more than one last name, but then there's a lot of things in this life I don't understand. You can call me Humphrey."

"Pleased to meet you, Mr. Humphrey."

"Like I said on the telephone, Mr. Silvester isn't here. He's off riding around some foreign place where it's warm, in his yacht. I've never seen it, but from what I hear, it's pretty fancy. Anyway, I keep an eye on things here for him, and he did tell me to sell off any of the stock I could find a buyer for. He's tired of raising horses and wants to retire, or so he says."

"Is that all you have available?" Percy asked, looking out at the horses they had seen on the drive in.

"Oh no, I've got the best ones in the barn. Brought 'em inside so you could get a good look. You said you wanted some mares and a stallion, didn't you?"

"That's right. Is the barn suitable for my lady friends?"

168

Humphrey turned to the motor in surprise, as if he hadn't noticed the women before. "Well, look at all the ladies. I didn't know Englishmen kept harems," he said with some amusement.

Percy laughed heartily at that. "I can only wish that one of these lovely ladies was my wife, but sadly, they are all just friends." He opened the back door. "Won't you join us? Mr. Humphrey says we can view some horses in the comfort of his barn." As Anna and Elizabeth climbed out, Percy walked around and opened the front door for Rosemary.

Rosemary, Elizabeth noted, managed to stumble, and Percy had to catch her by the arm.

"Are you all right?" Percy asked in concern.

"I don't know. The ground is so uneven here. Perhaps I should take your arm just to be sure," she said, giving him her best helpless-female-in-distress look.

"Of course," Percy said, offering it to her. They strolled slowly toward the barn with Humphrey, leaving Anna and Elizabeth to follow, unassisted on the uneven ground.

"I'm so very glad I'm not in love with Percy," Anna remarked, linking arms with Elizabeth.

"You should be," Elizabeth replied.

Gideon flagged down a cab and gave the driver Logan's address. Logan had gone to the bank after their meeting with Elizabeth yesterday to draw out the cash for Noelle's—or the Spanish Prisoner's—passage. This morning they were going to use the money Logan had collected to make the arrangements.

Elizabeth had been adamant that Gideon go with Logan to make sure he followed her instructions to the letter and didn't allow sentiment to dissuade him. If this wasn't done correctly, she had warned him, the whole plan would fail.

When the cab reached Logan's house, Gideon asked the driver to wait and went to fetch Logan. A maid answered his knock, but before Gideon could tell her what he wanted, he heard angry shouting coming from the parlor.

"Is that Mr. Carstens?" Gideon asked the maid, whose pinched expression revealed her discomfort.

"He has a visitor," she said, glancing anxiously in the direction of the noise.

Gideon pushed past her, ignoring her sputtered protest. The parlor doors were closed, but Gideon didn't hesitate. He threw them open to find Sergeant Kellogg berating Logan. Both men froze in surprise at the intrusion.

"What's going on here?" Gideon demanded.

Sergeant Kellogg's face was scarlet, his hands clenched into fists, and Logan looked pretty angry himself.

"Sergeant Kellogg is intruding where he has no business," Logan said stiffly.

"That is not true," Kellogg said. "This is very much my business." He still wore his uniform, Gideon noticed, although it was no longer as neat and clean as it had been, as if he'd been wearing it for many days without washing or ironing it.

"What is it you consider your business?" Gideon asked mildly, hoping to calm Kellogg.

Kellogg drew a deep breath, Gideon was pleased to note. "Helping the young lady. She sent the letters to me, after all. I feel it's my duty to make sure she is treated fairly."

"Do you have any reason to think Mr. Carstens will not treat her fairly?"

Kellogg opened his mouth to reply but no sound came out. He closed it with a snap and straightened his shoulders, tugging his uniform jacket down in what appeared to be a habitual gesture. "I would hope the captain would honor his obligations to her."

"Hasn't he told you that he intends to do just that?" Gideon asked.

"I certainly did," Logan said, managing to sound both outraged and insulted. "But for some reason, Sergeant Kellogg isn't satisfied."

"What . . . what you're going to do, that's not what she wanted," Kellogg said a little desperately.

"I thought she wanted Mr. Carstens to send her money for her passage to America," Gideon said.

"She asked for a lot more than that," Kellogg said, aggrieved.

"And I explained to you that it would take some time for Mr. Carstens to obtain that much money," Gideon said. "But it appears she didn't need that much just to escape from France after all. Her first request was much more reasonable."

"But he's not even going to send her that much," Kellogg protested.

"I think the important thing is to get Miss Fortier safely to America," Gideon said in his sensible lawyer's voice. "Wouldn't you agree, Sergeant Kellogg?"

"I . . . I guess you're right," Kellogg admitted reluctantly.

"And Mr. Carstens has told you he intends to do that. So why are you objecting?"

Kellogg's lips tightened with suppressed fury. "She said she wanted me to handle the arrangements."

Gideon glanced at Logan, who appeared to be as puzzled by Kellogg's demand as Gideon was. "I can appreciate your sense of duty, but what difference can it make who handles the arrangements?" Gideon asked.

"I . . ." Kellogg's uneasy glance darted from Gideon to Logan and back again. "I would like to make sure the young lady receives all the help she needs."

Gideon could understand that, although most

men would be more than happy to be relieved of any responsibility toward a woman with whom he had no real connection. "Your devotion to duty is commendable," Gideon said, only a little sarcastically. "Perhaps if you go with us, you can witness what Mr. Carstens does. Logan, would you mind if Sergeant Kellogg accompanied us on our rounds today?"

Plainly, Logan wanted to send Kellogg to the devil, but he said, "If he insists."

"All right, then. That should prove to you that everything has been done properly, Kellogg. I have a cab waiting outside," Gideon said. "Shall we go?"

Kellogg looked far from pleased, but he didn't object. The two men collected their coats and hats and followed Gideon out to the cab. Gideon noticed that Kellogg's overcoat was also a little the worse for wear. He wondered what the man's living arrangements were now that he had been discharged from the army.

The three men crowded into the back seat of the cab, with Kellogg in the middle, and Gideon gave the driver their destination, the port in Hoboken.

"Why are you going there?" Kellogg asked in apparent alarm.

"To purchase a ticket for Miss Fortier," Logan said, not bothering to hide his annoyance.

"But she said to wire the money directly to her so she could buy it," Kellogg said.

"We felt it would be more practical for Mr. Carstens to purchase her ticket here, so he'll know when she is arriving and can meet her ship," Gideon said as reasonably as he could under the circumstances. "There won't be time for her to send a letter giving him that information."

"But she'll also have to get from . . . from where she is to the port," Kellogg said, just as reasonably.

"And I'll wire her money directly for a train ticket and any other expenses she might have," Logan said.

"To the address she indicated?" Kellogg asked suspiciously.

"Where else would I send it?" Logan asked.

"I . . . I read her letter to you, Captain. I know her family disowned her and she's gone to Paris."

This time it was Logan's face that was red with fury. "You would do well not to insult me, Sergeant. I have every intention of fulfilling my responsibilities."

That seemed to placate Kellogg, and he settled back into his seat a bit, although he didn't relax completely. When they reached the offices of the steamship company, the three of them went to the ticket windows. Gideon stood back while Logan chose the nearest available window to make his purchase, but Kellogg stuck right by Logan's side as he conducted his transaction. Logan ended up buying a ticket on a ship that left Brest on Monday.

"Will there be any problem with her picking up the ticket at the port in France?" Logan asked. Elizabeth had been very clear about this part of it.

"Not if she has identification," the clerk said.

"What if she doesn't?" Kellogg said, earning a scowl from Logan and the clerk as well. "The situation in France is very unsettled since the war ended," he explained. "She may have lost her papers."

Gideon thought that unlikely, but he held his tongue.

"You can arrange a code word then," the clerk said, making it clear this was irregular and probably meant extra work on his part.

Luckily, the wire services also required a code word be used when picking up money that had been transferred, and the letter writer had provided the one she would use.

"The code word is 'mercy,' " Logan said.

The clerk raised his eyebrows but he dutifully wrote it down. "We will wire this to our offices over there and the ticket will be waiting for . . ." He glanced down at the form Logan had just filled out. "Miss Fortier."

Kellogg didn't seem happy about any of this, but since it wasn't really any of his business, Gideon saw no reason to be concerned.

"Where are we going now?" Kellogg asked.

"We are going to the nearest Western Union Office," Logan said. "I suppose you'll want to make sure we actually do it, too."

"I'd like to go along, if you don't mind," Kellogg said. He really was an annoying character. He must have been a very good sergeant for Logan to put up with this.

Their cab was waiting and it took them back into the city and the nearest telegraph office. Once again, Logan made the arrangements, with Kellogg looking over his shoulder the whole time. Kellogg seemed pleased when he saw that Logan was wiring Noelle an additional one hundred dollars. It was far more than she'd need for train fare to the coast, but it showed a generosity that did him credit, even though they were almost positive the person to whom he was sending this money was not Noelle. Logan also sent Noelle a cable at the Paris address she'd given in the most recent letter, telling her in as few words as possible to pick up the ticket and the money he'd wired. The cable was hideously expensive, but necessary if Noelle was to know what to do. A letter would take too long to reach her.

When they were finished, Logan turned to Kellogg. "I hope you are satisfied with the arrangements, Sergeant."

"Very much so, Captain." But Kellogg didn't look satisfied. He looked oddly worried.

176

Why should he be worried? Logan had done what the letter writer had asked.

But no, now that Gideon thought about it, he hadn't done exactly what she'd asked. As Kellogg had reminded them, she had wanted far more money and she'd wanted Kellogg to handle everything. But what would he have done differently from what they had done? Gideon wanted to ask, but if this were a swindle, as they suspected, Kellogg wouldn't dare tell him anything at all. They'd just have to wait to see what developed. At least if it were a swindle, Logan had only been cheated out of two hundred dollars.

"I'm sure Miss Fortier will be grateful for your help, Kellogg," Gideon said by way of dismissal.

"You should've done what she asked the first time," Kellogg said with what sounded like bitterness. "She wouldn't've had to tell you about the baby."

Logan gaped at him in astonishment at the misplaced criticism, and Gideon grabbed his arm before he could instinctively defend himself against such a scurrilous charge. "That's water under the bridge, Kellogg, and you have no right to question Mr. Carstens's actions. He did what he thought was right. Can we drop you somewhere?"

"No, I'll . . . I'll be fine on my own from here."

177

He didn't look like he'd be fine at all, but Gideon wasn't going to argue with him.

"I . . . I appreciate your concern for the young lady, Sergeant," Logan said, surprising Gideon. Logan must have a great deal of residual goodwill for Kellogg to actually thank him for all of this. "It does you proud."

"Uh, thank you, Captain," Kellogg said as if not quite certain of Logan's sincerity. "It's . . . I'm just glad I could help."

Kellogg quickly took his leave and scurried away, disappearing into the surge of pedestrians crowding the sidewalk.

"I hate to think he was less than honest after all we went through together in France," Logan said, staring after him.

"Perhaps we'll find a logical explanation for this when that ship docks," Gideon said. "Come on, let's get ourselves some lunch before I have to go back to my office."

"What beautiful horses," Rosemary said, not for the first time, as they were enjoying lunch at a country inn not far from the Happy Hills horse farm. Roast chicken and fried potatoes and glazed carrots had satisfied their hunger. A roaring fire in an enormous stone hearth helped chase the chill that seemed to have crept into Elizabeth's bones, but she wasn't complaining. Everything was going much too well.

"Yes, they were beautiful," Percy agreed, although he did not seem to share her enthusiasm.

"Surely, you're going to buy them all," Rosemary said. "I can just picture you riding that stallion across your estate."

"He really was a beauty," Anna agreed. "I don't know much about horses, but anyone can see that."

"I don't know much about horses, either," Elizabeth lied, "so I wouldn't dream of advising you, but I can see you're concerned about something, Percy. What is it?"

"I had no idea how much it would cost to refill my stables. I suppose horses have become scarce here in the United States as well because of the war."

"Everything was scarce because of the war," Anna said, "but I suppose England suffered far more, since you were fighting so much longer than we were."

"I suppose you lost a lot of your tenants as well," Elizabeth said.

"The wives and daughters worked very hard to keep the farms going," Percy said with a rueful smile. "We desperately needed the crops to feed the soldiers, you know, but you're right, the rents were affected, and now so many of the men won't be returning . . ." He shook his head with regret for all the lives lost. "But I'm sure the estate will recover quickly, and it's not that I don't have the funds. It's just that I didn't arrange for enough capital to cover both the horses and the cost of shipping them home."

"But surely, you can make some arrangements," Elizabeth said.

Percy smiled bravely. "I can, but I'll have to return to England to do it. Things are rather chaotic at home now, you see, and these things must be done in person."

"But you can't return to England so soon," Rosemary said with obvious alarm. "We've hardly had a chance to get to know you."

"I promise not to leave until after your party, at least," Percy said with a forced smile. "I'm looking forward to meeting your Logan and Elizabeth's Gideon."

"And who knows," Anna said, "you might meet some heiress and fall in love and her father will give you the horses as a wedding gift."

"Does that sort of thing still happen in America?" Percy asked, highly amused.

"Not as much as it used to, but I'm sure it still could," Anna said. "Don't set your hopes on me, though. I'm not an heiress."

"And Rosemary and I are already engaged," Elizabeth said, earning a frown from Rosemary. "Perhaps Rosemary could help you find a suitable bride, though. She seems to know all the best families."

Rosemary did not look at all pleased by

Elizabeth's suggestion, but she had a smile for Percy. "Would you really consider taking an American bride, Lord Percy?"

"If my heart demanded it," he said, laying a hand over the organ in question.

"And how would you entice her to return to England with you?" Anna asked.

Percy sighed, as if he were already in love. "I would tell her all about Hartwood. Elizabeth, you're an American girl, so you would know what would please my prospective bride. What impressed you most about my family's estate?"

Elizabeth wanted to pinch him, but she said, "I must confess, I never imagined being in a house with more rooms than I could count, and every one more beautiful than the last. The room I slept in—they always gave me the same one when I visited—was only one of dozens of guest rooms. It overlooked the lake, and I used to sit on the window seat and imagine I was the princess who lost her golden ball in the water and had it retrieved by a frog who claimed to be a prince."

"Would you have kissed the frog?" Anna asked.

"I certainly would have," Elizabeth assured her, then closed her eyes as if she were picturing Hartwood itself. "Oh, and the public rooms were gorgeous, too. Rich, dark woods and all that enormous furniture. There's actually a full suit of armor in the entrance hall. The first time I saw it, I thought there was a man inside. I was terrified!"

Percy laughed along with the other women. "And did you enjoy our little rides around the estate?"

"Of course. The grounds are delightful, as Percy has mentioned. The gardens are very formal, not like the ones here in America. Tell me, have they gone to ruin because of the war?"

"I'm afraid we weren't able to keep them up with all the men gone into the army," Percy said with regret. "Perhaps my heiress bride will oversee their restoration."

He gave Rosemary a big smile and she returned it. "Perhaps she will."

The waiter came to clear the table and then served them large wedges of warm apple pie with cheese for dessert.

"What arrangements are you going to make about the horses, Lord Percy?" Anna asked when they had begun to sample the pie. "If you wait until you get back from England, they might be sold."

"I will need to return to the farm at least once more before I make a final decision, of course. I'll want to ride them and have someone who is an expert examine them, too. It's very important that they are in good health for the voyage. Tell me, Miss Westerly, is your father an expert on horses, by any chance?"

"Heavens no," she said with a laugh. "Why would he be?"

"I thought perhaps he enjoyed horse racing. So many Americans seem to."

"Father isn't much of a gambler, I'm afraid."

"That's too bad. Perhaps he can recommend someone to me then."

"You can ask him at my party," Rosemary said, obviously happy for another opportunity to mention the event.

"And if he can't help, I'm sure Logan or Gideon would be happy to," Anna said. "Although that's still two days away. I hope no one buys the horses before you can get back to them."

"Don't be silly, Anna," Rosemary chided. "There are thousands of horses Lord Percy could buy in America. We'll make sure he doesn't return to England without some."

Elizabeth greeted Gideon with a kiss when he arrived on Friday evening to take her to Rosemary's party.

"You look beautiful," Gideon said when he stepped back to catch his breath.

She turned completely around, letting him admire her from all possible vantage points. She knew the royal-blue color of her gown looked fabulous on her. "I hope I won't outshine Rosemary."

He gave her a disapproving look. "You

don't hope any such thing, and of course you will."

"You may be a little prejudiced."

"I may also be right." He helped her with her coat, and while she was winding a scarf around her throat, he said, "When are you going to tell me the purpose of this party?"

"It's to welcome Logan home." She tried an innocent expression, but he didn't seem to be fooled.

"I already welcomed Logan home, and so did everyone else."

She pretended to consider this as she pulled on her gloves. "Perhaps Rosemary just wanted an excuse to show off her new friend, the Earl of Hartwood."

"That does sound more like Rosemary, but why would anyone care about this earl?"

"Don't tell me you can't guess. Americans love British aristocrats, and we haven't seen many of them these past few years because it was too dangerous to travel between England and America during the war. Those awful U-boats and mines, you know. Rosemary has captured one of the first British aristocrats of the year, though. This is bound to get her mentioned in all the gossip columns."

"Why would she want that?"

Elizabeth wanted to kiss him again because he really was the most sensible man she knew. "I have no idea, but apparently, it is very important to her. Shall we go?"

Gideon tucked her hand into the crook of his arm and escorted her out to the cab that was waiting for them. When they were on their way, Elizabeth turned to Gideon. "I hope you and Lord Percy will be good friends."

He turned to her very slowly and very suspiciously. "What does that mean?"

"That means I'm sure you'll make him feel welcome and give him all the assistance that he needs."

"What kind of assistance will he need?"

"Probably very little, but one never knows."

"I'm not going to—"

"—lie. Yes, we know, but just don't offer any unsolicited opinions."

"Opinions about what?"

"About anything."

Gideon sighed. "I'm going to be very sorry I attended this party, aren't I?"

"Oh no. I think you're going to enjoy yourself immensely."

He thought about this for a few minutes as the cab threaded its way through the evening traffic. "Do I already know this Earl of whatchamacallit?"

"Hartwood. It's possible he will be somewhat familiar to you."

"Just familiar?"

"But of course you have never met the earl."

"Are you sure?"

He knew her too well. "You have never met him as the earl."

"I see. I think."

"Of course you do, darling."

"And you already know him."

"We've known each other for years. Since childhood, in fact."

"Through your father."

"Yes. And you don't have to lie, I promise. You can just avoid Lord Percy if you like. In fact, you should be looking after poor Logan, because I'm afraid Rosemary will neglect him shamelessly."

"At his own welcome home party?" Gideon scoffed.

"If you doubt me, you are underestimating Rosemary."

"And Lord Percy, too, probably."

Elizabeth patted his arm in approval. "Most probably."

Elizabeth and Gideon were among the first guests to arrive. He introduced her to Rosemary's parents, whom Elizabeth recognized from church. Mrs. Westerly was a once-handsome woman who had thickened with age but had failed to accept her maturity with grace. Her mustard-yellow gown would have looked better on a much younger—and less sallow—woman, but she was gracious and welcoming and seemed fond of Gideon. If she eyed Elizabeth a little too critically, Elizabeth was used to that from society matrons. Those with marriageable daughters were always evaluating the competition.

Mr. Westerly was a bluff, portly man who spoke too loudly and eyed Elizabeth with more interest than a middle-aged married man should have shown.

Logan was genuinely glad to see them both, while Rosemary greeted them perfunctorily and then returned to watching for the arrival of the real guest of honor.

"Have you heard anything from France?" Elizabeth asked Logan when Rosemary had stepped away.

"Nothing. I keep reminding myself that the crossing can take as long as ten days each way, so even if Noelle answered my letter immediately, her reply couldn't possibly have arrived yet. But still . . ."

"Waiting is so difficult," Elizabeth said. "But you've done all you can. Gideon told me you'd sent the money and the steamship ticket."

"Yes, although Gideon has warned me not to be too optimistic."

"And rightly so. You haven't mentioned any of this to Rosemary, have you?" Elizabeth asked.

He looked horrified. "Of course not. I don't want to hurt her."

187

"That's very kind of you," Elizabeth said quite sincerely, earning a questioning look from Gideon, which she pretended not to see. Logan was a true gentleman and deserved the very best in life. "Where are your parents? I'd like to say hello."

Logan took them off to greet his parents, whom Elizabeth also knew from church. Then Gideon introduced her to some of the other guests as more people arrived. They were chatting with someone Gideon had just prepared a will for when they sensed a ripple of excitement going through the crowd.

"Who is that?" the man with whom they had been talking asked.

Elizabeth and Gideon turned to look. As she had suspected, it was Anna and the earl. Anna wore a simple gown in Alice blue, which was no longer a fashionable color but was very flattering to her complexion. Her gown didn't matter at all, however, since no one except Elizabeth had even noticed her. The earl wore evening clothes, like all the other men, but he wore his with somewhat more flair. His jacket was cut in a decidedly different style, and he had a satin opera cape lined in bloodred satin draped over his shoulders. He carried an ebony cane with a silver lion's head as a knob. His dark curls were elaborately arranged and his short beard had been waxed to a little point beneath his chin.

"Good Lord," Gideon muttered, and she didn't dare look at him for fear she might laugh.

"Yes, Lord Percy," she said with as much dignity as she could muster because he really was quite a sight.

Rosemary could not have been more pleased, if her expression was any indication. She had swooped in to claim him, tucking her hand into his arm and leading him to her parents who greeted him with an embarrassing level of enthusiasm. No one seemed to notice that they had left Anna standing quite alone.

Elizabeth hurried over to her, Gideon on her heels.

"Isn't he amazing?" Anna said, apparently not at all disturbed by the rude way Rosemary had treated her.

"That isn't the word I would have used," Gideon said.

"Hush," Elizabeth said. "You promised to be nice."

"I did no such thing."

"But you will be," Anna said with certainty. "Because you want to watch this as much as I do."

Gideon started to deny it, but Elizabeth said, "You aren't going to lie to Anna, are you?"

Gideon glared at her, making her smile in triumph.

"Come along, Anna," Elizabeth said. "You need

to speak to our hosts even if they have so rudely ignored you."

Anna made her way over to where the earl was still being welcomed by Mr. and Mrs. Westerly and thanked them for inviting her. They gave her a cursory greeting, and the earl made an effort to include her, but Rosemary was having none of it and dragged him away to introduce him to the rest of her guests.

Anna was still staring after them when a female voice said, "Did you come with the earl?"

CHAPTER EIGHT

A nna turned to find a rather determined-looking young lady staring intently at her as Gideon and Elizabeth hurried over to join them. At first glance, the young lady seemed to be just another guest, but then Elizabeth realized her gown, while attractive enough, had probably been purchased at the Macy's department store rather than custom-made for her by a society modiste.

"Yes, I did arrive with the earl," Anna said a little uncertainly.

"Would you tell me about him?" the young woman asked, pulling a small notebook and a pencil from the purse that dangled from her wrist.

"Who are you?" Gideon asked a little rudely.

She didn't seem the least bit offended. "I'm Carrie Decker with *The World*. I don't have to mention your name if you don't want me to, but our readers are desperate to know more about the earl and why he's in America."

"The earl's visit is hardly something *The World* would be interested in," Gideon said dismissively.

But Elizabeth laid a hand on his arm. "You're right, of course, darling, but I don't think Miss Decker reports the news."

Miss Decker smiled her gratitude.

"Are you a gossip columnist?" Anna asked in apparent shock. Her acting skills were improving daily.

"I'm a society reporter," Miss Decker said without so much as a blink. She'd been insulted before and by far more formidable foes than Anna Vanderslice. "Miss Westerly invites me to all of her parties, and she especially wants me to report that the earl attended this one, but no one else here seems to know anything about him."

Elizabeth was very much afraid she heard Gideon actually groan, but hopefully, Miss Decker would just think he was jealous of the attention the earl was garnering. She turned to him. "Perhaps you should find Logan and make sure he is feeling appropriately welcomed home. We wouldn't want him to be neglected."

Gideon gave her a look that warned of many difficult questions to come, but he muttered, "If you ladies will excuse me," and hurried off.

"What do you want to know about the earl?" Anna asked.

But Elizabeth gave Anna's arm a warning squeeze. "Perhaps we can find someplace more private to discuss this."

"The library," Miss Decker said knowingly and led the way.

They made their way slowly, because more than one person wanted to question Anna about the earl. Since these were merely curious inquiries about how she knew him or who he was, the conversations were brief, and Anna managed not to reveal anything that would spoil Carrie Decker's story.

The library was a poorly named room, since it contained only a few books, and those appeared to never have been opened. The lingering aroma of cigar smoke told them that Mr. Westerly probably used it as his private refuge. How Carrie Decker knew about it was anyone's guess.

Anna and Elizabeth sat down in the two oversized armchairs beside the fireplace and Carrie pulled a chair over from the desk.

"Now, Miss Vanderslice," Carrie began.

"How did you know my name?" Anna asked with creditable alarm.

"Miss Westerly told me the earl would be escorting you."

"How efficient of her," Elizabeth said, and Anna had to cover her mouth to hide a grin.

"Miss Vanderslice," Carrie continued, undaunted, "how do you know the earl?"

"I only met him a few days ago. Miss Miles here introduced us."

Carrie's attention shifted instantly to Elizabeth.

"You introduced them? How do you know the earl?"

Elizabeth repeated the story she had told Rosemary, about Percy's American mother and her family moving to England and their many visits to Hartwood. Poor Miss Decker could hardly keep up, even though she took notes with admirable speed.

"Why is the earl in America in the first place, though?" Carrie asked when Elizabeth had run out of stories.

"I don't think we can tell you that," Anna said with a worried frown.

"Yes, we can," Elizabeth said, taking great pains to make Carrie suspicious. "He came to buy horses."

"Horses?" Carried echoed in confusion.

"Yes, the British army confiscated all the horses in his stables, and now he needs to replace them."

Anna nodded enthusiastically. "Yes, that's right. Horses." Plainly, they weren't telling her the whole story. She'd be an idiot not to notice.

"You don't expect me to believe an earl came all the way to America just to buy some horses," Carrie said.

Anna and Elizabeth exchanged a look. After a moment of awkward silence, Anna said, "He also needs a bride."

"A bride?" Plainly, they could not have said

anything that pleased Carrie Decker more. "Are you saying you are engaged to the earl?" she asked, her eyes lighting up like Chinese lanterns.

"Heavens no," Anna said with a laugh. "He's looking for an heiress."

"An heiress?" Carrie said with a frown.

"Yes," Anna said with some authority. "English-men have been coming to America for decades looking for rich wives to help them restore their estates. It stopped because of the war, but now that the war is over . . ." She let the sentence dangle provocatively.

Carrie was scribbling frantically in her note-book. When she finally looked up, she said, "And you aren't engaged to the earl?"

"I already told you, I'm not an heiress. Besides, I'm not interested in moving to England, but I'm sure he'll find someone who is."

"Do you have any idea who that might be?" Carrie asked hopefully.

Anna sniffed. "Not at all."

"He only just arrived in the country," Elizabeth said. "But if you mention that he's looking for a wife, I'm sure he'll find one pretty quickly."

Carrie obviously thought so, too.

Elizabeth decided they had spent enough time with Carrie and made their excuses to return to the party. They had hardly returned before another reporter approached them. This time they withdrew to a corner of the dining room, where Elizabeth amused herself by making up a completely different story about how she knew the earl. They'd met at a fox hunt when he'd saved her from a runaway horse. Only the conclusion was the same, that the earl was shopping for horses and a bride.

"Why did you tell that woman a different tale?" Anna asked.

Elizabeth gave her an approving smile for using grifter slang. "Just to keep things interesting."

Before Anna could ask her anything else, another reporter approached them, and Elizabeth made up another story. By the time they had been interviewed by the fourth reporter, Anna was completely bewildered.

"I hope that's the last of them," she said, shaking her head. "I almost told that last woman that Percy came here so he could marry a horse."

"She probably would have printed it, too," Elizabeth said.

"But won't the last three reporters be upset when they find out their stories are wrong?"

"Anna, my sweet, none of the stories are true. They are merely different."

Anna blinked. "Oh yes, I guess I forgot."

"And they won't be upset because the stories are different, either. All the newspapers will think their version is the truth and that the others got it wrong. Let's go see what Percy is up to. I haven't even said hello to him."

Elizabeth was happy to see that Percy was conversing with Gideon and Logan.

"My dear girl," Percy said by way of greeting. He swept her an elegant bow and raised her hand to his lips.

Gideon, to his credit, simply shook his head in mock despair.

"I see you've met my fiancé," Elizabeth said, "and our guest of honor."

"Yes, Mr. Carstens has been telling us how Paris fared in the war. I'm so glad to hear it survived unscathed."

"Where have you ladies been?" Gideon asked with more than idle curiosity. "Surely that woman didn't keep you all this time."

"It seems Rosemary invited more than one," Elizabeth said.

"More than one what?" Logan asked.

"Society reporter," Anna said. "I had no idea this was such an important social event."

"It's not," Logan said with a frown. "Or at least it shouldn't be."

"But Rosemary does so enjoy seeing her name in the newspaper, doesn't she?" Anna asked sweetly.

Logan was still frowning, but before anyone could reply, Rosemary appeared at Percy's elbow. "Did I hear my name?"

"We were just saying how happy we are that you invited us," Elizabeth said.

Rosemary didn't even glance at her. She only had eyes for Percy. "Would you escort me in to dinner, Lord Percy?"

"I would be honored," he said, nodding to the rest of them before allowing Rosemary to lead him away.

"Don't worry," Anna told Logan. "He'll be going back to England soon."

Elizabeth was pleased to note that Logan didn't look a bit worried, though. "Perhaps we should all go in to dinner."

"Yes, we should," Logan said. "Anna, may I take you?" Gideon offered Elizabeth his arm—since they weren't married yet, he could still escort her.

As they made their way through the crowded rooms, they stopped a few times to chat with friends, and by the time they entered the dining room, Percy and Rosemary had filled their plates from the massive buffet and moved on.

After dinner, the four of them moved upstairs to the ballroom, where a small ensemble was playing dance music. Lord Percy had to share his favors with as many ladies as possible, since everyone wanted to dance with the earl, but Rosemary kept her eye on him, ready to intervene if any of them tried to monopolize his attention. He did manage to claim Anna for a dance or two, and finally he escaped long enough to claim Elizabeth.

"You cut a fine figure, Lord Percy," she said. He really was a good dancer, a skill that served a man well if he wanted to succeed in society.

"High praise indeed, my lady." He smirked.

"How is your hunt for horses going?"

"Amazingly well. Mr. Westerly has offered me his advice, and he has promised to go out to the farm with me."

"I thought he didn't know anything about horses," Elizabeth said.

"I find that the more ignorant a man is on a particular subject, the more eager he is to give advice on it."

Elizabeth had made the same observation. "Rosemary seems quite taken with you."

"Now you are teasing me, my dear Elizabeth. Miss Westerly is already engaged and I have no hope of winning her heart."

Elizabeth just smiled.

Elizabeth found herself warmly greeted when she entered the offices of Devoss and Van Aken the following Monday morning. Smith came forward, a puzzled frown marking his homely face.

"Is Mr. Bates expecting you, Miss Miles?"

"No, he isn't, and that is because I have an appointment with Mr. Devoss."

"I see," he said, plainly not seeing at all. He must have thought he should have been informed as to why Gideon's fiancée wanted to see the senior partner in the firm. She saw no reason to enlighten him, though.

One of the other clerks escorted her down the hall to Mr. Devoss's office. He rose and came around his desk to greet her. "What a pleasant surprise, Miss Miles," he said, taking the hand she offered. "I wasn't expecting to see your name on my list of appointments today. Surely, Gideon can give you all the legal advice you might need."

"I'm sure he could, but I have some business that only you can help me with, Mr. Devoss."

"I certainly will do my best. Please, sit down."

He offered her refreshment and saw her seated comfortably in one of the large chairs chosen specifically to accommodate portly gentleman of comfortable means who needed help planning their estates. When tea had been brought and the pleasantries dealt with—Mr. Devoss took more than a passing interest in the well-being of Gideon's mother, of whom he was quite fond— Mr. Devoss said, "Now how can I assist you, Miss Miles?"

She glanced over her shoulder, making sure the office door was closed, because she really didn't want anyone to overhear this conversation. "Gideon told me that you are associated with the League."

"The American Protective League, you mean?" he asked in surprise. "Yes, it is my great honor to have been selected to serve them during the war."

"Gideon also told me that you were very helpful when he, uh, discovered some people who were, shall we say, not exactly loyal to the United States."

"I was able to pass the information along to the proper authorities, yes," he said proudly. "That is what League members are trained to do."

Elizabeth pretended to consider this and fiddled with her spoon, giving her tea a stir it didn't need before finally bringing herself to say, "If I were to give you some similar information, would you still be able to take it to the proper authorities?"

Mr. Devoss frowned and shifted uncomfortably in his chair. "Perhaps you are not aware that the American Protective League was officially disbanded shortly after the Armistice was announced."

Rats! That wouldn't do at all. She needed a group of overly enthusiastic spy catchers who were notorious for accusing innocent people of imaginary disloyalty. The League had been doing that practically since the moment the United States entered the war, so she had assumed by now they'd be experts at it.

"But . . ." Mr. Devoss said, raising her spirits instantly.

"But what?" She smiled hopefully.

"The New York branch of the League was

granted special permission to continue our work by the Military Intelligence Division."

"How interesting," she said, trying not to sound too enthusiastic.

"Yes, because of New York's unique . . . situation." He dropped his gaze to his desktop and squared his desk blotter, even though it was already perfectly squared.

"What situation is that?" she asked with just the right level of alarm.

"Nothing about which you need be concerned," he hastily assured her. "But New York has so many . . . immigrants."

New York had always had many immigrants, starting with the first Dutch settlers who had purchased the island from the natives for a string of beads and named it New Amsterdam. Ever since, wave after wave of people had flocked here from other countries, bringing their food and their customs and their languages. Why should this suddenly be a matter of concern to the League or anyone else?

"Immigrants?" Elizabeth echoed, not even having to pretend to be confused.

Mr. Devoss was nodding his head. "We're still keeping an eye on the Germans, of course. We don't know what someone might do in a misguided attempt at revenge, but with the war over, what we really need to be concerned about is the Bolsheviks."

"Bolsheviks? Aren't they in Russia?"

"Yes, and they are trying to overthrow their government and bring anarchy to their country. They are now active in several other countries, and we know they have many supporters here in America, too."

"Really?" Elizabeth couldn't imagine a bunch of wild-eyed Russians trying to bring a revolution to this country.

"Indeed. They are raising money here for the revolution in Russia, and they're talking about starting the same violence in America. In view of what we managed to uncover during the last months of the war, the MID gave us permission to continue our investigations even though the rest of the League has officially disbanded."

"How fortunate." Elizabeth tried to sound happy, even though he had crushed her hopes. "So you aren't concerned about the Germans anymore?"

"Well . . ." Mr. Devoss straightened his blotter again. "Actually, some League members believe that the Bolsheviks are being financed by the Germans."

"Really?" This was good news indeed, no matter how preposterous. By all accounts, the German government had practically bankrupted itself with the war.

"Yes, there is some evidence to support this, so naturally, we're still concerned with the activities of German Americans who may not be loyal to the United States."

As disconcerting as it was to learn the League was going to continue their ham-handed quest for traitors, Elizabeth had to also feel relief. "So if I brought you some information about . . . about someone betraying our country, you would be able to take action?"

Mr. Devoss frowned again, and this time Elizabeth was very much afraid he was going to completely dash her hopes. "Perhaps you saw the list of un-American Americans that appeared in the newspapers a week or so ago."

"I . . . Yes, although many of those people were listed in error, as I understand it."

"Yes, I'm afraid that is correct. Mr. Stevenson was, perhaps, a bit overzealous in his reporting to the Overman Committee."

"What is the Overman Committee?"

"A Senate Committee investigating . . . Well, they started out investigating one thing that led to other things and now they are investigating how the Bolsheviks are influencing American labor. In any event, Mr. Stevenson had prepared a list of over two hundred individuals with connections to various anti-war organizations. Senator Overman deleted the names of those who had obviously been listed in error, but he allowed the rest of the names to be published."

"But some of those remaining names were also

listed in error," Elizabeth said as tactfully as she could.

"Yes, which is why Secretary of War Baker has finally ordered the League to cease all operations, even here in New York, as of February first."

"February first? But that was two days ago."

"Yes."

"Then the American Protective League no longer exists at all?" Could Devoss be any more infuriating?

"No," he said, but added before she could despair, "but if you have information, I can assure you that other groups are still working to protect Americans."

"Other groups?"

"Yes. The Union League Club here in the city has appointed Mr. Stevenson to an official position, and we are planning to continue the work of the American Protective League, although it will be unofficial. So I would be happy to help if you have uncovered someone who is disloyal to our great country. Just give me his name and tell me what you know about him."

"I'm sorry, but I'm not ready to do that yet," Elizabeth said with an apologetic smile. "I mean, I have only heard rumors, and I don't want to report someone who has done nothing wrong."

"Miss Miles, if you suspect treachery, you had best turn the matter over to professionals immediately. You have no training and may inadvertently put yourself in danger. I would never forgive myself if anything happened to you."

"Believe me, I have no intention of putting myself in danger, Mr. Devoss. And what I've heard is only a rumor, as I said. I suspect that if I remain silent but interested, I will eventually learn something of importance, and when I do, I will immediately notify you."

"But the Club could do an investigation and—"

"Please, Mr. Devoss, you must trust me. This rumor is like a wisp of smoke and will vanish if anyone shows too much interest. Just give me a little time. As I said, I will come to you immediately when I have anything worth reporting."

Mr. Devoss sighed. "I suppose that if you won't tell me anything more, I will simply have to trust you, but you must promise not to take any chances. Gideon would never forgive me if I didn't at least warn you."

"I appreciate your concern, Mr. Devoss, and Gideon will, too. If you are worried for my safety, imagine how he feels. Believe me, he won't allow me to put myself in any danger." Or at least not if he knows about it.

"These are serious matters, Miss Miles. Entire countries will rise and fall during our lifetimes, and we must be vigilant."

"I promise to be vigilant, Mr. Devoss." She would be, too. Her very life depended upon it.

• • •

Oscar Thornton was lingering over his lunch in the hotel dining room, wondering how he was going to fill the long afternoon ahead of him, when a bellman entered the room carrying a silver tray. The bellman glanced around and then headed straight for Thornton's table.

Thornton frowned. He could already see the envelope that lay on the tray. He tipped the bellman a nickel and checked the return address. It was stationery from a hotel in Brownsville, Texas, which was just across the border from Matamoros. Vane must have written to him from there, but why had he written a letter instead of sending a telegram?

He'd already heard from Vane by telegram a few days ago that he'd arrived safely in Brownsville, so surely this was a message letting him know that Vane and Berta were on their way to New York. Maybe he was just saving money, since their voyage would take much longer than a letter would to arrive.

He tore open the envelope and read the scrawled handwriting twice before muttering a curse. Vane had written a letter because he couldn't explain the situation in a ten-word telegram. He also couldn't risk putting information in a message others would see, because the news was not good.

Vane had found a boat he could buy, but hiring

a crew who wouldn't ask questions had been far more expensive than he had expected. Also, he'd had to bribe far more people than he had planned to get the proper papers for Berta's departure. He needed five thousand more to get her safely away, but after that, the boat would sail directly to New York and they would arrive in less than two weeks after Vane received the additional money.

Thornton wanted to curse out loud, but they frowned on that in hotels like this, and he didn't want to get thrown out. The other thing that kept him from cursing—aloud, at least—was Vane's report that Berta had shown him her stash of securities, and they were worth almost eight hundred thousand dollars, not five as Vane had originally estimated. That meant his share would be almost two hundred thousand, plus he would get back all the money he'd advanced Vane. As annoying as this was, five thousand more was a small investment compared to what he would make on this deal. Who knew rescuing refugees could be so profitable? Maybe he should put an ad in the newspapers offering assistance.

At least he now had something to do this afternoon. He strolled down to his bank where the president welcomed him into his office. "I thought I'd see you sooner than this, Mr. Thornton," Diller said, shaking his hand and motioning for him to be seated. "Or at least see Mr. Vane and his cousin. But perhaps they decided to use another bank."

"I'm sure Vane will bring his cousin here, but she hasn't arrived in New York yet."

Diller frowned as he sank back down into his own chair. "She hasn't? I thought Vane said . . . But maybe he didn't say where she was. Do you know?"

"No, he didn't tell me, either," Thornton lied. Saying Berta was in Mexico would sound suspicious. "Someplace in the South, I think."

"It's odd she didn't come directly to New York when she fled Europe. Where did you say she was from?"

"I didn't say, and I'm not really sure."

"Her name sounds German, doesn't it?" Diller mused.

"I'm sure a lot of rich Germans escaped with their fortunes," Thornton said. "Who can blame them?"

"Who indeed?" Diller agreed with forced cheer. "But you didn't come here to discuss Mr. Vane's business, I'm sure. What can I do for you?"

"I need five thousand dollars in cash."

"I trust you are going to make good use of it," Diller said a little uneasily.

"Of course I am, and I assure you that when I make my profits, I will bring them right back here to invest."

But Diller didn't seem reassured. "Forgive my

curiosity, but does this withdrawal have anything to do with Mr. Vane and his cousin?"

"Is that any of your business, Mr. Diller?"

"Certainly not, but . . . How well do you know Mr. Vane?"

"Pretty well. We've done business before."

"Successfully?" Diller asked, still frowning.

Not successfully, Thornton remembered bitterly, but that hadn't been Vane's fault. "I trust him, if that's what you mean."

This news seemed to placate Diller, at least a little. "I'm glad. One hears stories, and I'd be remiss not to warn my customers."

"I'm not an easy man to fool, Mr. Diller," Thornton said. Once burned, twice shy, after all.

"And then there's the issue of another large cash withdrawal catching the interest of the government."

"Why would the government care what I do with my own money?" Thornton scoffed.

"Well, not the government itself, but the American Protective League. They get suspicious if someone withdraws a large sum of money."

"How would they even know?"

Mr. Diller shrugged apologetically. "They have sp— I mean agents everywhere. I'm sure several of our tellers are members of the League, although they tend to keep that affiliation a secret."

"But I thought the League disbanded after the

war. Why would they still be looking for German supporters?"

"I don't know, but they are still active in New York. Or someone is, at least. All those men who were so vigilant during the war haven't stopped looking for foreign agents. They may question you about your withdrawal."

That could be a problem, but then how would they know what he had used the money for? He would simply lie and say he invested it in a business deal with Vane. Vane would back him up. "They are free to ask me anything they like. I'm certainly not going to be funding any German spy rings."

Diller smiled. "That wouldn't be likely to earn you much of a profit, either. I'm sorry if you feel I was overstepping, but I try to protect my customers whenever I can."

"You may have customers who need protection, but I'm not one of them. Now do you have the cash on hand or will I need to come back for it?"

Gideon stood up when Smith escorted Elizabeth into his office. He had been as surprised as Smith to learn Elizabeth had an appointment with Devoss, so he had instructed Smith to waylay her before she could leave and bring her to see him.

"What a pleasant surprise to see you in the office today," he said with a smile that felt only slightly strained.

Elizabeth, of course, apparently felt no guilt at all about her surreptitious appointment. "I'm glad to see you, too, darling."

Smith saw her seated and offered her refreshment, which she declined. They both waited until Smith had withdrawn. Gideon then gave her a long moment to speak, and when she didn't, he felt compelled to say, "I understand you had an appointment with Mr. Devoss this morning."

"Yes." She seemed more amused than anything. "I hope you aren't thinking I'm giving him my business instead of you."

"Then I can assume you didn't ask him to draw up your will."

"Do you think I should?" She sounded genuinely concerned.

"Everyone should have a last will and testament, particularly someone who has a lot of money," he felt compelled to say. He knew perfectly well that Elizabeth had more money than he liked to think about.

"Then I should have asked Mr. Devoss about it, I suppose. I assume you can't do it, since you'll be my beneficiary."

He was trying hard not to grind his teeth. "No, I can't do it for you."

"I wish I'd thought of that. It would have made Mr. Devoss much less suspicious."

"What does he have to be suspicious about?" Gideon asked in alarm.

"Well, perhaps not suspicious exactly. He's just worried that I'm putting myself in danger by investigating a bunch of German spies."

Now he was more than alarmed. "And are you?"

"Probably. Why else would I need Mr. Devoss?"

"Elizabeth, you can't investigate German spies. The war is over."

"You're right, of course, as Mr. Devoss pointed out to me. Apparently, we're more concerned with Bolsheviks now."

"And you aren't going to investigate Bolsheviks, either."

"No, I'm not. Not real ones at least."

Gideon opened his mouth to reply but then closed it with a snap when her meaning sank in. "You're running a con." It wasn't a question.

"Not me. I'm completely reformed now."

"But the earl . . ."

"Nothing to do with me."

He gave her a skeptical look.

"I'm just observing, as are you."

He couldn't argue with that. "Is this about Thornton, then?"

"Nothing to do with me, either. The Old Man is taking care of Thornton."

"Then why are you discussing German spies with Devoss?"

"Just exploring some possibilities. Did you

know that the government disbanded the League when the war ended?"

"I may have read it somewhere."

"But they didn't disband it in New York City. We are, apparently, a special case."

"Special how?"

"We have a lot of immigrants who, Mr. Devoss assures me, want to cause a revolution here like the one in Russia."

"That's ridiculous."

"I'm sure the czar thought it was ridiculous, too, and look what happened in Russia."

He couldn't argue with that, either. "All right, so you're investigating imaginary Bolsheviks now?"

"Oh no, I'm stuck with Germans, or rather the Old Man is, but luckily the League thinks the Germans are financing the Bolsheviks."

"Why does the Old Man need to be stuck with anybody?" Gideon asked, thoroughly confused.

"Because, darling, we must rid ourselves of Thornton once and for all. If he . . ."

To his horror, Elizabeth's voice caught, and he realized she was suddenly on the verge of tears. He jumped up and hurried around his desk, taking her hand in his. "What is it, darling? What's wrong?"

She had lifted her free hand to her lips and pressed her fist there, as if she could hold back her emotions with it. After a moment, she lowered her fist and looked up at him with shining eyes and a wavering smile. "I'm sorry. I don't know what came over me."

Still holding her hand, Gideon pulled the other client chair closer and sat down beside her. "Darling, I know this must be difficult for you. Thornton wanted to kill you and Jake just a year ago."

"Yes, and he probably still longs for revenge, even if we pay him the blackmail he asked for. That is why we've been trying to figure out how to ruin his credibility, so even if he does decide to tell people the truth about me, no one will believe him."

She looked so stricken, Gideon thought his heart would break. "What if I told you it wouldn't matter to me even if everyone believed him?"

"I do love you so very much, my darling, and I appreciate your devotion, but yours isn't the opinion that matters."

"Whose opinion could possibly matter more than mine?" he challenged, feeling very virtuous.

"Everyone's, I'm afraid. What happens when we are snubbed by all your friends? What happens when your clients no longer trust you because you're married to a woman who steals for a living?"

"But you don't—"

"Mr. Devoss would regret it very much, but he would have no choice but to let you go. You know it's true. And your poor mother wouldn't be able to go anywhere without being laughed at and—"

"Elizabeth, stop. Not all my friends would snub me, and I'd simply find other clients and—"

"Would you? Are you sure? New York is a big city, but New York society is a small town where everyone knows everyone else. How could some of your friends support you without being snubbed themselves?"

"I think you're making way too much of this, darling. And if it were as bad as you imagine, we'd just pick up and move out West somewhere and start over."

"Would we?" she asked with a sad smile. "You'd leave your home and your family and everyone you've ever known?"

"Of course I would."

But she shook her head. "How could I ask that of you?" Her eyes were shining again. How could he bear it if she cried?

"You wouldn't have to ask me. I'd do it gladly." He would, too, but he could see she didn't believe it.

"Oh Gideon, I love you so dearly for saying that, and I know you really believe it, but how can one person sacrifice everything for another without at least some regret? And how long until that regret turned bitter and soured our love?"

He wanted to argue with her, but he could

find no words. He just shook his head in silent denial.

She smiled at that. "So you see, we have to stop Thornton somehow, because if we don't, we'll never be able to live in this town."

CHAPTER NINE

B olsheviks?" the Old Man asked. He and Elizabeth were sequestered in her bedroom at Cybil's house, hoping to finish their meeting before the guests began to arrive for the Monday evening salon. She was recounting her earlier conversation with Mr. Devoss.

"Yes, those Russian revolutionaries."

"I know what Bolsheviks are." All good con men kept abreast of current affairs. You never knew when something in the news might work into a con. "What makes Devoss think they're a problem here, though?"

"Some fellow from the League decided they were and told some committee in Washington City. You know how these things happen. The country is already in a tizzy about German saboteurs, so it was an easy connection to make, I suppose."

"And the Germans are supposedly financing the Bolsheviks," he mused in wonder.

"Which probably isn't true," Elizabeth felt compelled to say.

"Not that it matters. If people believe it, then

it's true for them. It's a pity about the League, though. They had already proven very useful."

"I'm sure all the people they falsely accused of disloyalty are heartbroken," Elizabeth chastened him.

"Yes, that was too bad, but I think we can make do without them. What was the name of the new group?"

"The Union League Club. They aren't exactly a group. It's really a men's club. Gideon says they aren't ordinarily a bad bunch."

"Oh yes, Teddy Roosevelt's club. They sponsored the Harlem Hellfighters, I believe," the Old Man recalled, naming a unit of Black soldiers who had distinguished themselves in the war.

"And now they're sponsoring a bunch of spy hunters," Elizabeth said with a sigh.

"We have to keep our country safe," the Old Man said with a smirk. "Don't worry, I know all about them. How are things going for you?"

"Fine as far as I know, but I don't always know, since I have to rely on what others tell me. Being retired from grifting has its disadvantages."

"Everything I hear is good, so don't worry." He studied her for a long moment. He was sitting in her one comfortable chair and she was perched on the stool from her dressing table. "Are you sure you can leave all this behind, Lizzie? Won't you miss the excitement?"

She smiled. "I hope not, although I officially

gave up the grift a year ago, and here I am, up to my neck in cons again."

He smiled back. "I guess that proves we don't really do it for the money."

"No, it's for the thrill. I've always known that, and oddly enough, it's even more thrilling when you do it to help someone else than it is when you're just doing it for yourself."

"Is it?" he asked as if the concept were completely new to him. "I'll have to try it sometime."

She didn't point out that he was currently doing just that.

Elizabeth wasn't exactly sure what she hoped to learn from Carrie Decker, but the reporter probably knew a lot more about Rosemary Westerly than Elizabeth was likely to find out just from seeing Rosemary socially. New York society was, Elizabeth knew, an endless source of gossip, but she had not yet been admitted into that elite realm. Her marriage to Gideon would give her a place there, but she knew she would need years before she would really be accepted, if she ever was. And if Thornton did his worst, well . . . It just didn't bear thinking about.

"What are we going to ask her?" Anna said, interrupting Elizabeth's dark musings. They were in the parlor of Cybil's house, awaiting Carrie's arrival. Last night at the salon, Elizabeth had invited Anna for afternoon tea, and she'd been grateful that Anna's Tuesday class schedule had allowed her to attend.

"We want to find out what she knows about Rosemary, of course, but we can't start with that. We have to make her think we are interested in something else entirely."

"Maybe you should be interested in winning her over so she won't report bad things about you," Anna said. "Like the arrangement Rosemary made."

"Or at least like we think Rosemary has made. Anna, you're brilliant."

Anna ducked her head with feigned modesty. "I've gotten much smarter since I started college."

"I don't know about that, but you've certainly gotten more devious since meeting me."

"Oh, I'm smarter, too. I can't believe how much I never knew before. The women at Hunter know everything."

Elizabeth doubted that very much, but she wasn't going to say so. Anna really had changed since she and Elizabeth had first met, and college was only one of the reasons. "I think you were always smart, Anna, but being a society girl never gave you an opportunity to show it."

"You're right about that. Sometimes . . ." Anna's eyes filled with tears.

"Are you thinking about David?" Elizabeth guessed, since that was the only time Anna ever wept.

"I just wish he could see me now."

"He'd be very proud of the woman you have become," Elizabeth said loyally.

"Do you think so? He'd be surprised, at least." She pulled out a handkerchief and dabbed at her eyes.

"Pleasantly surprised, I'm sure," Elizabeth said. "I know Gideon is, and Jake, too. They are both impressed by how far you've come. David would be, also, and you should be very proud of yourself, at least."

Anna smiled at that. "Then that's what I'll be."

Elizabeth quickly changed the subject, and she and Anna chatted about possible things they could discuss with Miss Decker until the doorbell rang.

Elizabeth greeted her visitor and escorted her inside. Miss Decker seemed a bit uncertain, but she allowed Elizabeth to take her coat and joined Anna in the parlor while Elizabeth went to get the tea things. They talked about the winter weather while Elizabeth served them tea and tiny sandwiches and the iced tea cakes she had found at a nearby bakery.

"I don't often get invited for tea," Miss Decker said at last, allowing her skepticism to show.

"I'm sure you don't," Elizabeth said. "I suppose a lot of people actually try to avoid you."

Miss Decker's sardonic smile was her only reply.

"Miss Miles is rather new to society," Anna said. "I tried to tell her that most people don't try to befriend newspaper reporters, but she said she wanted to follow Rosemary Westerly's example."

As Elizabeth had hoped, Miss Decker seemed to know exactly what Anna was talking about. "Miss Westerly is . . . well, she's rather a special case."

"I thought so," Elizabeth said. "It just seems sensible to befriend reporters, though. If they're going to write stories about us anyway, why not make as good an impression as possible?"

"Of course, that's not why Rosemary befriended you, is it?" Anna said.

Miss Decker turned to Anna in surprise. "I . . . I don't know what you mean."

"Don't be coy, Miss Decker." Anna picked up a sandwich and eyed it critically before taking a bite. She let Miss Decker stew for a long moment while she chewed and swallowed. "We know why Rosemary is so eager to keep you supplied with gossip."

"We don't report gossip," Miss Decker tried.

"News, then. Whatever you call it. We know about Rosemary, though."

"But you couldn't," Miss Decker said in dismay.

"Why not?" Elizabeth said.

"Because . . . No one knows." She didn't seem certain of that, though.

"And it wasn't in the newspaper," Elizabeth guessed.

"Something like that would never be on the society page."

"Do you think it would be on another page?" Anna asked before taking another bite of her sandwich.

"Heavens no. No one wants to read about suicide." Miss Decker instantly realized her mistake and gave a little squeak of distress before covering her mouth.

Anna, Elizabeth was pleased to note, did not even blink. "You're right, of course. One hates reading about suicide. So painful for the family. So awkward for Rosemary."

"She didn't . . . It was a terrible mistake," Miss Decker insisted. "She honestly thought the young lady had behaved . . . indiscreetly."

"Did she now?" Elizabeth said. "How can you be sure?"

"Because she was so upset when . . . when it happened. She was practically hysterical. I . . . Well, I actually felt sorry for her."

How interesting.

"And I suppose she was desperate for you to keep her name out of it," Elizabeth said. "Did she actually beg or just bargain?"

Miss Decker stared at Elizabeth in surprise. "A . . . a little of both."

"And we know what the bargain was, don't we?" Anna said with complete confidence, although they were still just guessing. "She would keep you supplied with society gossip—"

"News," Miss Decker insisted.

"Society news," Anna corrected herself, "and you would protect her from disgrace."

"But someone found out," Elizabeth said. "How else to explain the two broken engagements?"

"I couldn't possibly say," Miss Decker's mouth said, although her eyes spoke volumes.

"Could you say, Anna?" Elizabeth asked.

Anna pretended to consider, or maybe she wasn't pretending. She would know a lot of society gossip just from having lived among those people her entire life. Maybe she could actually piece everything together. "Harvey Urquhart was Rosemary's first beau," Anna remembered.

Elizabeth watched Carrie Decker's face. She showed no reaction at all. "Were they actually engaged?"

"Not formally, no. In fact, Logan is her first official fiancé, although her parents had high hopes for the two previous suitors. Rosemary had just made her debut when she took up with Harvey, if I remember correctly. She's a few years older than I am, so I wasn't out yet myself."

Carrie Decker calmly took a sip of her tea.

"Why didn't it work out?" Elizabeth asked.

"Everyone was very discreet, of course, but we all just assumed he got to know Rosemary better and that scared him off."

Carrie Decker didn't even bother to hide her smirk.

"And the second one," Elizabeth prodded.

"Felix Young," Anna reported.

"Not formally engaged, either, I take it," Elizabeth said.

Anna glanced at Miss Decker, who watched her expectantly. "No, although Rosemary was hinting rather broadly. She had high expectations. Felix's family had invited her to a house party at their country house, as I recall."

Miss Decker's eyebrows rose, but she still did not speak. She took a bite of her tea cake instead.

"There was a terrible accident," Anna said, all teasing gone from her voice as she obviously remembered this old event with new horror. She must have realized it was much worse than she had ever suspected. "They managed to keep things very quiet, didn't they?"

"Money changed hands, I'm told," Miss Decker said with a trace of bitterness. "Death certificates can be altered so a person can be buried in hallowed ground."

"But the Youngs aren't Catholic," Anna said, "so it was mainly to protect her reputation."

"And the family's, too," Miss Decker said.

"Poor Daisy," Anna said, her eyes growing moist at the memory.

"And Rosemary Westerly had told you about Daisy," Elizabeth said. "About her indiscretion. Did you really report it?"

"It was a scandal," Miss Decker defended herself. "A young girl and an old man like that."

"Old man?" Anna challenged.

"He was forty if he was a day, but we weren't going to print their names. We never use names when it's a scandal."

"And yet everyone always knows who it is, don't they?" Elizabeth said.

Miss Decker had no answer for that. To her credit, she looked ashamed.

"The part I can't understand is why Rosemary thought she should expose a young woman who was going to be her sister-in-law," Elizabeth mused.

To Elizabeth's surprise, Carrie Decker's lips stretched into a mirthless grin. "You must not know Rosemary very well, then. She never gave a thought to the havoc she might wreak on others, or even on herself. She just enjoys causing people pain."

"You sound like you know her well," Elizabeth said.

"We were at school together, at least until my father died and I had to leave. After we lost all our money and I had to get a job, Rosemary forgot she knew me."

"Until she needed to spread some gossip," Elizabeth said. "That's why she chose you to tell, isn't it?"

Miss Decker's face twisted with distaste. "She said she came to me because we were friends, but we were never friends. She enjoyed lording it over me, how she was a rich debutante and I was a struggling reporter. I didn't want to publish the story, because it would destroy the young woman and also just to annoy Rosemary, but she threatened to take it to another newspaper, so my editor told me I had to. Then Daisy . . . died."

"And Rosemary came to you in tears and begged you not to tell anyone she gave you the information," Elizabeth said.

"And once again, money changed hands. Rosemary's father paid my publisher, although I'm sure they would both deny it. But I knew the truth about what happened, and Rosemary promised that she would repay me for my silence with a wealth of stories about other people, which helps me keep my job."

"But she gives her stories to everyone now," Anna said. "Do they all know her secret?"

"I don't think so. I think she decided she likes the attention, so she started whispering in other people's ears, and before you know it, she's the darling of all the gossip columnists."

"News," Anna corrected her, making her blush.

"I'm curious about why you decided to meet with us today," Elizabeth said.

"I thought you might have some more news for me. The things you told me about the earl were wonderful. My editor wants everything I can find out about him."

"I will be happy to tell you everything I know," Elizabeth said quite honestly. "Unfortunately, I haven't learned anything new since Friday night."

"But you'll tell me first when you hear something?" Miss Decker asked.

"Oh yes," Elizabeth promised. She would be happy to.

Anna could hardly contain herself after Miss Decker had gone. "I always wondered about poor Daisy. They said it was a boating accident."

"What happened?"

"That's what is so strange. They said she went out in a rowboat alone. What girl does a thing like that?"

"No girl does a thing like that. Have you ever tried to row a boat?"

"No, that's why God gave us men, to do the hard work."

"I suppose the boat overturned or something," Elizabeth said.

"That was the story. She couldn't swim and her clothes dragged her down and it was a tragic accident."

"What about the scandal? Didn't people put the two together?"

"Some probably did, but Miss Decker was right about them using initials in the newspapers. The story could have been about anyone, and after Daisy died, no one wanted to speculate anymore, at least not in public. It was too ghoulish."

Elizabeth nodded. "And even if they did talk about it, how would anyone know it was Rosemary who gave Miss Decker the story in the first place?"

"They wouldn't, unless Carrie Decker told them."

"And she would have nothing to gain and everything to lose by doing that, since she would lose her best source, and others who gave her tips would be nervous that she might expose them as well," Elizabeth said.

"From what she said, she might also have lost her job, but she did seem pleased that we had guessed the truth at last."

"That you guessed the truth, at least," Elizabeth said with admiration. "Do you have any idea who the older man might have been?"

"None, but I was young then. People wouldn't have talked about such things in front of me."

"Gideon might know, or his mother."

"I'm not sure what good it would do us to find out," Anna said. "It's too late to help Daisy."

"I was just thinking we might have an ally if

we need one, but even if we can't find him, we can still get a little revenge for Daisy."

"Exactly what do you think Miss Decker can do for us?"

"Oh, any number of things, but we'll have to see how our little plans work out. I also had high hopes for the American Protective League, but it seems to have died a rather ignominious death."

"What good news!"

"It would be if I didn't need them. The Old Man doesn't think it will be a problem though, because Mr. Devoss has found an equally questionable group who may be able to help."

"I'm so glad you were able to join me today," Rosemary told Elizabeth. They were once again at Delmonico's for lunch. This time they had actually planned to encounter the earl, however.

Or at least Rosemary had planned it. She couldn't be seen alone with him, though, so she had invited Elizabeth to join her. Anna would probably have classes on a Wednesday afternoon, but Elizabeth suspected Rosemary hadn't even considered inviting her. Anna was a single woman who might represent competition. Rosemary didn't know that Anna had absolutely no interest in the earl or any other man. But Elizabeth had already declared herself to be uninterested in the earl, and since Elizabeth and the earl were such good friends, it was only natural they should meet for lunch.

"Thank you for inviting me," Elizabeth replied.

"It was Lord Percy's idea," Rosemary said, effectively erasing any goodwill Elizabeth might have felt for her. Fortunately, that wasn't much.

Rosemary looked remarkably good in a suit designed in the new military fashion. The tan color flattered her somehow, and her angular frame filled out the suit just the way it was intended to do. Even her hat had a military jauntiness to it, with a sprig of peacock feather to add some feminine flare. Elizabeth had chosen a gray velvet dress so she wouldn't outshine Rosemary, at least not too much.

The earl only kept them waiting a few minutes before making his appearance. He wore one of the new trench coats, although his was much fancier than Gideon's. The earl had added brass buttons bearing some elaborate crest, and gold epaulets shimmered on the shoulders. Today he carried a cane with a gold knob. Or maybe it was only brass. Elizabeth thought he looked ridiculous, but Rosemary seemed impressed.

He greeted each of them with a kiss on the hand and tipped the maître d' to give them a good table.

"What have you been up to, Percy?" Elizabeth asked when the waiter had taken their orders.

He and Rosemary exchanged a guilty glance, and the color rose in Rosemary's cheeks. Oh dear, they'd obviously been up to no good!

"I've been seeing the sights and meeting new people," Percy said. "Rosemary has been kind enough to take me under her wing."

"I merely suggested to some of my friends that Percy would make an interesting addition to their guest lists."

"But it's only been a few days since your party," Elizabeth said in surprise.

"And I haven't dined alone a single time since then," Percy marveled. "Miss Westerly seems to know everyone in the city."

Rosemary did like to give that impression.

"I wonder that Logan is so willing to share you, Rosemary."

She gave Elizabeth a tolerant smile. "He doesn't mind in the slightest, and of course he's much too busy to squire me around everywhere I need to go. His father has put him to work again, you see."

How convenient that Logan couldn't accompany his fiancée to events Rosemary didn't want him attending. Elizabeth turned to Percy. "I suppose Rosemary is introducing you to a lot of eligible young ladies."

Rosemary's smug expression vanished, but the earl merely shrugged. "These things take time, don't you know? One can't be expected to find a suitable bride at a single social event."

"But surely you've met at least one young lady you'd like to see again," Elizabeth prodded.

The earl gave Rosemary an appraising look. "Perhaps I have."

Rosemary returned his gaze unflinchingly. "I should hope so."

Elizabeth needed all her acting skills to pretend she didn't notice the undercurrent of longing running between her two companions. Who would have imagined that Rosemary would be so easily wooed?

The waiter arrived with the first course of their lunch. When he had served it and retreated, Elizabeth said, "I saw a friend of yours yesterday, Rosemary."

"Really? Who?"

"Carrie Decker."

Luckily, Rosemary didn't have anything in her mouth because she might have choked. "Where on earth did you encounter her?" she asked when she had regained her composure.

"She came to see me. She seemed to think I might know something more about the earl here." Elizabeth gave him a dazzling smile.

He frowned in return. "Is this a person I have met?"

"She's a society reporter for *The World*," Elizabeth said before Rosemary could reply. "I don't know if you have actually met her or not, but she was asking all kinds of questions about you at Rosemary's party."

Percy was not pleased. "Really, I was quite surprised to see my name mentioned in the newspapers. My visit here was supposed to go unnoticed."

"Unnoticed by whom?" Elizabeth asked with interest.

Percy glanced at Rosemary, who was also quite interested in his answer. "I told you when we met here the first time that I'm doing some work for my government."

"Even still, unless you're a spy, I can't think why you should remain unnoticed," Elizabeth said.

"That's because you know nothing about international diplomacy," Rosemary scolded her. "Lord Percy is involved in some delicate negotiations."

"If you wanted to keep his visit a secret, you shouldn't have invited so many gossip columnists to your party," Elizabeth said.

Rosemary's eyes flashed, but she knew better than to cause a scene in a public place.

Percy reached over and patted her hand where it had formed into a fist on the table. "Now, now, you didn't realize at the time, my dear."

Elizabeth couldn't keep her eyes from widening, but she managed not to say anything at this expression of intimacy.

Rosemary drew a calming breath but still turned angry eyes on Elizabeth. "What did you tell Carrie?"

"Nothing about Percy, if that's what you're worried about. I had already told her everything I knew about him, though."

"And everything you didn't know about me, if you were the source of all those fairy tales the other newspapers told about me," Percy said with a small smile.

"I thought you would enjoy that," Elizabeth said. "But I am sorry if I interfered with something important. You should have told me it involved international diplomacy."

"No harm done, I'm sure," Percy said with more hope than confidence. "Let's not spoil our lunch with arguing."

"Certainly not," Rosemary said, although she didn't look like she would be able to enjoy anything at all. Plainly, she thought Elizabeth had done this to get back at her for revealing Elizabeth's engagement, which was a perfectly natural assumption for her to make.

Elizabeth smiled as if she were making an effort to be pleasant. "In any event, Carrie Decker asked to be remembered to you, Rosemary."

All the heightened color that had been so unbecoming drained from Rosemary's face. "Did she?" she asked stiffly.

"Yes." Elizabeth pretended not to notice

her discomfort. "She said you were at school together."

Percy seemed delighted by this. "This woman is your friend? America is such a strange place. I had no idea that society girls could become newspaper reporters."

Rosemary's expression could only be described as pinched. "They don't, as a general rule, but Carrie . . . her father died and the family was ruined."

"Ruined?" Percy echoed, confused.

"Without her father to earn money, they became poor," Elizabeth explained. "So Carrie had to get a job."

Percy shook his head in disapproval. "This is why the English method is so superior. When a man dies, his oldest son inherits the estate and the income that goes with it. We never have to depend on employment or worry about becoming poor just because someone dies."

Rosemary's expression went from pinched to adoring in about two seconds. "You're right, that is a far superior system."

Elizabeth could have pointed out some flaws in that system, but she didn't want to spoil the mood. "Yes, England has many advantages over America. For example, it's an ocean away."

"Why would that be an advantage?" Rosemary asked, still staring adoringly at Percy.

"For many reasons, I suppose," Elizabeth said.

"For instance, if you had a secret you didn't want anyone to know, going to live in a country halfway around the world would be a definite advantage."

Rosemary's head jerked, but when she turned to Elizabeth, she saw no accusation in Elizabeth's expression, only pure innocence. Elizabeth wasn't going to suggest that Rosemary had a secret she would travel thousands of miles to hide. When Rosemary turned back to Percy, she seemed to see him in a whole new light, a light that made him even more attractive.

Gideon was finishing up for the day, glad that Friday was almost over and looking forward to a quiet evening with Elizabeth, when an aggrieved Smith appeared in his office doorway.

"Who is it this time, Smith?" Gideon asked with a sympathetic smile.

"Mr. Thornton, sir. He said you wouldn't mind seeing him for a few minutes, although I doubt that very much."

Gideon's good mood evaporated in the heat of his rage, but he couldn't allow himself to show Thornton how disturbing his presence was. "You're right, Smith, I do mind, but I'll see him. Make him wait for a few minutes before you show him back, though."

That would let Thornton know he hadn't intimidated Gideon and also give Gideon time to get his temper under control. When Smith finally brought Thornton in, Gideon was able to look up with only mild annoyance at the interruption.

"Thornton," he said by way of greeting, making no move to stand or shake hands.

"Bates," Thornton replied. He took one of the client chairs without being asked.

Smith gave a long-suffering sigh before withdrawing, closing the door discreetly behind him.

"What do you want?" Gideon asked, being as rude as his position allowed.

"I want my money."

Gideon gave him a long stare. "The month isn't up yet. Not even close." Which wasn't what he wanted to say, but there was nothing to gain by arguing with the man.

Thornton shrugged. "I know. I just wanted to remind you, in case you'd forgotten."

"Not likely."

"I'm assuming you told Miss Miles about my previous visit."

"Of course I did."

"Good. I wouldn't want you protecting her. She should know that her actions have consequences."

Gideon had to clench his teeth to keep from saying what he thought of Thornton. The man had confessed to murdering his wife, his men had nearly beaten Jake to death, and he had intended to kill Elizabeth. How dare he judge her?

"I assume Miss Miles is taking steps to procure my money."

"Assume whatever you like."

Thornton smiled at that. "Then I'll assume that when I return on February twentieth, you will have a quarter of a million dollars for me. In cash. Oh, and I'd like Miss Miles to hand it to me herself, in person."

Gideon's fury roared in his ears, but he managed to keep his voice level. "That is also not likely."

"Then let's call the whole thing off. I'll just notify the police and the newspapers that Miss Miles is a con artist who stole money from me."

That was a horrifying thought, but Gideon recognized it for what it was. He gave a tiny shrug. "If you're willing to exchange a quarter of a million dollars for a little petty revenge, then suit yourself, Thornton, but I'm guessing you'd rather have the money. Either way, you won't be seeing Miss Miles."

Now Thornton was angry. He probably hadn't expected Gideon to call his bluff. "Who is she cheating this time? It must be good if she's getting that much money from him."

"I don't have any idea what you're talking about," Gideon said, because he did know she wasn't cheating anybody. Or at least not that he knew of.

Thornton laughed at that, a bitter sound deep

241

in his chest. "I'm sure you don't. She's good though, so I'll keep my options open until the twentieth. If I get my money, neither of you will hear from me again."

But Thornton had already warned him that he would always be a threat to them, hadn't he? "We'll never hear from you again?" Gideon echoed. "Isn't that what blackmailers always say?"

"What does that mean?" Thornton demanded, apparently insulted.

"You know what it means."

"Are you calling me a blackmailer?"

"I believe when someone demands money in exchange for not harming another person, the law calls that blackmail."

Color flooded Thornton's pudgy face as he leaned forward menacingly in his chair. "Call it whatever you want, Bates. Just get me my money."

CHAPTER TEN

❧❦❧

Elizabeth and Gideon had hardly had time to rise from their pew at the end of the Sunday service when Logan Carstens accosted them. He had scurried over from where he'd been sitting with Rosemary and her family before most of the congregation had managed to close their hymnals.

"Can I have a word?" he whispered almost desperately to Gideon.

"Good morning, Logan," Mrs. Bates said. She'd been sitting with them and was still gathering her things.

"So nice to see you, Mrs. Bates," Logan said in an attempt to appear normal, although his voice betrayed his anxiety.

Mrs. Bates glanced at each of them, reading their expressions, and then rose. "I'll just go say hello to Rosemary, shall I?"

"Yes, please," Logan said, stepping aside so she could make her way into the aisle.

"And why don't we move out of the way so everyone else can leave," Elizabeth said, leading the two men to the side aisle at the other end of the pew, which hardly anyone used, since people rarely chose to sidle down it to sneak out of the church quickly.

Logan couldn't help a glance over his shoulder to make sure Mrs. Bates was indeed distracting Rosemary. "Did you see the newspaper this morning? Noelle's ship is docking tomorrow."

"That's at least a day early, isn't it?" Gideon asked.

"They must have had a good crossing. I should meet the ship, shouldn't I?" Logan asked somewhat hopefully.

"Of course you should," Elizabeth said, "although you do remember that you probably won't find Noelle on it, don't you?"

"Yes, yes," Logan said so impatiently that Elizabeth knew he still at least half believed those letters had been from the woman he loved.

"And we'll go with you," she added.

Gideon looked at her in surprise, and Logan immediately objected. "That isn't necessary—"

"Of course it is. What are you going to do with Noelle if she does arrive? Take her home to your parents?"

Logan just stared at her, dumbfounded.

"Elizabeth is right," Gideon said, probably because he knew how much she liked it when he acknowledged this. "And you wouldn't want to give her the wrong impression of what you expected from her by putting her in a hotel."

"But what difference will it make if the two of you are there?" Logan asked, obviously still not thinking straight.

"We will serve as chaperones, and if Noelle does indeed arrive tomorrow, I can take her home with me. That will be completely proper and she will be reassured about your intentions, at least."

"I couldn't ask you to do that, Elizabeth," Logan said.

"You didn't ask me. I volunteered. Tell him again that I'm right, Gideon."

Gideon grinned at that. "She's right, so there's no use arguing. What time shall we meet you at the dock?"

They had just arranged the time and place for their meeting when Rosemary came up. Mrs. Bates had done an admirable job of distracting her, but her powers were not without limits, and Rosemary must have sensed something of importance happening without her. "What are the three of you cooking up?" she asked with forced cheerfulness, but Elizabeth could see the concern in her eyes. She must be worried that Elizabeth would tell Logan how much time she had been spending with Percy. Rosemary obviously had no idea that Logan wouldn't care.

"We were just trying to convince Logan that the two of you should have dinner with us sometime soon, but he says you don't have a free evening for weeks," Elizabeth said as if she hadn't already discussed Rosemary's busy social calendar with her and Percy a few days ago.

"I'm sure we can find some time before your wedding," Rosemary said without much conviction. "Logan, are you joining us for Sunday dinner? Mother needs to know."

"I . . . I promised I'd dine at home today," Logan said. He really was a terrible liar, but Rosemary didn't seem to notice. He obviously didn't want to spend the day with Rosemary when he was anticipating Noelle's imminent arrival. "My parents have been complaining they haven't seen nearly enough of me since I've been back."

"Then you must stay home," Rosemary said, almost relieved. "Your parents' feelings must come before mine." For some reason, she didn't want Logan to attend. Could she have invited Percy to Sunday dinner? Anything was possible. "Come along, Logan. We need to speak to some people before they leave."

Logan waited until Rosemary had turned away to mouth, "Thank you," and then followed after her.

"Was that wise to say you'd take in Noelle?" Gideon asked when they were gone.

"Noelle isn't going to be on the ship, Gideon. Please tell me you understand that."

He sighed. "I guess I do. I just hate to see Logan disappointed."

"So do I, but there's still a chance for them if she receives his letter. In the meantime, we need to find out who really did send those letters to Kellogg and who used the ticket Logan sent. The only chance we have of doing that is meeting the ship."

"And what if nobody used the ticket? What if someone just cashed it in for the money?"

"Then we'll have wasted a trip to Hoboken, but I have a feeling that someone did use the ticket, and I want to be there to find out who it is."

The cabdriver hadn't been happy about driving to Hoboken. They could have taken a train, but the day was blustery and Gideon didn't want to make Elizabeth walk outside any more than was necessary. A cab would drop them right at the dock.

Logan was already there when they arrived. He had been pacing, and even when they joined him, he couldn't stand still. He kept bouncing on the balls of his feet and peering out at the bulk of the ship coming ever closer to the pier.

"What will I do if it's her?" Logan asked suddenly. "I mean, I'm still engaged to Rosemary. Noelle knows that. Surely, she won't expect . . . But what will she expect?"

"The letters said she knows you won't marry her," Elizabeth said reasonably. "Even the one that claimed she is having a baby."

"I know what she said, but . . . What will become of her if I don't marry her?"

"I don't know. Do you think she expects to become your mistress?" Elizabeth asked baldly, shocking Gideon.

Logan blushed furiously. "I'd never do that to her."

"Of course you wouldn't," Gideon said, patting his friend on the back reassuringly while shooting Elizabeth an exasperated glance.

Elizabeth was unrepentant. "I think you needed to hear yourself say it, Logan. You would never dishonor Noelle because you love her, so stop talking nonsense. If she does walk down the gangplank, there is only one thing you can do, and you know what it is."

Suddenly, all the tension seemed to drain out of him, and his whole body stilled. He turned his clear gaze to Elizabeth. "Yes, I do know what it is. I'll marry her, no matter what."

Elizabeth rewarded him with a dazzling smile. "We'll remember you said that."

Gideon had no idea what she had just done, but Logan had transformed from despair to determination in a matter of moments. He had also sworn to marry Noelle in spite of his engagement to Rosemary, something Gideon would have bet that Logan wouldn't even consider. So much for honor. Or dishonor. Or anything at all.

They went inside and found some hot coffee

248

and waited until the ship had docked. Then they went back outside to watch the crew lower the gangplank and so Logan could see the passengers gathered on the deck. Many of them were searching the crowd below for loved ones who had come to meet them. Those who succeeded were easily identified from their frantic waving and even shouting, as if anyone could be heard above the din of the gathered crowd.

At last the gangplank was in place, and passengers began to disembark. Gideon found himself studying every female who came down, even those who were clearly too young or too old to be Noelle, and those who came arm in arm with a gentleman because who knew what might happen on a sea voyage? He knew he was wasting his time. He had no idea what Noelle even looked like, but it seemed important somehow to help Logan find his lost love.

Many of the men were in uniform, so the ship must be delivering troops as well as commercial passengers, and in the end the troops far outnumbered the civilians. The crowds on the dock had thinned as people left with the passengers they had come to meet, so they had no trouble at all watching the last of the passengers disembark. A woman clutching a bundle to her chest was making her way slowly down the ramp, and beside him Logan gasped.

"Is that her?" Gideon asked.

"No, but I know that woman."

"Who is she?" Elizabeth asked.

"She's . . . She's Kellogg's girl."

Suddenly, everything made sense. "Kellogg tricked you into paying her fare," Gideon said.

"But why didn't he just bring her with him when he came home?" Elizabeth asked. "Didn't the army allow the men to marry and bring their brides home for free?"

"No, not . . ." Logan turned to Gideon. "Remember I told you I was in charge of approving the marriages for the men in my company?"

"You mean the men had to get approval to marry?" Elizabeth asked in amazement.

"Yes, because . . . Not all of the women were like Noelle. Some of them . . . Well, some of them were prostitutes who just wanted to get to America. Others were, well, less than virtuous at least. One woman they told us about married a dozen soldiers just to get their allotments. Most of my men were mere boys, away from home for the first time and lonely and innocent. They were too easily fooled, so I had to make sure the women were, uh, respectable before I could give my approval."

"And Kellogg's young lady wasn't respectable," Gideon guessed.

"More than one of the men told me the rumors that she had been selling herself long before the Americans got there. Kellogg was especially eager to marry her because she was with child, but he had only known her a month or two and she was plainly much farther along than that. I couldn't . . . I had to protect my men. I had to refuse him permission even though he was besotted with her and there was the child to consider."

The woman wore a coat, so Gideon couldn't really judge if she was pregnant or not, but as they watched, Kellogg emerged from the remnants of the crowd and hurried toward her. He still wore his bedraggled uniform, and when he would have thrown his arms around the woman, she stopped him with a gesture and held out the bundle for him to see.

"That's a baby," Gideon realized.

"Good heavens, so it is," Elizabeth said.

Logan sighed. "And Kellogg hasn't even known her for six months."

"Come on," Elizabeth said. "Let's see what they have to say for themselves."

Elizabeth had to admit the plan had been clever, if poorly executed. As they approached, she could hear the woman speaking to Kellogg in French. She didn't understand the words, but she recognized the tone. The woman was cajoling him, charming him, trying to convince him to be excited about the child who appeared to be sleeping inside his bundle of dingy rags.

"Kellogg," Logan said sharply, and Kellogg almost snapped to attention. They both turned in surprise. "What is the meaning of this?"

Kellogg, bless him, refused to be cowed. He straightened his shoulders and faced his angry captain with anger of his own. "This is my fiancée, Mademoiselle Segal. You will remember her, I'm sure, Captain."

To his credit, Logan ignored the sarcastic tone and tipped his hat. "Miss Segal, welcome to America." He sounded only a little sarcastic in return.

"No thanks to you, Captain," Miss Segal said.

"And this is your child, I assume," Logan said.

"My son," Kellogg said as if he really believed it. Perhaps he did.

"Congratulations," Elizabeth said, deciding to take charge before this became a masculine battle of wills that no one would win. "Miss Segal, welcome to America."

"And who are you?" Miss Segal asked with a suspicious frown but in nearly perfect English.

Logan cleared his throat. "May I introduce my friend, Gideon Bates, although Kellogg has already met him, and his fiancée, Miss Elizabeth Miles."

"Nice to meet you," Kellogg said to Elizabeth without much enthusiasm and turned back to Miss Segal. "Oriel, let's go."

"Where are you going?" Elizabeth asked, still

smiling cheerfully, although her cheeks were feeling a bit tight.

Kellogg just stared back at her uncertainly, but Miss Segal said, "Phillipe is taking me to his home."

Elizabeth had already noted that Kellogg was still wearing his uniform a month after he had been discharged from the army. It was a bit worse for wear and none too clean, as if he had worn it every day out of necessity. She had also been reading the newspapers, so she knew enough about the plight of returning soldiers to guess his situation. "Sergeant Kellogg, is your home a suitable place for a woman and a new baby?"

"I . . ." He looked at each of them in turn, carefully avoiding meeting Miss Segal's eye. "I have a room."

"In a rooming house?" Elizabeth said, keeping all judgment from her tone. "Does your landlady know Miss Segal and the baby will be sharing it with you?"

"A room?" Miss Segal said. She was not happy. "Just one room?"

"I haven't been able to find a job," Kellogg said, suddenly furious.

"And that's why you had to lie to Mr. Carstens and steal money from him to pay Miss Segal's fare," Gideon said. Elizabeth was proud that he'd managed to say it without the slightest trace of criticism.

"I didn't have any choice, and it's all your fault, Captain Carstens," Kellogg said. "If you'd let me marry Oriel in France, the army would have brought her over when I came."

"I see," Logan said mildly. "So that's why you felt justified in stealing from me."

"You owed me."

"Just for curiosity," Elizabeth said, "whose idea was it to ask the captain for the money?"

Kellogg was obviously new at this business, and he gave himself away—or rather he gave Oriel away—by glancing at her.

"Please," Miss Segal said quickly, managing to sound a little pathetic. "The cold, it is not good for the *bébé*."

"May I make a suggestion?" Elizabeth said.

Everyone looked at her as if she were crazy, even Gideon. She'd have to speak to him about that later.

Hearing no objections, she said, "Since you and Miss Segal are not yet married, it seems unlikely your landlady will welcome her and her child." Judging from his frown, Kellogg had already considered this, but he had no alternative to offer. "Forgive me for being so forward, but are you in a position to make other living arrangements for Miss Segal, Mr. Kellogg?"

"I told you, I don't have a job," Kellogg said grudgingly.

"Then may I offer to take Miss Segal home

with me as my guest? Miss Segal, I live with my aunt and her friend in a large house. You and your baby would have your own room to sleep in and the use of the rest of the house. You'll probably only need to stay for a few days, until Sergeant Kellogg can make other arrangements and you can marry and move in with him. What do you think?"

Plainly, she thought a lot of things, but she knew a good offer when she heard one. "You are very kind."

"Not at all. You and Sergeant Kellogg may not deserve consideration after you cheated Mr. Carstens, but there is no reason your innocent baby should suffer."

Kellogg had stiffened at this, but Miss Segal merely smiled. She plainly thought Elizabeth was a gullible do-gooder who would be a pushover.

That was just fine with Elizabeth.

Since Logan had driven his father's motorcar to the docks, he offered to drive everyone to Elizabeth's house in Greenwich Village. Gideon could have returned to his office—he probably had work to do—but Elizabeth was pleased to note he chose to accompany them as well. He was obviously much too curious about Elizabeth's motives to be left out now.

Gideon sat up front with Logan while Kellogg sat in the back with the women and the baby.

Logan, Elizabeth was happy to see, seemed to be taking this whole thing rather well. He hadn't even expressed dismay at not finding Noelle on the ship, but oddly, he hadn't expressed any anger over being cheated, either. In Elizabeth's experience, this wasn't natural, so she'd ask Gideon to deal with Logan later.

Oriel spent most of the trip babbling in French to Kellogg and trying to get him to admire the baby. Plainly, he didn't want to show any emotion in front of Gideon and Logan, but he was slowly softening.

Oriel seemed very pleased at the accommodations and equally willing to stay as long as it took Kellogg to make whatever arrangements an unemployed ex-soldier could be expected to make. She was in America with a roof over her head, which was more than she had any right to expect from her luck so far in life, so she was satisfied.

Elizabeth left her and Kellogg alone in the parlor while she showed Logan and Gideon out. She closed the doors to give the couple some privacy.

"Are you sure you want that woman here?" Gideon whispered with some concern when they were in the foyer. Logan seemed equally confounded.

"Don't worry about a thing. I think Miss Segal and I will get along famously."

Gideon looked determined to worry anyway, which probably wouldn't hurt him. Then he turned to Logan. "What about you? Are you going to turn them into the police?"

But Logan shook his head. "I'm afraid Kellogg is right, this really was all my fault."

"But you did what you thought was right," Gideon said.

"And who am I to decide what's right for other people? I can't even decide that for myself. So no, I'm not going to report them to the police. They'll have enough problems without that. I'll consider the money a wedding present to them and a lesson to me."

"You are very kind," Elizabeth said in a fake French accent, making both men laugh. "But don't tell Kellogg just yet. Let him stew for a few days, which will be a lesson to him."

She sent the men on their way, and then went to the kitchen to make some sandwiches. Kellogg and Miss Segal would probably be wanting lunch, and that would also give her something to do while she allowed the two lovers some time to discuss their situation. She hoped Kellogg would make that situation very clear to her, because it would make Elizabeth's job so much easier.

After a surprisingly short time, she heard the baby begin to fuss and then the front door opened and closed. Moments later, the baby abruptly silenced, and Elizabeth went into the

257

parlor to find Oriel alone and nursing the baby.

"Is Sergeant Kellogg gone?" Elizabeth asked.

"He is eager to find a place for us to live," she said.

"I'm making some sandwiches. I can bring one out here to you, if you're hungry."

"I am always hungry. This little one must eat constantly. Mostly, I am thirsty, though. Can you also bring me a drink?"

Elizabeth prepared a tray with a sandwich, a pot of tea and a glass of water. Oriel drank the water gratefully, using her free hand while she held the baby to her breast with the other, then started nibbling at the sandwich.

"Is that really Sergeant Kellogg's baby?" Elizabeth asked after a companionable silence.

"He is now," Oriel said without a trace of shame.

Elizabeth smiled. "It was a clever plan, but you should have just asked for the five thousand dollars."

"Ah, Phillipe, he is so *stupide*. He was supposed to show that letter only. I explained everything and wrote the letter for him before he even leaves France. But he is worry, so I write the other letter, for a smaller money, in case the captain refuses because it is too much money. I mail them both so they look like they come from that other woman, but I mail them at the same time, you know?"

"Yes," Elizabeth said because she did know. "And Kellogg was afraid to ask for so much money the first time, so he gave the captain the other letter. But mentioning a baby was a mistake. You see, the captain knew he couldn't have fathered a child with Noelle."

Oriel sighed as only French women can sigh. "*Merde*. Now I am here, at least, but he has no money at all. I thought all Americans are rich."

"Even so, you're better off here than in France, I imagine."

"Oh yes. Things are very bad there."

"And I think a woman of your talents will do very well in America. In fact, I think I can help you make some money to get yourself started. Do you by any chance speak German?"

Percy Hyde-Langdon was finding New York society incredibly boring. How many games of cards (where the stakes were so low) could one play without losing one's mind? How many vapid debutantes could one charm without losing interest in the entire sex? How many times could one flirt with Rosemary Westerly without becoming physically ill? He tried to remind himself it was for a good cause, but he'd never been very concerned with good causes, so he'd fallen back on duty. Duty was a cruel mistress, he was learning. Perhaps it would build character.

If only he were really interested in improving his character.

"Is it true that you're looking for a bride, Lord Percy?" the young woman sitting to his left at the card table asked. What was her name again?

How many young women had asked him that question in the two and a half weeks since Rosemary had set out to introduce him to New York society? "One mustn't believe everything one reads in the newspapers," he said with a teasing grin.

"Then you aren't interested in finding a bride?" she pressed, her disappointment obvious.

"Why do you care, Cecily?" the young man sitting to Percy's right asked. He sounded resentful, and Percy couldn't blame him.

Cecily blushed. "I only care because everyone is interested in Lord Percy."

"Only because Englishmen were so scarce during the war, I imagine," Percy said modestly.

"You underestimate your appeal, Lord Percy," Rosemary said archly. "And if you were to look for a bride in this country, I'm sure you would have your pick."

Percy bestowed his most charming smile upon her. "I suppose most men would find that information gratifying, but alas, I am only interested in one American lady, and her affections are otherwise engaged."

Cecily and the young man—Robert? Rodney?

260

Who cares?—were deliciously scandalized by this revelation, and Rosemary blushed becomingly.

"Really, Lord Percy, you are such a tease," Rosemary claimed, taking her turn to distract everyone.

But the seed was planted. Now Percy only had to wait to see if it took root.

He didn't need to wait very long. Since they were gathered at Rosemary's parents' home, it only took another hour for Cecily and Roger—that was his name—to decide their evening was complete when yet another game of cards had concluded. Rosemary saw them out while Percy gathered the cards and shuffled them unnecessarily.

"I suppose I should be on my way as well," he said perfunctorily when she returned.

"Heavens no," Rosemary said. "Come and sit with me awhile. We hardly ever get a moment alone."

Indeed, they had not. Rosemary's parents saw to it that she was always properly chaperoned, and she also managed to never be quite alone with him even when she did succeed in escaping their observation. Tonight, however, her parents seemed to have retired for the night and she had closed the parlor doors when she returned from seeing out her other guests.

She sat down on a love seat situated close

to the fire, which had died down to a flicker. Percy stopped to throw a couple logs onto it before sitting down beside her. She had left only enough room for him, so they were quite close. She smelled of roses, which he supposed was appropriate.

"What you said tonight," Rosemary began, staring into the fire, which was surging to life around the added fuel. "Did you mean it?"

"I said many things tonight," Percy said with a noncommittal smile. "If you're asking about the compliments I paid Cecily, I'm afraid they were not all completely sincere."

She smiled a little at that, still looking at the flames. "No, I mean . . . what you said about your interest in one American lady."

Percy sighed. "Oh yes, that. I realized at once that I had been too forthcoming."

"Then you really are interested in an American lady. May I ask her name?" This time, Rosemary turned to him, her gaze as sharp as a knife, although her words were smooth as silk.

"You must know already to whom I referred." His tone, he was happy to note, was just a shade tragic. "You have led me on unmercifully."

"Then why haven't you said anything?"

"Do you have to ask? It is, as I said, impossible because you are engaged to another man."

Plainly, this fact annoyed her as much as it did him. "And if I were no longer engaged to Logan?"

He sighed again. "Rosemary, my dear, I could not possibly expect you to do such a thing. What kind of a man would even ask it of you?"

"A man who was in love," she said quite confidently.

"Does love excuse bad behavior in America?"

She smiled at that. "Love excuses every kind of behavior in America, but you are probably correct that it isn't really proper to ask a lady to break her engagement. Let me ask you a different question. If I had not been engaged when we first met, would you have behaved differently?"

"Now that is a question I can answer honestly. I would certainly have behaved differently. I would have sought you out and courted you, as is proper and correct. I have thoroughly enjoyed the time I have spent with you since I arrived in New York, but it has, I must confess, been an exquisite form of torture to be with you while knowing nothing can ever come of it."

"And if I had not already been engaged, would something have come of it?" Rosemary asked with shocking frankness.

He smiled sadly. "My dear Rosemary, that would have depended entirely on you, since a man can only ask. The woman makes the final decision, after all."

"Does that mean you would ask, if I were free?"

He reached for her hand but stopped himself,

because he had no right to touch her. "You are a cruel woman to tease me like this."

"But I'm not teasing, Percy," she said, dropping his title to show that she was serious. "I have long since regretted my decision to accept Logan's proposal. The war has changed him. He's always so serious now."

Percy wasn't sure how she would know that Logan was changed, since she'd spent precious little time with him, but he had to agree that Carstens did seem rather serious. "And one does so hate to cause a soldier distress after what they all went through in the war."

Plainly, that was not what Rosemary wanted to hear.

"But," he continued seamlessly, "it would be wrong to marry out of duty rather than affection."

"That is exactly what I was thinking," Rosemary said. "How much better it would be for us—for all three of us, I mean—if I were to end my engagement with Logan."

Percy gazed at her with genuine admiration. He seldom met a woman so practical and also so self-serving. "I can't think of anything that would make me happier."

"Then I shall take the earliest opportunity to speak with Logan," she said. "You may kiss me now."

Percy managed to hide his surprise at her boldness. "I would like nothing better, my darling, but I have no right to even touch your hand as long as you are promised to another. Rest assured, however, that I will kiss you thoroughly and make my offer for your hand with the utmost dispatch as soon as I return from England."

Her expression was almost comical. "Return from England? What do you mean?"

He smiled sadly again. "You recall that my original plan for coming to the United States, in addition to doing some diplomacy for my country, was to purchase breeding stock for my stables. I did not arrange for sufficient capital for that endeavor, so I must return to England to correct that oversight."

"You can't mean you're traveling all the way back to England just so you can buy some horses," Rosemary practically screeched.

Percy couldn't help wincing just a bit. "I'll only be gone a month at the most. By then the news of your broken engagement will have grown old and no one will think it the least bit odd when I begin to pay you court."

"I don't care if they think it odd or not," she pouted. "I don't want to wait a month."

"But I'll have to return to England sooner or later because I must buy some horses to replenish the stables at Hartwood. I told you—"

"And I told you that you can't go back to England now. If it's just a matter of money, my father will buy the horses for you."

Percy expressed an appropriate amount of shock at such an idea. "I can't believe your father would be willing to do any such thing."

"He would if we were going to be married," Rosemary said, obviously figuring it out as she spoke. "He could . . . It would be a wedding present."

"Like a dowry?" he asked, still uncertain.

"Yes, like a dowry."

"Have you spoken to him about this?" Percy asked doubtfully.

"Not yet, but he never denies me anything, and if I'm going to marry an earl, he'd be so pleased that he'll give me anything I want. He can easily afford a few horses."

"I couldn't possibly accept such a gift," Percy claimed.

"Nonsense. I'll explain everything to my father—"

"After you have broken your engagement, I hope."

"Yes, of course," she said, although she clearly hadn't thought that necessary. "As soon as I speak to Logan, I will discuss this with my father. My parents will be delighted!"

"As will I, my darling," Percy said, daring to take her hand in both of his. "When I arrived here, I had no idea I would meet the love of my life."

"And I had no idea I would become a countess!"

CHAPTER ELEVEN

O scar Thornton had just returned to his hotel, having attended a matinee at the movie theater. Charlie Chaplin had managed to entertain him with a series of ridiculous antics, but now he faced an evening of utter boredom unless he could find something else to distract him. Only one more week until he could demand his money from Elizabeth Miles. Then he could leave New York for a place where he would be appreciated simply for being rich, which was probably any city other than New York because here you had to be at least a millionaire to get noticed.

Making money would be more difficult now that the war was over, but there were always opportunities for a man who kept his eyes open. He'd be more careful in the future, too. No one was going to take advantage of him ever again.

He stopped at the front desk to pick up his room key, and the clerk also handed him an envelope. "This came for you while you were out, Mr. Thornton."

He'd been expecting to hear from Vane. The

man had sent him a second telegram, acknowledging receipt of the five thousand dollars he'd requested and confirming that he and Berta would be sailing for New York very soon. That had been a week ago, so he expected to see them in New York around the same time he got his money from Bates. This wasn't a letter from Vane, however. This was a plain envelope with just his name written on it.

The paper, he noted, was expensive and was that a hint of perfume? He'd been careful not to express interest in any of the respectable females he had encountered in New York, and the less-than-respectable ones he had visited wouldn't be sending him notes on expensive paper.

More than curious now, he carried the envelope up to his room where he could read it in private. No sense giving the staff anything to gossip about. A perfumed note was more than enough.

In his room, he slipped off his coat, kicked off his shoes, and poured himself a glass of whiskey before sitting down to open the mysterious missive.

"Dear Mr. Thornton," it began. "We have not met, but my cousin has told me much about you. I am grateful for the help you have given me, and I now must impose upon you one last time. After an unfortunate incident, I am unexpectedly in New York and find myself without friends and temporarily without funds. My cousin said

I could depend upon you for assistance until he arrives with my belongings. Can you meet me in the tea shop across the street from your hotel on Thursday afternoon at four o'clock? I will be sitting alone and wearing a dark blue dress." It was signed, "Berta Volker." Unlike her cousin, she had not yet adopted the Americanized version of her name, apparently.

Thornton stared at the note for a long time trying to figure out what could have gone wrong and why Berta would be in the city already and without Vane or her "belongings," by which she obviously meant the securities. Finally he realized it was almost four o'clock, and if he wanted to see Berta Volker for himself and get some answers, he should get over to the tea shop. He winced at the thought of going into one of the places where women could meet without the need of a male escort. That meant he'd probably be the only man there, but if Berta was a respectable woman—and he had every reason to believe she was—she'd be guarding her reputation. That explained why she hadn't made any attempt to meet him at his hotel.

With a weary sigh, he gathered his shoes from where they'd landed and put them on again. He should be eager to meet Miss Volker. She was going to help restore his fortunes. He only wished he didn't have such a bad feeling. She wasn't supposed to be in New York yet, and she definitely wasn't supposed to be in New York without Vane.

The tea shop was exactly what he'd expected, small and depressingly feminine. Fortunately, it was nearly empty this time of day, since most women were at home at this hour, preparing supper for their husbands. A lone female in a blue suit sat at a table in the far corner. She looked up expectantly when he entered and gave him a tentative smile.

Ignoring the disapproving frown from the woman behind the counter, Thornton made his way over to the table. "Miss Volker?"

"Mr. Thornton, so good of you to come," she said in passable English, although her accent was noticeable. "Please sit down. Would you like some tea?"

She had ordered a pot and had a half-empty cup in front of her. An empty cup sat in front of his chair. "No thank you. What happened? How did you get here without Vane?"

She glanced around, as if checking for eavesdroppers. Then she picked up the pot and filled his cup. "For appearances," she murmured. She was younger than he'd expected, probably in her twenties, although she'd plainly seen some hard times and was thinner than American women tended to be. The war had been hard on everyone, he supposed. She wasn't a pretty woman, but not bad looking either. Her clothes were new but not expensive.

"Leo bought a boat. Did he tell you?" she said softly.

"Yes, he said that was the safest thing to do."

"The crew, they were hard men, but they left us alone. Everything was fine until we stopped in . . . I think the place was called Charles Town."

"Charleston probably," he said, thinking of the Southern port.

"Yes, that is it. We needed fuel and food. I was going to stay in my cabin so no one would see me, but Leo comes. He tells me the captain has heard they are going to search the boat and he is afraid they will question my papers. He refuses to take me any farther."

"Didn't Vane offer him more money?" Thornton asked angrily.

"Vane?" she echoed in confusion.

"Leo. He changed his name from Volker to Vane."

"He did? He did not tell me this."

"It doesn't matter. What happened then?"

"He told me to pack a small bag and then he took me off the boat before the men came to search. He took me to a train station and bought me a ticket for New York. No one even asked for my papers after that, so I arrived here safely."

"And where is Vane? And your . . . your

luggage?" Mainly the trunk with the false bottom, although he didn't say that.

"He said he would keep it safe. No one would find my . . . my valuables, and his papers were good so no one would stop him."

Of course his papers were good. "When is he going to arrive?"

"He says next week, first or second day. He says to tell you he will come to you immediately, but until then, I have no money."

"Did Vane, I mean Leo, send you off with nothing?" Thornton asked skeptically.

"He gave me a little money, what he could spare, but I have spent it all. I only had a small bag with me, so I needed clothes, and the hotels here cost so much."

She was right, they did. She'd have to eat in restaurants, too. Silently cursing Vane, he said, "How much do you need?"

Berta looked away and shuddered. "This is so difficult. At home, I never think about money."

Which was a nice situation to be in. "You need to think about it now."

"I hate to ask because you have given so much already. Leo should be the one asking."

He certainly hadn't hesitated to ask before. "But he isn't here."

"I think . . . I will need five thousand dollars."

Thornton managed not to laugh in her face. Just what hotel was she staying in? And how long did

272

she think it would take Vane to get here? "You shouldn't need that much for a week, even in New York. Five hundred should be more than enough."

"I do not understand American money. How much is five hundred compared to five thousand? Leo said I should ask for five thousand."

"You should only need a couple hundred at most for your hotel, and your meals will be another hundred. That should still give you some spending money, too."

"But I need new clothes. I cannot wear clothes like this at the Waldorf," she sniffed, flicking the collar of her suit disdainfully.

"Is that where you're staying?" he asked in surprise.

"Leo tells me it is the best hotel. I always stay in the best hotel."

God deliver him from rich women. "You still don't need five thousand dollars to live in New York for a week."

"Herr Thornton," she began stridently, but he silenced her with a gesture.

"No German, please," he whispered urgently.

She sniffed. "As you say, Mister Thornton, I cannot be seen dressed like an *armselig*. Did Leo not tell you I am wealthy woman?"

"He did, which is the only reason I agreed to help you," he said baldly.

"I see. Leo is not very good, is he?"

Thornton didn't know what she meant by that, so he said nothing.

"I tell Leo I will give him half of my fortune if he bring me to America. He tell me he is giving you half of his part. Is this right?"

"Yes, it is."

"Then I will change my mind. You are the one who helped me the most, so I will give you half of my fortune if you will help me now."

"That's . . . very generous," Thornton said with some surprise.

"I have no choice. You can see that, I think."

He did see it. "What about Leo?"

"I will repay what he gave me to escape Germany. He will be happy with that."

Thornton doubted it very much, but he wasn't going to stand up for Vane. "All right."

"And you will give me five thousand dollars."

Thornton could have agreed, but he saw no point in giving her more than she could possibly spend. In another week, she'd have her securities back and be able to cash them in, which would make her rich enough to buy whatever she liked. Since everything he gave her was now coming out of his share—although his share was twice as big as before—he had no intention of spending any more of it than necessary.

They negotiated back and forth, and in the end he agreed to twenty-five hundred. The bank was closed, so he arranged to meet her there the next morning. In the meantime, he gave her two hundred in cash, which was all he had in his wallet. At least she wouldn't go hungry.

Elizabeth had just returned from shopping, with a fresh supply of food for her houseguest, when the doorbell rang. Oriel and her baby were already noticeably healthier from just a few days of adequate nourishment. Cybil and Zelda were completely enamored with the baby, whose looks had improved considerably as his little face had filled out. They didn't seem to mind at all when the baby woke them up in the middle of the night, screaming to be fed. Zelda even took a turn walking him when he refused to settle down again, and Oriel was obviously grateful for the help. Elizabeth couldn't help thinking Oriel would be glad to leave the entire care of the baby to someone else, but no one could feed him except her, so she didn't have that option.

The doorbell rang again before Elizabeth even had a chance to set her purchases down in the kitchen. "Coming," she called, hurrying to answer the door. She saw no sign of Oriel or the baby, which meant that he was probably asleep upstairs. Elizabeth nearly ran to prevent her eager visitor from ringing yet again and possibly waking him up.

Seeing a man's silhouette through the window, for a moment she thought Gideon might have come to call, but when she opened the door, Logan Carstens stood on her porch. She would have been concerned except for the fact that he was grinning like a lunatic and holding up a piece of paper.

"Noelle wrote back to me!" he cried.

"Shhh!" she cautioned, waving him inside. "Don't wake the baby."

Logan's smile vanished for a few seconds. "Hasn't Kellogg claimed them yet?"

"Not yet."

She had just closed the door behind him when they heard Oriel coming down the stairs. She was dressed to go out. "You are here, good," she said to Elizabeth. "I must leave." Then she saw Carstens and turned up her nose, muttering something in French.

But Carstens was in too good a mood to be disturbed by anything she might have to say. "Good morning, mademoiselle. You are in good health, I hope."

Oriel frowned at that. Plainly, she wasn't prepared to deal with courtesy from him and certainly not cheerfulness, so she chose to simply ignore him. She turned back to Elizabeth. "I will return soon. Little Phillipe, he will sleep now."

"I hope so," Elizabeth said as Oriel let herself out of the house.

"Where is she going?" Carstens asked.

"To do some shopping, I think," Elizabeth said

276

vaguely. "Now come in and tell me what Noelle has to say."

His good mood restored, Carstens removed his hat and coat, hung them in the hallway, and followed Elizabeth into the parlor. They sat together on the sofa beside the fire, and he tried to hand her the dog-eared envelope. "Here, read it for yourself."

"I don't read French, remember?"

"She wrote in English, mostly anyway."

Elizabeth pulled the letter from the envelope. "How long has it been?"

"Since I mailed my letter? Almost a month to the day. This came in yesterday's mail, but I didn't see it until last night. Rosemary had invited me to supper, so I didn't get home until late."

"Was Lord Percy there?" Elizabeth couldn't resist asking.

Logan's smile dimmed a bit. "No. In fact, I was the only guest, and after supper, Rosemary took me into the parlor and broke our engagement."

"She did?" Elizabeth cried, hardly able to believe it. "Did she give you a reason?"

"Oh yes," Carstens reported with satisfaction. "She said that I'm a changed man since I returned from the war, and she doesn't feel she knows me anymore. She thought it best to release me so we can both find partners more suited to us."

"Partners?" Elizabeth echoed. "Did she really say that?"

"I'm afraid so. She has changed, too, it seems."

"And how fortunate that she has. She has saved you the trouble of breaking the engagement yourself."

"She has, and Elizabeth, I would have had to break it, no matter how ungentlemanly that would be. I knew it the instant I saw this letter from Noelle."

"So you have no regrets?"

"None at all. I went to see Gideon first thing this morning, to tell him the news, and he sent me straight here because he knew you'd want to hear it, too. Go ahead, read the letter."

Elizabeth started reading. She had to stop several times where Noelle used a French word to ask Logan its meaning, but long before she'd reached the end, she had gotten the underlying meaning. "She is quite clever, isn't she?"

"No more clever than you are, I expect. The letter you composed for me was so subtle and discreet, in case she really had written demanding money from me."

"And lying about the child, but you knew she wouldn't have done a thing like that, didn't you?"

"In my heart, yes, I did. I suppose I was just desperate to hear from her in any way at all, so I was willing to believe even that."

"Fortunately, you don't have to now. So here

she says she is puzzled about who could have written you such a letter and signed her name."

"And now we know the answer to that question," Carstens said with a note of triumph.

"Yes, we do, but she was nevertheless pleased to hear from you. And she is concerned about your welfare and obviously missed you very much, but how interesting that she manages to convey all of that without once asking for anything in return."

"She would think I'm still engaged."

"And perhaps even married by now, I suppose. What are you going to do?"

"I've given it a lot of thought. I hardly slept at all last night, as you can imagine, and I've decided I'm going back to France."

"You are?" she asked in surprise.

"Yes. I can't just write and ask her to come here. I've got to show her my intentions are honorable, and ask her parents for her hand, and marry her there, with her family and friends to see it. I've got to do this properly."

"Oh, Logan, how could she refuse a man who would do all that?"

"I certainly hope she couldn't."

"When are you leaving?"

"Tomorrow."

"My goodness!"

"I don't see any reason to wait. I've already told my parents. They were a little stunned, I think, but also somewhat relieved that I won't be marrying Rosemary, if the truth were told."

"That isn't surprising."

"Oh, Elizabeth, how can I ever thank you?"

"I didn't do very much at all," she said quite modestly, because others had actually done most of the work, "but if you want to express appreciation, bring Noelle back here in time for my wedding."

Berta was already waiting for him when Thornton entered the bank that morning. She did not look happy or nearly as grateful as Thornton would have expected. Didn't she realize he could refuse to give her so much as a penny? He should have thought of that last night, before he gave her the cash from his wallet.

"You are late," she said, rising imperiously from the bench upon which she had been sitting.

"No, I'm not," he said, somehow managing not to pull out his pocket watch to prove it. What did it matter? There was no sense in antagonizing her any more, at least until he had her money in his possession. "Let's go see the bank president."

She seemed mildly impressed by that and allowed him to escort her to Diller's office. Diller was obviously pleased to see them, jumping to his feet. "Is this . . . ?"

"Yes, Miss Berta Volker," Thornton said. He

introduced Diller, and Berta acknowledged him with a small nod.

"I'm very happy to make your acquaintance, Miss Volker. I understand you've just arrived in New York. How do you like it?"

"I do not like it at all," Berta informed him. "But I do not have any choice."

Diller seemed a little taken aback but he rallied quickly. "Please sit down. May I offer you some refreshment?"

"No," Thornton said, but Berta simultaneously said, "Yes, some tea."

Diller sent his secretary to fetch some tea while Thornton and Berta sat down in the client chairs.

"May I assume that you have brought your securities with you, Miss Volker?" Diller said hopefully.

"You may not," she snapped.

Diller, astonished, turned to Thornton for an explanation.

"There was some . . . some trouble. Miss Volker had to come on ahead, but her cousin is bringing them. He should be here in a week or so."

"What kind of trouble?" Diller asked uneasily.

Berta turned to Thornton, her gaze icy. "Why must this man know all of my business?"

"He's just trying to help," Thornton said impatiently. That was a thankless job, however, as he was learning.

"Then tell him how he can help, so we can

leave," she said. "I have an appointment with a dressmaker, and I do not want to be late."

Diller was thoroughly confused by now and Thornton tried a reassuring smile. "Miss Volker needs some funds to cover her expenses until her cousin arrives, and I'm going to advance her some money. I'd like to have twenty-five hundred in cash."

"Twenty-five hundred?" he echoed, a bit surprised.

"Yes. Is that a problem?"

"No, not at all," Diller said. "Let me just . . . I need to instruct my staff." He got up and left them alone in the office.

"I do not like that man," Berta informed him.

Thornton was pretty sure Diller didn't like her, either, but he didn't say so.

While they were waiting, a young man brought in a tray with tea things on it and a single cup of tea. He set it on the edge of Diller's desk closest to Berta. She made a little show of adding sugar and then taking a sip. "Ach, it is cold," she declared, setting the teacup down and pushing the tray away.

Why on earth had Leo Vane been so eager to help this nasty woman?

Well, that was a stupid question. For the same reason that Thornton was still willing to help her. With any luck at all, he'd only have to see her once more, when she cashed in her securities and they divided the proceeds. When that was done, his responsibility would be over. She'd lose Vane's assistance, too, once he realized she'd made a new deal with Thornton. Thornton was actually looking forward to that revelation.

"Mr. Thornton?" Diller said from the office doorway.

Thornton looked up.

"May I ask you to come with me for a moment? There are some papers to sign."

Berta made to stand as well, but Diller stopped her.

"I only need Mr. Thornton. Just make yourself comfortable, Miss Volker. We won't be gone long."

Diller led Thornton into a neighboring office and shut the door. The man whose office it was had left, so they were alone and Thornton saw no papers needing a signature. "I had a clerk add up your recent withdrawals, and they total twenty-three thousand dollars, including today's. I know you assured me that you trust this Vane fellow, but that is a lot of money."

What Diller didn't say was that it was also a rather large percentage of the funds Thornton had deposited here. Diller couldn't know this was all the money Thornton had, and Thornton wasn't about to tell him that. Better to give the impression he wasn't at all concerned. "It's nothing compared to what Miss Volker is worth."

"And you are certain she or Vane will repay you?"

"She will more than repay me. She is going to give me half of her fortune in exchange for the assistance I have given her."

Diller's frown deepened. "Mr. Thornton, that seems, uh, overly generous, don't you think?"

"For what I've done to help her? Not at all. Without me . . . Well, the less you know about it, the better. I know you're trying to do your job, Diller, but this is my money and my business. Just give me the cash and we'll be on our way."

Diller didn't look convinced, but he said, "As you wish."

A few minutes later, Thornton was back in the office with Berta and a now-smiling Diller when a clerk brought in an envelope containing the money. He handed it to Thornton who tried to give it to Berta.

"Count it," she ordered. "I do not understand your money."

Thornton counted it and realized he should have asked for some extra for himself, since he'd emptied his wallet last night. He thought about slipping some bills out of the envelope but figured she'd throw a fit if she saw it. Satisfied that the amount was correct, he handed the envelope to Berta who slipped it into her purse.

"I can go now?" she asked.

"Why yes, you can," Diller said. "It was a

pleasure to meet you, Miss Volker. I hope to see you very soon along with your cousin, Mr. Vane."

"That is not his proper name," she said, rising from her seat. She turned and walked out without so much as a glance at Thornton, which was just fine with him. He'd be pleased not to ever see her again if it wasn't for her money.

"She's not what I was expecting," Diller said.

"She's not what I was expecting, either," Thornton agreed.

"What happened to Vane?"

Thornton explained briefly.

"Do you mean she's in the country illegally?" Diller asked, alarmed.

Thornton wanted to swear at himself for revealing too much. "No, Vane was just afraid they might stop her when they saw she was from Germany. Everything is fine," Thornton lied.

Diller still didn't seem convinced, but luckily, he was also not inclined to get involved any deeper in other people's problems. "Just be careful, Mr. Thornton."

Hadn't he just promised himself he would be?

Elizabeth was rather relieved when Oriel returned to the house. She had half expected Oriel to disappear, leaving her helpless infant behind for Sergeant Kellogg or, even worse, Elizabeth to deal with. Thankfully, Oriel did feel some

285

responsibility for the child, even if it wasn't always obvious.

"What did the captain want?" Oriel asked when she'd answered Elizabeth's questions about her errand.

"His fiancée has broken their engagement, so he is returning to France to marry the girl he met there."

Oriel shook her head. "*Vive l'amour*," she said with no enthusiasm.

"I'm sure they'll be very happy."

"For a while," Oriel conceded. Plainly, Oriel had no romantic illusions.

"And what are you going to do now?"

"I will tell Phillipe that if he finds work, I will go with him. If not, I will go without him."

They hadn't seen Phillip Kellogg since the day he left Oriel here, so Elizabeth thought it unlikely they would have a happy ending together. "How will you live?"

"The same way I always have, only I think it will be easier here."

She was probably right. "Now that you're back, I have an errand of my own to run, and tonight I'm going to have supper with my fiancé to celebrate Valentine's Day. Would you tell my aunt where I've gone if she gets home before I do?"

"*Mais oui*. It will give me a reason to stay here another day." She would be using whatever excuse she could find to stay on, Elizabeth predicted.

Elizabeth's errand took her to the Upper West Side where the Westerly family lived in their new mansion. She knew that Friday was Rosemary and her mother's "at home" day when they would be receiving callers. Had word gotten out about the broken engagement yet? If so, they would be swamped with curious visitors, and Elizabeth was determined to be one of them.

But when she arrived, a maid admitted her to the parlor, where she found only Rosemary, her mother, and Lord Percy.

Percy jumped to his feet and hurried over to greet her. "Elizabeth, how delightful to see you." She imagined it was delightful, if he'd been keeping company with Rosemary and Mrs. Westerly for very long. He kissed her hand, earning a black look from his two hostesses.

"Percy, what a surprise. Aren't you afraid you'll wear out your welcome here?" she teased.

Rosemary laughed at that, a forced laugh that sounded a little bitter to Elizabeth. "We never get tired of Lord Percy's company, do we, Mother?"

"Not at all, dear," Mrs. Westerly said with some pride. Plainly, she had high expectations for Percy.

Mrs. Westerly invited Elizabeth to sit, so they all did. A moment of awkward silence fell before

Elizabeth turned to Rosemary. "I was surprised to hear about you and Logan."

"Were you?" Rosemary said. "I thought perhaps you had noticed that . . . Well, that things between us had changed."

"I don't think I saw the two of you together enough to really know," Elizabeth said ingenuously.

"Yes, well, that was part of the problem. Logan always seemed to have something else to do. It became evident to me that I would not be the most important person in his life."

And Logan certainly wasn't the most important person in hers, but Elizabeth just smiled sympathetically. "It's good you discovered that before it was too late." She turned to Percy. "How much longer will you be with us, Percy?"

"What do you mean by that?" Mrs. Westerly asked with a frown.

Both women were glaring at her. She pretended to be puzzled at their reaction. "I thought Lord Percy said he must return to England soon to make some arrangements about the horses he wants to buy."

"Fortunately, that will no longer be necessary," Percy said with a lazy smile.

"Then you won't be buying the horses after all?"

"Lord Percy has made other arrangements to purchase them," Rosemary said smugly.

"Is that so? Well, I must say, I'm happy to hear it. That means we will get to see even more of you. Do you think you'll be staying in the country through March? I'd love to have you attend my wedding."

"I would be honored, my dear friend," he said.

Elizabeth managed an apologetic look for Rosemary. "But you won't be attending, will you, Rosemary? You would have come with Logan, but now . . ." She turned her sad face to Mrs. Westerly. "We're just having a small ceremony at home with family and a few close friends, so the guest list is very limited."

"I'll be sorry to miss it," Rosemary said without a trace of regret.

"It really is too bad you wasted all that time planning your own wedding," Elizabeth said.

"Oh, I don't think it was wasted," Rosemary said, and suddenly she and her mother were both smiling again.

"Really? You can't mean you expect to be planning another one anytime soon. I'd think that a broken engagement would put you off the thought of marriage at least for a while. But then this isn't your first broken engagement, is it?"

Rosemary's smile vanished again. "I have only been engaged once."

"Oh yes, the others were just . . ." Elizabeth dismissed the two previous suitors with a wave of her hand.

Percy, she noticed, was eyeing her with dismay. Perhaps she was going too far.

"But I don't know why I should be surprised that you have another suitor already when Logan is leaving for France tomorrow," she continued, changing tactics.

"France?" Mrs. Westerly echoed in surprise. "Why on earth would he be going back to France?"

"To be married, of course."

Plainly, Rosemary and her mother had no idea, and even Percy looked shocked.

"Who would he marry in France?" Mrs. Westerly wanted to know.

"Oh dear, I thought you must have heard by now," Elizabeth said with just the proper amount of dismay.

"Heard what?" Rosemary demanded. "And who would Logan be marrying?"

Elizabeth managed an apologetic wince. "The young lady he met when he was in France. They fell in love and . . . Well, how silly of me to think you would know about her. It's not likely a man would tell his fiancée a thing like that, is it?"

"Not likely at all," Percy agreed stiffly.

"But Logan had every intention of fulfilling his obligation to you, Rosemary," Elizabeth hastily assured her. "You have to admire that in him, don't you? He's so honorable. But as soon as you released him from his obligation, he . . . Well, he's going back to France."

"To be married," Rosemary said faintly.

"The cad," Mrs. Westerly said.

"Do you think so?" Elizabeth asked. "I'm so new to New York society that I wasn't sure how it would look. I mean, it was Rosemary who broke the engagement, wasn't it?"

"Of course it was," Rosemary said.

"But now people might think Logan threw her over for this French girl," Mrs. Westerly said, earning a scowl from her daughter.

"Surely not," Elizabeth said. "Not if Rosemary is going to be married herself. Or did I misunderstand?"

Rosemary looked as if she would like to strangle Elizabeth, but her mother was more than capable of handling the situation. "It would not be proper to announce an engagement so soon after ending one."

"I see. That seems reasonable. And in the meantime, Rosemary can enjoy receiving sympathy from her friends for Logan's caddish behavior."

"No one enjoys receiving sympathy," Rosemary pointed out. She certainly wasn't enjoying this conversation.

"You're probably right. But at least you will have Percy here to help you through the awkward times. Imagine if he'd returned to England."

"And I will be here for you, my dear Rosemary," he promised.

Rosemary seemed only mildly comforted by that thought.

"I really must apologize for breaking the news about Logan so clumsily," Elizabeth said. "As I said, I'm new to New York society, so I'm not sure how these things are done. But I am sure that as soon as Rosemary announces her new engagement, everyone will forget about Logan deserting her for this French girl, won't they?"

Rosemary and her mother exchanged a look and reached a silent understanding in a matter of seconds. Then they both turned to Percy who stared back with an oblivious smile.

"Yes," Rosemary said with satisfaction. "Everyone will forget all about that French girl."

CHAPTER TWELVE

Percy hated the motorcar he'd been using. He much preferred something flashier, but it was far too cold this time of year for an open car. He certainly didn't want Mr. Westerly to freeze to death, at least not until he'd provided the money Percy needed. Westerly nodded his approval when they turned into the gate of Happy Hills Farm on Monday morning.

"Nice-looking place," he remarked.

Percy had managed to convince Rosemary he should discuss the horses with her father before he asked for her hand. Otherwise it would look like he was marrying Rosemary for the money. Since he was, that was the last thing Percy wanted the old man to think.

"Wait until you see the horses," Percy said. "Rosemary says you're somewhat of an expert, so I value your opinion."

"I don't like to brag, but I'm sure I can help you make your decision. My, that's some fine-looking horseflesh," he said, turning to see the horses grazing peacefully in the paddock.

They did look good, Percy had to admit, but

the ones in the barn would look better. He pulled the motorcar to a stop. By the time he and Mr. Westerly were out of the motor, Humphrey had emerged from the barn. Today his ratty wool coat had straw stuck to it here and there. He sauntered over.

"Good morning, Mr. Hyde-Langdon," he said.

Percy returned the greeting and introduced Mr. Westerly.

"Is this the fellow who's gonna help you choose your horses?" Humphrey asked, lifting his disreputable hat to scratch his head.

"He is indeed. I hope you've gathered up your best stock for him to see."

"All my stock is good," Humphrey insisted, a little insulted.

"I'm sure it is," Mr. Westerly said jovially. "Let's take a look, shall we?"

Humphrey led the way and brought out each animal in turn. The stallion was a bit unruly, so they contented themselves with a look into the stall. The mares all pranced prettily and meekly submitted to an examination of their hooves and teeth.

"Fine animals," Westerly proclaimed more than once. He had no fault to find with any of them, as Percy had expected. Rosemary had, of course, warned him that her father knew nothing about horses.

While Humphrey was putting the last mare

away, Percy told Westerly which animals he was considering purchasing. One stallion and a half-dozen mares seemed like a good start, Westerly agreed, and he confirmed Percy's selections. A brief discussion with Humphrey revealed the price of each animal. Mr. Westerly felt obliged to negotiate the prices, and Humphrey felt obliged to reduce them a bit, although Percy realized he was still overcharging them.

After arranging to return soon to make the actual purchase, Percy and Mr. Westerly left in search of the inn where Percy had dined with the ladies previously.

Over lunch, Percy told Westerly all about Hart-wood and how anxious he was to restore it to its former glory.

"The war was hard on everyone," he explained. "Even though England itself saw no fighting, almost every able-bodied man was in the army, and the women worked in the factories, so the farms were badly neglected."

"Which is why America had to provide so much food for you folks," Westerly said. "It's good to see one of you at least is spending a bit of coin over here in return."

"And that is my problem, Mr. Westerly. You see, I didn't explain everything to Rosemary because one doesn't bother women with such matters, but the truth is, my tenants were all in the army, the men at least, and a lot of the younger women went to the city for better jobs, so we weren't able to cultivate all the farms and I didn't collect much in rents over the past four years. I told Rosemary I needed to return to England to arrange for more funds to buy the horses, but the truth is, I don't actually have more funds. I really need to return to sell some of my property so I can afford to ship the horses back."

"I did think it was strange when she told me you had to go back to England to arrange for a letter of credit. But now that the war is over, your tenants will return, won't they?"

"Those who can," Percy said sadly, remembering all the boys who would never return from the war. "But it will take a while for us to get back to where we were when the war started."

Westerly nodded sagely. He might not know anything about horses, but he did know a thing or two about money. "I'm guessing you'll need a big investment to get the place back on its feet."

Percy smiled gratefully. "How pleasant to deal with a man who understands finance, Mr. Westerly."

"I know you have to spend money to make money, son, and luckily for you, I've got some to spend. Now I know you've got your eye on my little girl, so I think we might be able to make a deal."

Percy winced a little at his frankness. The English handled such things with more delicacy, or at least Percy assumed they did. He'd never bargained for a bride before. "Yes, buying the horses is the least of it. Shipping them will be quite costly, and I'll need to hire some men to accompany them, since I plan to stay on in America for a while."

"Yes, until the wedding," Westerly said with a booming laugh.

"I'm afraid you have spoiled my little speech, sir. I was planning to ask your permission to marry your lovely daughter when we concluded our business."

"I suppose that's how they do it where you come from, but in America, the girl makes up her own mind, and we both know Rosemary has made up her mind to have you. I don't have much to say about it except to pay the bills. I just need to know what that bill will be."

Percy shifted uneasily in his chair. "I can give you a detailed accounting. In addition to the horses, we'll need to repair the outbuildings and replace the equipment. A lot of it was confiscated for the war effort."

"Did they use plows in the war effort?" Westerly asked, plainly amused by his own joke.

"I understand they melted the equipment down to make military machinery."

"Of course they did. Did the same thing here, too. I'm just pulling your leg, son. What else do you need?"

"Workers, of course, and—"

"Just give me a round number, why don't you?"

Percy leaned back in his chair and studied Mr. Westerly's jowly face for a long moment while he mentally multiplied his round number by two and divided it by four to convert it to English pounds and added a little to make it come out even. "I think thirteen thousand pounds should cover my expenses and return Hartwood to a manor worthy of your daughter, Mr. Westerly."

"And how much would that be in real money?" Westerly asked, signaling the waiter to refill his coffee cup.

Percy pretended to consider. "About fifty-two thousand American dollars, I think, although your banker could surely—"

"That's fine, son. We'll make it an even fifty-five. Rosemary is going to want a nice ring to show off, and you'll want to take a wedding trip somewhere."

Percy could only blink in surprise.

"Now don't think I just fell off the turnip truck. I'm going to make this all legal and official. You'll sign a promissory note for the whole bundle."

Percy didn't have to feign dismay. "Mr. Westerly, I cannot hope to repay you for decades."

But Westerly was still smiling. "Don't worry, son. The note will become null and void the minute you marry Rosemary. Let's just call it an incentive to make sure you toe the mark. My little girl has been disappointed too many times. I want to guarantee the knot gets tied good and tight this time."

Percy smiled with relief. "Mr. Westerly, I would like nothing more."

Mr. Westerly clapped his hands together. The sound made Percy jump. "By God, Vanderbilt had to pay two-and-a-half million to buy his daughter a duke, and I got an earl for my girl for only fifty-five thousand!"

Thornton had taken to reading the newspapers in the lobby. At least there he might meet someone and have a conversation. Not that he'd met anyone he wanted to ever see again, but it was somewhat better than sitting in his room alone, at least. Only a few more days until he collected his money from Bates, and Vane should also be arriving soon with Berta's trunk and her fortune. Then he could leave this town behind.

For the past few days he'd been trying to decide where he would go first. Maybe he would take a run down to Cuba where it was warm. With the war over, ships were running everywhere now. He didn't want to go on a tramp steamer, though. No, he wanted one of those luxury ocean liners. Or had the navy claimed all of them for troop transports? He'd have to look into that.

"Thornton?"

He looked up to find Leo Vane standing over him. "You're back," was all he could think to say.

Vane glanced around as if worried they might be overheard. "We need to talk. Can we go up to your suite?" He did not look like a man who had just completed a successful venture.

"Of course," Thornton said with a frown.

Vane still wore his overcoat and carried a valise covered with stickers from many ports of call. Thornton saw no sign of a trunk, but Vane had probably moved the securities to the valise. You couldn't carry a trunk around New York City. They took the stairs up to the second floor, and Thornton let them into his suite.

Vane set down the valise and started taking off his coat. "Could I have a drink?"

It was still early in the day, but Thornton could see Vane needed it. He poured two glasses. Vane sank into one of the chairs and accepted a glass gratefully. He took a long sip.

"I didn't expect you so soon," Thornton said, sitting down in the other chair.

"Yes, it would have taken me a few more days if I'd come all the way by boat, but I had to get off in Charleston."

"I know. Berta told me, but she said you would be staying on the boat."

"Berta? Have you seen her?" Vane asked in surprise.

"Yes, she sent me word when she arrived in the city, like you told her to, and she told me what happened and that you'd put her on the train and would be coming later on the boat."

Vane's puzzled frown was worrisome. "What are you talking about?"

"I'm talking about Berta, your cousin," Thornton snapped, losing patience. "She said you sent her ahead so she would be safe, and you were bringing the securities."

But Vane was shaking his head. "You couldn't have seen Berta."

"But I did. She's here in New York and staying at the Waldorf."

"No, she isn't. She's in Charleston, South Carolina, and she's in jail."

"Jail?" Thornton echoed. "She can't be in jail."

"But she is. We had to put in at Charleston because something went wrong with the boat. The engine or something. We had to wait a few days to get it fixed, and the authorities came aboard to check for contraband and found Berta."

"But they couldn't have found her. She's here, I tell you. I saw her."

"And I'm telling you, they found her, and they also found the false bottom in the trunk. She had . . ." He looked away and took another long sip of his whiskey.

"She had the securities, yes, I know. Did they find them?"

"Yes, but she also had some papers, instructions."

"What kind of instructions?"

"Instructions on what to do with the money. Who to give it to after she cashed in the securities. It wasn't her money at all. It was for the Bolsheviks."

"Bolsheviks?"

"Yes, the Germans and the Russians formed a pact when Russia withdrew from the war. The Germans are financing the revolution in Russia, and they're going to finance one here, too."

"That's ridiculous!"

"But it's also true. Berta confessed everything after they arrested her and she saw that they knew it all anyway. She's trying to save her own neck. They're going to take her to Washington, DC, to testify at some congressional committee."

Thornton took a sip of his own drink, thinking one of them was very confused. "But Berta is here, in New York. She said you took her off the boat when you heard the authorities were going to search it and put her on a train. She got here last . . . Well, she contacted me last Thursday. I'm not sure exactly when she arrived."

"That woman couldn't have been Berta."

But Thornton wasn't going to be fooled. If Elizabeth Miles had taught him nothing else, he now knew a lie when he heard one. "If she wasn't

302

Berta, how did she know all about you and the trunk and the securities?"

"I have no idea, but she couldn't have been Berta, because last Thursday, Berta was in a jail in Charleston. Here, look at this." He jumped up and grabbed his valise, setting it on a table and opening it to reveal a jumble of clothes and a newspaper on top. He pulled out the newspaper and slammed the valise closed. "I knew you wouldn't believe me, so I brought this."

The newspaper was from Charleston, South Carolina, and dated last Thursday. On the bottom of the front page was a picture of a middle-aged woman who looked frightened to death and who also looked nothing at all like the woman he had taken to his bank last week. The caption read, "Alberta Volker." The headline read, "German Operative Caught Sneaking into Country to Fund Sabotage." He skimmed the article and then went back and read it more carefully, unable to believe it the first time. The report said the police had arrested a woman who was trying to enter the United States illegally with over half a million dollars that she was going to use to fund a Bolshevik revolution in America. She had been working in league with a man named Leopold Volker, alias Leo Vane, who was now wanted for questioning by federal authorities.

Thornton was so enraged, he could hardly focus on the words. "How did you . . . ?" He had to stop and clear his throat because his fury was literally choking him. "How did you escape?"

Vane had dropped back into his chair, and he pulled out a handkerchief to wipe his forehead. "It was pure luck. I'd gone ashore to buy some things for Berta. She was staying on board because we didn't want anyone to see her and ask questions about why a woman was traveling on a boat like that. I think the captain must have betrayed us. At any rate, these men came aboard, and they took Berta and all her belongings. I guess that's how they finally found the false bottom in the trunk, or maybe she told them about it. It seems she told them everything else."

"But not my name. I'm not mentioned here."

"I don't think she knows your name. I just told her . . ." He stopped to rub his forehead as if it ached. It probably did. "I told her an associate was helping me. She wanted to know where I'd gotten the money to buy the boat after I told her I was broke."

"So the police aren't looking for me?"

"I don't think so."

"But if they're following you, you've led them right here," Thornton said, not bothering to hide his anger.

"No one was following me. Do you take me for a fool?" Vane asked, outraged. "I stayed in Charleston for a few days so I could be there if they let Berta go, but after this story, there was nothing else in the newspapers about her. I didn't dare make inquiries because I knew they were looking for me, so I caught a train and came back here."

"You idiot," Thornton said, although his heart wasn't really in it. He was thinking about all the plans he'd made, how careful he had been, and all of it for nothing. He felt as if a boulder had settled in his stomach.

"What else could I have done? Someone betrayed us. That's the only explanation." Vane drained his glass and got up to serve himself another, but he stopped halfway to the sideboard where the whiskey sat. "But what about . . . ? You said you'd seen Berta. You said she's here in New York. Maybe they did let her go."

Thornton shook his head as he contemplated this final blow. He pointed to the photograph on the front page of the paper he still held. "That woman wasn't her."

"That . . . That's not a good picture of her," Vane said, determined to find a solution. "And you said she knew all about me and the trunk and . . . How could anyone else know all those things?"

"I don't know. How did the captain know Berta was a German operative?"

"I . . ." Vane ran a hand over his face and finished his trip to the whiskey bottle. He poured a generous amount and took a large gulp before returning to his seat. When he'd had a chance to think a bit, he said, "What did she want, though? This woman, I mean. The real Berta had all the securities."

"She wanted me to give her some money of course. She said you'd sent her off with just a few hundred dollars. She was staying at the Waldorf, and she needed some nice clothes."

"And you gave her money?" Vane asked, as if that was the most amazing part of this whole fiasco.

Thornton glared at him until he cringed a little. "Of course I gave her money. You'll be interested to know that she and I struck a new deal."

"What kind of deal?" Vane asked uneasily.

"She said because I was the one who had helped her the most, she was going to give me half of her fortune and leave you out altogether."

"Why, that ungrateful little—"

Thornton's bark of laughter stopped him. "She wasn't the real Berta, you fool. You just said so yourself. That woman didn't have any money to share at all except what I gave her."

"How much was that?"

"Twenty-five hundred."

Vane whistled in amazement.

"She asked me for five thousand, so it could have been worse."

They sat in silence for a long moment as they considered what they had lost.

"It must have been the captain," Vane said at last. "He was always hanging around, talking to Berta. He spoke German, too. I didn't realize it at first, so he probably overheard us talking. And we made a stop in Florida on the way. He must have contacted that woman then."

Thornton made a rude noise. "How likely is that?"

"He could have told her about you. She could have taken a train to New York to get there ahead of us."

"How could he have known what to tell her though? I thought you didn't tell Berta about me," Thornton said, angry all over again.

He drained his glass again. "I guess I must have."

"Which means the real Berta knows about me, too."

Vane started to deny it, but he couldn't, as he realized the truth of it.

"What are you going to do now?" Thornton asked.

"I'm going to leave New York as quickly as I can. Maybe I'll go to Canada until this blows over."

"Is it likely to blow over?"

"It could. Everyone was crazy over German spies during the war and now they're after Bolsheviks and it will probably be somebody else by next month. What will you do?"

"I'm not going to do anything. I have a . . . a business deal going here. I have to stay until Thursday, and then I'll be able to go wherever I want." Cuba was looking better and better, even if he had to take a tramp steamer.

But not until he got the money from Bates.

Elizabeth was surprised to find Oriel entertaining a visitor when she returned from what had become her regular morning shopping trip for food. She was especially surprised to see that the visitor was Sergeant Kellogg. He had taken pains with his appearance today, and he was wearing civilian clothes. He jumped to his feet when Elizabeth entered the parlor, still wearing her coat and carrying her heavily laden market basket.

"Hello," Elizabeth said tentatively. The baby was nowhere in sight, which meant he was probably sleeping upstairs. "How nice to see you, Sergeant Kellogg." Hopefully, her tone conveyed the disapproval she felt for his having completely disappeared for a week.

"I've been busy, looking for a job," he said. "I didn't want to come back until I had a place for Oriel and the baby to live."

"Am I to understand that you have found work, then?" she asked. A glance in Oriel's direction confirmed that she seemed very pleased about something.

"I have. In fact . . . Well, I was just telling Oriel that the captain found a place for me in his father's company."

"That was . . . thoughtful of him," Elizabeth said.

Kellogg had the grace to look a bit chagrined, but he said, "He told me he might not have ever gone back to France for Miss Fortier if I hadn't . . . I mean, if Oriel hadn't sent those letters."

Which was more than generous of Logan, but Elizabeth didn't bother to point that out. Very few men would help a man who had cheated him. Kellogg must know that.

"I just came by to tell Oriel to pack her things because I found a place for us to live. I'll come back this evening when I get off work to get her and the baby."

"Are you satisfied with this arrangement, Oriel?" Elizabeth asked.

"*Mais oui*, I am."

"Turns out Oriel has a little money left over from what the captain sent her, so that will help, too," Kellogg reported.

"How fortunate," Elizabeth said, exchanging a knowing glance with Oriel who obviously knew how to keep secrets. "Perhaps Oriel told you that we have a salon here on Monday evenings, so don't be alarmed if you see a lot of people here."

"She told me, but I should get here before it starts."

"We shall miss Oriel and the baby," Elizabeth lied. "I know my aunt and her friend have become very attached to little Phillipe." That much was true, anyway.

"And I will miss their help with the baby," Oriel said. "I am in your debt, Miss Miles."

"I was happy to be of assistance," Elizabeth said with a smile.

Oriel smiled back. "And so was I."

Oscar Thornton spent the rest of the day stewing over the fiasco with Vane and his cousin Berta. He'd pored over all the New York newspapers, looking for any mention of her arrest but found none. He did see stories about the congressional hearings being held in Washington City. Vane had said they were taking Berta there to testify, but so far, he had seen no mention of Berta or of the search for Vane himself. If Vane went to Canada, they were unlikely to find him in any case.

If only Thornton knew whether Berta was going to implicate him. Vane had been so sure she didn't even know his name, but someone had known it. That someone had known all about Vane and Berta and her trunk and her securities, and that someone had also known exactly where to find Oscar Thornton. So now he had to worry about federal officers tracking him down and arresting him for aiding a foreign agent while at the same time being furious that some completely different woman had tricked him into giving her twenty-five hundred dollars.

Vane had suggested that Thornton destroy any papers he had that would indicate he had provided Berta with assistance. Those papers were, of course, the promissory notes he and Vane had signed in which Vane agreed to repay the money Thornton had advanced for Berta's rescue and to give Thornton half of his share of Berta's fortune. With Berta in jail and her fortune confiscated, Thornton had no hope of collecting on any of these debts, so he burned the papers without regret. When they were ashes, he knew nothing could connect him with that plot except the word of a woman who may or may not even know his name.

Thornton gave a moment's thought to the bank president, Diller, but he'd never volunteer to explain how his bank became involved in a plot like this. And the woman who had pretended to be Berta was equally unlikely to come forward, since she was nothing more than a crook.

By evening, Thornton's white-hot rage had settled into a smoldering lump in his chest. He was furious at Vane and certain the man had done something stupid to cause the betrayal and subsequent arrest of his cousin. The fortune at least had been real enough. He'd seen part of it with his

311

own eyes, hadn't he? He also couldn't believe a mere female could have planned to outsmart both him and Vane to get herself to America and then make off with the entire fortune to give away to some Russian revolutionaries. That never could have happened. Even that vixen Elizabeth Miles had needed help from her brother. No, Thornton would have figured it out and gotten at least his original share if the government hadn't stepped in when they did. The loss of the twenty thousand dollars in expenses burned, but that, at least, had been his choice. A man had to be willing to take chances if he wanted to win big, and Oscar Thornton had never been afraid to take chances.

No, what burned was the money he'd given that woman, even though it was a much smaller amount. Who on earth was she and how had she found him? Who knew enough about Vane and his cousin to trick him like that?

Thornton tried to make sense of Vane's theory, that the captain of their boat must have eavesdropped and learned of the plan. Vane would have had to discuss every detail with Berta on the boat and then mention not only Thornton's name but also his hotel. Otherwise, how would the other woman have found him? Now that he thought it through, he realized Vane's theory was ridiculous.

No, the information must have come directly from Vane, from him telling someone the sad story of his cousin Berta the way he'd told it to Thornton. Then that person had to find out somehow that Thornton was helping Vane. But hardly anyone even knew Thornton was in the city. He tried to think of everyone he'd seen during his stay here.

Vane knew, of course. He'd chanced to see Thornton in the hotel dining room. And Diller, the banker. He actually knew almost all the story, but why would he have sent a woman to bilk Thornton out of such a relatively small amount of money and then warn Thornton not to give it to her? Bates knew he was in town, of course, but he knew nothing about Berta and her fortune. How could he?

And Elizabeth Miles knew. He hadn't seen her, but he'd felt her presence every moment he'd been here. She had cheated him twice already. He was sure of it. The first time there was no doubt. She and her so-called brother had tricked him out of fifty thousand dollars. Then there was the government deal that went so very wrong. He had never figured out how she was involved, but he was sure she was. Hadn't she made him think her dead so he would never seek revenge? That was an elaborate charade for an innocent person to concoct.

Thornton went over and over his short list of prospects far into the night, first pacing his room and then tossing restlessly in his bed until the winter sunrise lighted the artificial canyons that served as streets in New York City. By then he had finally found the link: Leo Vane had been Leopold Volker. Over a year ago, Volker had sold Thornton a warehouse full of rifles that vanished when the army had interrupted his deal with a retired general and confiscated everything. That was the deal he'd been sure Elizabeth Miles had planned.

Thornton had remembered that connection when he first encountered Volker/Vane down in the hotel restaurant, but he hadn't considered it a problem because Vane hadn't been involved in the final part of the deal that had gone so horribly wrong. But what if he was involved somehow? What if he was part of it and what if he had engineered this whole deal with Berta and . . . ?

But no, the story was in the newspaper. That part was real enough, and the real Berta was in jail. Vane would hardly have planned something like that. But Vane was very likely to have told someone else about Berta and her fortune, someone here in New York, before he even went to Mexico. He'd been ready enough to tell Thornton everything, and Diller, too. Thornton had no reason to think he was the first person Vane had asked for help. What if Vane had confided in someone less trustworthy? Someone connected to the army swindle. Someone who would figure out a way to trick Thornton out of five thousand dollars? Maybe the fake Berta had only gotten half of that from him, but she'd wanted more. Even what she'd gotten was a tidy sum for a few hours' work.

It all came back to Elizabeth Miles. She was responsible for everything that had gone wrong in his life. He should never have walked away that last day. He should have made sure she was dead. He should have had one of his men make sure. If he'd done that, none of this would have happened.

Suddenly, getting the money from Elizabeth Miles seemed like the most important thing he could do. The deadline was only two days away, but it might not be safe for him to wait around even that long. If Berta had told the government about him, they could be looking for him at this very moment. The Miles girl should have the money by now anyway. All he had to do was find her and get it, and once he did, he'd make sure she would never cheat him again.

The problem, of course, was that he had no idea where to find her. His men might have been able to find her, but he'd let them go months ago, after she'd cleaned him out in that deal with the army and he could no longer afford to pay them. No, he'd have to find someone who knew where she lived. Bates knew, but he'd never tell. He'd protect her to his dying day.

Thornton could stay in town until their

wedding. The location would probably be in the newspapers, but that was too public and much too long to wait. If he didn't leave town and Berta told the congressional committee about him, he might be in jail himself by then.

But he did know someone who could tell him how to find her, someone not very clever who could be tricked into telling before he realized Thornton's intent. And he knew exactly where to find him.

Thornton shaved and dressed carefully, then packed his bags so he'd be ready to leave the moment he returned with the money. Then he stopped for breakfast in the hotel dining room because it was still too early for his first errand. After breakfast, he chose to walk because the day was crisp and clear and the cold air helped him think. He needed a plan for getting the information he required, and by the time he reached the building he'd been looking for, he had one.

The building he sought was located just off Fifth Avenue, an old office building that no one had gotten around to tearing down and replacing with something new and modern. The wavy glass in the windows disgusted Thornton, as did the general air of age inside, created by the dark wood wainscoting and the ancient wallpaper.

To his surprise a girl secretary sat at the front desk in the suite of offices he'd entered. The war had changed a lot of things.

"Good morning," she said, looking down at her appointment book after greeting him. "Did you have an appointment?"

"No, I—"

"Our partners don't see anyone without an appointment, I'm afraid. If you'd like to schedule one—"

"I don't want to schedule one," Thornton said, trying to keep the impatience out of his voice. He'd obviously failed, if her startled expression was any indication. "I just need to see David Vanderslice for a few minutes."

"David Vanderslice?" she asked with a puzzled frown.

"Yes. Is he in or not?"

She bit her lip. "He, uh . . . he isn't in, I'm afraid. Perhaps one of our other partners can help you."

"No other partner can help me. I need to see Vanderslice. When will he be back?" He should have known. Men like Vanderslice kept banker's hours and only on the days they came to work at all. Perhaps he should have telephoned and made an appointment.

"I . . . Are you and Mr. Vanderslice friends?" she asked, still frowning. What was wrong with her?

"No, we aren't. Just tell me when he's coming into the office and I'll be back."

"He . . . I'm very sorry to have to tell you,

but Mr. Vanderslice is . . . no longer with us."

Why didn't she just say that in the first place? "Then tell me where his new office is and I'll go find him."

"He doesn't have a new office. He . . . I . . . I don't know how to tell you this, but Mr. Vanderslice is dead."

CHAPTER THIRTEEN

Dead? What do you mean he's dead?" Thornton demanded.

The girl flinched, but she was determined to maintain her composure. "He died. Last fall, I believe. That was before I came."

"In the war?" Thornton asked, trying to make sense of it. Vanderslice would have been the right age for that.

"No, uh, I believe it was the flu."

The flu? Thornton wanted to swear, but that would probably send the girl screaming for help. He glanced around and wondered if any of the other partners were even there. No sense causing a disturbance to find out. The girl wouldn't be any help anyway. The flu. What a disaster.

Totally frustrated, Thornton left the office without another word, leaving the girl gaping. Once out in the street, he started walking again, hoping the cold air would clear his mind. To his great relief, it did, because a few minutes later he remembered another person who could help him. She would be just as stupid as her brother and a girl to boot. He wouldn't even need to be clever to get her to tell him how to find Elizabeth Miles.

"That's quite a signature," the gentleman behind the large mahogany desk said, examining the papers Percy had just returned to him. They were at Mr. Westerly's bank, where he had taken Percy that morning to finalize the arrangements for Percy's "loan." "Why do you have two last names, Mr. Hyde-Langdon?"

"He's an earl, Gilbert. It's Lord Percy," Westerly corrected him with an unmistakable air of satisfaction.

"Lord Percy, then," Mr. Gilbert said, a little doubtfully. Percy thought he looked like an artist's version of what a banker should look like: corpulent, well dressed, and not quite bright.

"Hyphenated names are an old British custom. Aristocratic families with no male heirs who didn't want their name to die out would ask the man who married a daughter to add her name to his."

"I see," Gilbert said, still peering at Percy's signature. "Earl of Hartwood. Where is that?"

"In the Cotswolds," Percy said, knowing full well no American had any idea where that was.

"Yes, of course." Gilbert was still peering at the signature. "This is an unusual arrangement, I must say."

"Providing a girl with a dowry?" Westerly scoffed. "It's not unusual at all."

"I mean structuring it as a loan that will be forgiven upon marriage," Gilbert clarified. "I don't think I've ever seen anything like that."

"But surely it's perfectly legal," Percy said as if he really wondered.

"I suppose it is," Gilbert said without much enthusiasm.

"Then is everything in order?" Westerly said impatiently.

"What?" Gilbert looked up. "Oh yes, everything is fine. I suppose you'll want the money transferred into an account for Mr., uh, I mean Lord Percy."

"If you don't mind, old chap," Percy said before Westerly could express an opinion, "could I have it in cash?"

"Cash?" Gilbert actually blanched at the word.

"Yes, you see, I have several large expenses to take care of." He glanced at Westerly and said, "The horses." Then turned back to Gilbert. "And I will be taking the remainder of it directly to England, you see. Since the war, things are very uncertain, and I don't really trust the usual channels." Then to Westerly again, "I'll need the money to be available so the work can begin on my estate at once. I want the place in tip-top form when I bring my bride home."

"Oh yes, good idea," Westerly said, even

though he looked almost as shocked as Gilbert.

"Will that be a problem?" Percy asked with perfect innocence.

"Not at all," Gilbert said, still worried, "but aren't you concerned about carrying that much cash?"

"I've brought a friend along, and I have a motorcar, so I won't be trudging through the streets with a bag of money thrown over my shoulder, if that is what you're imagining."

The other two men smiled at Percy's little joke.

"And of course I want to visit a jeweler this afternoon," Percy added to Westerly. "Rosemary did say she wanted our engagement announced in next Sunday's newspapers."

"Why yes, she did say that, didn't she?" Westerly said, his good mood restored. Rosemary had actually said she wanted her engagement announced well before Logan returned from France with his new bride. Percy was only too happy to do his part.

"Then I'll have your money prepared," Gilbert said, rising ponderously to his feet. "I don't suppose you have something to carry it in."

Percy reached down and lifted the small valise he had brought with him. "Will this do? I'm afraid I don't know exactly how large a bundle it will be."

"I'm sure that will be adequate," Gilbert said a little stiffly. He took the bag with him.

"If you need a good jeweler, I can recommend some," Westerly said when they were alone.

"Thank you, Mr. Westerly. I would appreciate it," Percy said and listened with rapt attention as Westerly gave him the names of several jewelers Percy had no intention of visiting. When Westerly was finished with that, he proceeded to instruct Percy in the best method of shipping the horses, a subject he obviously knew nothing about, but Percy continued to listen in respectful silence.

After what seemed an eternity, Gilbert returned with the satchel. Westerly insisted on counting the money while Percy looked on, appalled. A British gentleman would never insult anyone by insisting on a count. Fortunately, it was a matter of only a few moments, since the bills were banded and labeled and there were only five bundles, each with a hundred one-hundred-dollar bills and five thousand in smaller bills. Percy would have fanned the strapped bundles to make sure all the bills were hundreds, but he could do that later.

When Westerly was satisfied, the men shook hands all around, and Percy excused himself. He had errands to run, he told them, although none of them included the shipping of horses or the purchase of an engagement ring.

The girl had finally arrived home. Thornton had been waiting for hours in the cold, walking up and down the block and disappearing around the corner whenever a passing resident gave him a suspicious look or the beat cop made his rounds.

He had known exactly where she lived because he'd been a guest in this house. An honored guest. David Vanderslice's valued client. He also knew the girl, not only from his previous visit here but because he'd seen her murder Elizabeth Miles. He would take great delight in terrifying her into giving him the information he needed.

She was, he noticed, carrying books as she made her way along the street to the house he remembered so well. She was a bit long in the tooth to be going to school, but maybe she'd had to get a job to support her family when her brother died. Maybe she was a teacher now. These old New York families had never been especially good at holding on to money, and Thornton knew a moment of satisfaction at the thought of this old Knickerbocker family having to earn their daily bread.

He picked up his pace, timing his arrival at her stoop just as she was unlocking the front door. Then he bounded up the steps, arriving as the door swung open. He pushed her inside and stepped in behind her, closing the door securely.

"What on earth?" she cried, catching her balance and turning to see who had pushed her. "Thornton," she said without as much surprise as he had expected.

"Yes, Thornton," he confirmed. "A pleasure to see you, Miss Vanderslice."

"Miss?" a voice said, startling them both. The maid had appeared, obviously drawn by the sound of the front door opening. She eyed them both with a worried frown. "Is everything all right?"

"Perfectly all right," Thornton assured her. "I told you I'd be back." But she looked to the Vanderslice girl for confirmation.

"I was here earlier," he hastened to explain before the maid could speak, keeping his voice friendly. "Your maid told me you'd be back this afternoon, so I returned just in time, didn't I?"

"Yes, you did," the Vanderslice girl said. "It's all right, Mary. I'll deal with Mr. Thornton."

The maid glanced at him, then said, "He asked for your mother when I told him you weren't here, but I didn't tell her."

"That's good. Thank you, Mary."

They waited in silence while the maid retreated back to the kitchen.

"Is something wrong with your mother?" he asked. He didn't care, but he needed to know if she was going to be a problem.

"She doesn't go out much since . . ."

"Since your brother died?" She flinched but said nothing. "I was sorry to hear that," he added quite honestly. Vanderslice's death was a great inconvenience.

She didn't look like she appreciated his sympathy though. "What do you want?"

"I want Elizabeth Miles."

That surprised her, but she said, "Then go find her."

"I don't know where she lives."

She smiled. "Then ask Gideon Bates."

"I'm asking you."

His fury must have finally registered with her because she frowned again. "What do you want with her?"

"I'm surprised you don't know. She owes me some money. A lot of money, and I need to collect it."

"I thought you were going to collect it on Thursday."

So she did know. How very interesting. "I need it now."

"And what if she doesn't have it now?"

"She'd better have it."

Miss Vanderslice seemed unmoved, which he found exceedingly annoying. "But if she doesn't, what will you do?" She held up her hand to stop him when he would have told her in no uncertain terms. "Yes, I know, men like you always threaten violence when they don't get their way, but in this case, violence won't get you anything at all. If you hurt Elizabeth, you might get some satisfaction, but you won't get your money, and isn't that what you really want?"

His anger was nearly choking him, but she was right, the money was the important thing. "How do you know she doesn't have it?"

"Because she's working a con on . . . on someone, and it isn't finished yet."

"How do you know that?" he scoffed.

"Because I'm helping her."

Now he was really surprised. The Vanderslices had really fallen on hard times if the daughter was reduced to being a con artist. "Who is she running the con on?"

"Does it matter?"

"Yes, it does, if you expect me to believe you."

She gave a long-suffering sigh. "On some British fellow. He's a duke, I think."

"A duke?" That sounded promising. "Where did she find him?"

"He's . . ." She hesitated, biting her lip. Plainly, she didn't want to say.

"Tell me," he demanded.

"He's going to marry one of her friends," she said reluctantly.

"One of her society friends, you mean?"

"Of course one of her society friends. He's a duke."

"And how much money is she going to take him for?"

"I have no idea."

"I thought you were helping her."

"I just help. I'm not . . . I don't do the actual con part of it."

Thornton somehow resisted the urge to shake her. "Take me to her."

"What?"

"Take me to Elizabeth Miles. I want her to explain what she's going to do, and then I want to be there when she does it."

"Are you out of your mind? You'll ruin everything."

He grabbed her wrist, still encased in the gloves she'd been wearing outside, and squeezed until she cried out with pain. "Take me to her, or I'll get your mother to do it, and I won't be nearly as nice to her as I was planning to be to you."

He released her and she staggered back, holding her wrist. Now she looked appropriately frightened. They could hear the maid's footsteps as she came running to see what was happening. "Tell her nothing is wrong," Thornton whispered.

"Miss Vanderslice, do you need me?" the girl asked anxiously. She could plainly see Miss Vanderslice was still holding her wrist, and her expression clearly said she was in trouble, but she said with amazing serenity, "No, I don't need you, Mary. Will you tell my mother I've gone out with a friend and I probably won't be home for dinner?"

"Are you sure, miss?" the girl asked, still eyeing Thornton warily.

"Yes, I'm sure. Come along, Mr. Thornton. Let's get this over with."

"You can just give me her address," he said, not relishing trying to control her as they moved through the city.

"I don't know the address. I'll have to show you."

Elizabeth had truly enjoyed her first day in a week without Oriel and a squalling baby in the house. She had gone for a fitting on her wedding gown earlier, which was a delightful creation she was truly going to love wearing, and now she could enjoy some peace and quiet. She couldn't help thinking about all the various schemes going on around her, but she wasn't involved in any of them at this point, so she could finally relax. That was why she groaned when someone rang the doorbell.

It was too early for Cybil and Zelda to be home from Hunter College, and besides, they would have used their keys. That meant the person at the door was a visitor. But perhaps Gideon had decided to stop by. That made her step light as she hurried to see who was there. The sight of two silhouettes on the glass slowed her a bit, but curiosity won the day and she opened the door to find her best friend and her worst nightmare.

Thornton gave Anna a shove, propelling her

through the door, before Elizabeth could even speak.

"I'm sorry," Anna said as Elizabeth caught her arm to keep her from falling.

"What's going on?" Elizabeth demanded. "What do you want, and why is Anna with you?"

"She had to show me where you live," Thornton said.

"I couldn't remember your address," Anna said a little plaintively.

Elizabeth knew that was a lie. Anna had probably heard Gideon give it to the cabdriver dozens of times when he escorted her here for salons. For some reason, her friend had deliberately chosen to accompany Thornton here, probably out of an unsubstantiated belief that she could be of some help. Elizabeth loved her for that.

"Then won't you come in?" Elizabeth said with false cheer. "Can I get you some refreshment?"

"Just go in and sit down and tell me all about this duke," Thornton said.

"Duke?" Elizabeth echoed with a frown.

"Don't pretend you don't know what I'm talking about. Miss Vanderslice told me you're conning some duke to get my money."

"I had to tell him about the duke," Anna said with apparent dismay. "He was going to hurt my mother if I didn't."

"I see." And she did. He would probably have hurt Anna, too. Anna was such a clever girl, though. Elizabeth would have to see that she got a cut of the score. She and her mother could certainly use the money.

Elizabeth gently took Anna's arm and led her into the parlor, leaving Thornton to follow. "Are you all right?" she asked.

"I think so," Anna said with a rueful smile.

The two women sat down on the sofa, and Thornton paced around the room for a few minutes before finally settling in a chair across from them.

"So, Thornton, tell me why you had to terrify my friend in order to find me," Elizabeth said. "Our deal was that I don't have to pay you until Thursday."

She watched the emotions play across his face and realized he was under some sort of pressure that he didn't want to admit, something that had nothing to do with her, or at least that's what he thought. "I decided to leave town early, and I figured you'd have the money by now anyway."

"But I don't have the money yet, as Anna probably would have told you if you'd given her a chance."

"I did tell him," Anna reported. "But he said he wanted to meet the duke and see him give you the money."

Now Elizabeth was sure she was even angrier than Thornton was. How dare he try to spoil

331

everything? "Honestly, Thornton, I thought you were smarter than that."

Which was obviously the wrong thing to say. His face, already ruddy from the cold, turned almost purple. "You little bi—"

"I mean, you can't be there when he gives me the money," she quickly explained, "because he isn't giving the money to me. He's giving it to someone else entirely."

"Who?" he demanded.

"Does it really matter? Besides, why should I tell you and risk that you'll barge in and ruin everything?"

"And how do I know there really is a duke at all? The only thing I'm sure of is that you're a liar and a good one, too."

"Because I'm not the one who told you about the duke in the first place," she reminded him. What on earth was she going to do with him now? She couldn't possibly introduce him to Percy. "Anna is the one who told you, and she is just a respectable young woman who usually tells the truth."

"She also pretends to murder people, so you'll forgive me if I don't trust either one of you," he said quite bitterly.

He was right, of course, and Elizabeth could almost feel sorry for him. "And you'll forgive me if I don't understand why you have suddenly decided that you can't wait two more days—until the deadline you yourself set, I might add—for the rather large sum of money I am taking great pains to raise for you."

"I . . . I have a business deal that needs my attention, and I have to leave town," he said uneasily.

"A business deal that will earn you more than the money you're blackmailing me for?"

"How much is it?" Anna asked with great interest. "He wouldn't tell me."

"A lot," was all Elizabeth felt comfortable saying.

"And is he really blackmailing you?" Anna asked.

"Yes," Elizabeth said at the same time Thornton said, "No."

"I see," Anna said.

"And you can't think I would fail to pay you," Elizabeth continued as if Anna hadn't interrupted.

"I certainly can," Thornton insisted. "You've cheated me before."

"And now you're blackmailing me for it," she reminded him. "I would be a fool to give you good reason to spread your gossip."

"Yes, you would. Now tell me where I can find this duke, so I can be sure he really exists."

Elizabeth felt an uncharacteristic surge of panic at the very thought. She glanced at Anna, who was obviously trying to figure out a solution to this situation as well. Unfortunately, she didn't know all the information. How foolish Elizabeth had been to not tell Anna all her secrets.

"Could we visit Rosemary and take him along?" Anna asked.

"Who's Rosemary?" Thornton asked eagerly.

"She's engaged to the duke," Anna said. "Or at least she intends to be."

"And why is this duke giving you money?" he asked Elizabeth.

"I told you, he's not giving it to me. Besides, he's an earl."

"A what?" Thornton asked, bewildered.

"He's an earl, not a duke."

"What's the difference?" Thornton asked.

"Who knows? But he's particular about it."

"And why can't you introduce me to him?"

"I don't . . . Because I can't think of a single reason why I would bring a total stranger to Rosemary's house to meet him, that's why."

"Maybe we could meet them someplace else," Anna said.

They couldn't meet Percy anywhere, but Elizabeth said, "Where?"

"I don't know. Delmonico's maybe," Anna said. "We could encounter him by accident like we did the first time."

"But the earl would have to be there in the first place, so we could encounter him," Elizabeth said. "How could we arrange that?"

"We could ask him," Anna said quite reasonably. "Or more logically, we could ask Rosemary." She turned to Thornton. "We could meet for lunch tomorrow."

"I need to see him tonight," Thornton insisted. "I'm not letting the two of you out of my sight until I do."

Elizabeth eyed his rather rumpled appearance. "Will they let you into Delmonico's dressed like that?"

The answer, of course, was no. Gentlemen dressed for dinner.

"And," Elizabeth continued, "we have no guarantee that Rosemary and the duke will be interested in meeting us at Delmonico's at all."

"I thought he was an earl," Thornton said sourly.

"I was just confused when I called him a duke," Anna said by way of explanation, although it explained nothing.

Elizabeth's mind had been racing throughout this entire inane conversation, and she thought she might have a solution. "I know, the earl has an appointment with Gideon tomorrow."

Thornton immediately perked up. "Is he giving the money to Bates then?"

"Don't be silly, of course not. Gideon would never participate in something illegal."

"He participated when you swindled me over the rifles."

"I had nothing to do with that, as you well know, and neither did Gideon."

"I know you were behind it somehow."

"No, you don't, which makes this whole blackmail scheme ridiculous, but here we are. I'm sorry, but I don't know any other way for you to meet the earl. You'll just have to wait until tomorrow."

"I told you, I have to leave town, and I'm not leaving you alone until I meet him."

Elizabeth gave him a pitying look. "Are you planning to stay here with me all night? And what about Miss Vanderslice? Is she free to go or are you going to keep her a prisoner as well? If you let her go, she will most likely contact Gideon or the police, perhaps both, and if you keep her here, I'm sure her mother will be concerned when she doesn't return home. Mrs. Vanderslice will probably telephone me to ask if I've seen her, and what shall I say? That we're being held hostage by Oscar Thornton?"

"You'll just tell her Miss Vanderslice is spending the night with you," he snarled.

"Why would she do a thing like that?" Elizabeth asked with genuine curiosity and continued without waiting for a reply, "And you may be under the mistaken impression that I live here alone, but I share this house with two college professors, both of whom are perfectly capable of summoning the police when they find a strange

336

man has forced his way into their home and is holding two young women as prisoners."

"Damn you."

"Did I mention they will be home any moment?" Elizabeth asked sweetly.

"All right, all right, when is this duke or whatever he is meeting with Bates?"

"One o'clock, I believe."

"But how will you arrange to meet him?" Anna asked.

He gave her a look that could have curdled her blood if she had been the least bit intimidated by him. "I'll just introduce myself." He turned to Elizabeth. "If he isn't there, I'll be back to find you, now that I know where you live."

"If he isn't there, it will be no fault of mine, I assure you. I want nothing more than to pay you off and be rid of you once and for all."

They all heard the front door opening.

"Elizabeth, we're home," Aunt Cybil called.

"We have company," Elizabeth called back, giving Thornton a phony smile.

He scowled in return. "I know where to find you." He moved toward the hallway and the front door, passing Cybil and Zelda without a word and completely ignoring their curious stares.

"Who was that?" Cybil asked, coming into the parlor without even removing her coat.

Only then did Elizabeth notice Anna was shaking. Or maybe she had just started shaking.

"Are you all right?" she asked, taking Anna's hands in hers. They were icy.

"I'm so sorry, Elizabeth," she said. "I didn't know what else to do. He forced his way into our house, and he wanted to know where to find you. He said he needed the money you were going to pay him right away and couldn't wait until Thursday."

"Are you going to pay that man money, Elizabeth?" Zelda asked in amazement.

"No, dear, I'm not." She turned back to Anna. "Did he say why he needed it early?"

"No, he didn't. I tried to convince him you wouldn't have the money until Thursday, so then he wanted to know who you were getting it from."

"So you told him I was conning a duke?" Elizabeth guessed, impressed.

"It was all I could think of, and I thought he'd believe a duke would have a lot of money. I tried to explain that he couldn't meet the duke because that would spoil everything, but he said if I didn't tell him where to find you, he'd do something to Mother. When I remembered what he had done to his wife . . ."

"You did exactly the right thing, except you should have just told him where I live instead of coming with him."

"I couldn't let you face him alone. I didn't know what he might do."

Elizabeth felt the sting of tears at Anna's courage. "And you thought you could protect me?" she teased.

Anna smiled wanly. "I don't know what I thought. I just hope I didn't make things worse."

"No, you were brilliant."

"May I assume," Cybil said, unbuttoning her coat, "that the man who just left is somehow dangerous?"

Zelda was still frowning with concern, obviously not certain if she should be upset or not.

Elizabeth gave them both an apologetic smile. "He's the man Jake and I conned in Washington City."

Cybil and Zelda knew the story, and they gasped in dismay, but Anna let out a yelp of distress. "You and Jake? Oh no! Don't tell me he knows Jake."

"I'm afraid he does." Which was the information Anna didn't have before.

Anna moaned, but Elizabeth squeezed her hands reassuringly.

"Don't worry, we'll work this out. I just need to make a few telephone calls."

Percy arrived at the offices of Devoss and Van Aken promptly at one o'clock on Wednesday afternoon. He had worn a particularly impressive suit cut in the Continental style and made of a

339

striking shade of blue wool. He'd chosen an ascot instead of a tie, and he'd wrapped a white silk scarf around his neck over his tweed overcoat. Today he carried his small valise and a walking stick with an elephant head on the knob, and he'd worn a monocle.

He strode into the building and stopped in the middle of the lobby, fully expecting to be greeted, which he was, although not by a clerk. Instead, a very ordinary-looking man jumped up from his seat in the waiting area and approached him.

"Earl, is that you?"

Percy affixed his monocle more firmly and examined the man from head to foot with undisguised disdain. "I do not believe I have made your acquaintance, sir."

"Oscar Thornton, at your service, Earl." Thornton thrust out his hand, but Percy merely glared at it.

"Lord Percy?" the clerk asked, scurrying out to greet him. He gave Thornton an uneasy glance and silently dismissed him. "I hope I haven't kept you waiting."

"Not at all, my good man. Not at all."

"Allow me to escort you back," the clerk said with another glance at Thornton.

"Thank you." Percy spared the upstart Thornton one more dismissive glare before following the clerk down the hallway. "Who was that man?"

he asked the clerk, knowing full well Thornton could still hear them.

"One of our clients," the clerk said, as he had no doubt been trained to do.

The clerk escorted him to Mr. Devoss's office after relieving him of his hat and overcoat. The two men greeted each other and shook hands. Devoss invited him to be seated and offered him coffee. Percy preferred tea, so that was brought after the weather had been thoroughly discussed.

"What brings you here today, Lord Percy?" Devoss finally asked when all the amenities had been dealt with.

"A matter of grave concern, I'm afraid, Mr. Devoss. Miss Elizabeth Miles suggested that I bring the matter directly to you, since it concerns the security of your nation."

"Miss Miles? You know her?"

"We are old friends, and she advised me that you were the person to see. She said she had mentioned the situation to you."

"Uh, yes, she did speak to me, but only in the vaguest of terms."

"Which would have been necessary at that point," Percy assured him.

"So it isn't a legal matter?"

"Not a personal one, no. Perhaps I should explain. You see, I came to America to represent the British government unofficially in some diplomatic matters. After I arrived and quite by accident, I came across some information about a plot to bring a German operative into the country."

"A German operative?" Devoss echoed with a frown. "How did you come to learn about this?"

"I cannot reveal my sources, but I assure you they are reliable. This woman was carrying—"

"It was a woman?" Devoss asked, hardly able to credit such a thing.

"All the better to travel undetected, wouldn't you say? A man named Leopold Volker was arranging to smuggle her into the country from Mexico. She was carrying a fortune in securities that she was planning to convert to cash and turn over to . . ."

"To whom?" Devoss prodded when Percy hesitated.

Percy looked over his shoulder, checking to make sure the door was securely closed. "To some Bolsheviks."

"I knew it!" Devoss practically crowed. "We've suspected this for months, that the Germans and the Russians had made a secret pact when Russia withdrew from the war."

"I know nothing of secret pacts," Percy hastily assured him. "I only know what I was told about this Volker. I understand the Bolsheviks are planning a revolution in this country, too, and the

342

fortune this woman was carrying was to be used to finance it."

"You say she *was* carrying," Devoss said. "Does that mean she no longer has it?"

"It means she was captured by the authorities when the boat that was carrying her from Mexico to New York had to stop in Charleston for repairs. They have seized the securities that were in her possession."

"Then the plot was foiled. That's good news indeed, Lord Percy," Devoss said.

"Not entirely. I mentioned that this Volker was assisting her. He was the one who helped her travel from Germany to Mexico, and then he purchased a boat and hired a crew to carry her to New York."

"It sounds like this plan was already well financed even without this woman's fortune," Devoss said with a worried frown. "Where did Volker get the money?"

"You are very clever to ask, Mr. Devoss. Volker had a wealthy patron who paid for the boat and the other expenses. When they captured the woman in Charleston, however, Volker escaped, and his patron is also still at large."

"That's very disturbing. Do you know where Volker is now?"

"No, but my sources tell me he may have gone to Canada."

"That's a pity. But if this plan was so well

organized, there must be others who will carry out their original scheme, and surely they are still in this country. We need to find them and stop them."

"You certainly do. Miss Miles told me that you are a member of an organization that can seek out these people."

"We have no legal authority, you understand, not the kind we had during the war, but we still know how to investigate these things, and we can bring the culprits to the authorities when we find them."

"Then Miss Miles was right to send me to you. I know this is a rather outlandish tale, and you would be right to doubt me, but I do have some proof about the German operative and her arrest." He opened his valise and pulled out a newspaper. He handed it to Mr. Devoss.

" 'Charleston, South Carolina,' " he read from the front page.

"The story is here." Percy pointed to the article and the photo of Alberta Volker.

Devoss read it quickly, muttering outrage as he did so. "This is horrifying," he said when he was finished.

"As you see, they were unable to capture Volker, and he is probably beyond your reach by now, but the other man, the one who funded the entire effort to bring this Miss Volker to America, is still here."

"This man Thornton, you mean," Devoss said, pointing to the name mentioned prominently in the article.

"Yes, and I happen to know that he is still in this country because I just met him in your front lobby."

CHAPTER FOURTEEN

Elizabeth had had a busy day, so she was thrilled to see Gideon, who had telephoned to say he was coming to visit her after work. Cybil had insisted he stay for supper, so they didn't have time for a private conversation until the meal was over. Cybil and Zelda went to do the washing up, leaving Elizabeth free to snuggle with Gideon in the parlor.

Unfortunately, Gideon was in no mood for snuggling, as Elizabeth had noted the moment he came through the front door.

"Did you remember that Oscar Thornton is showing up at my office tomorrow morning expecting me to give him a quarter of a million dollars?"

"I don't know why you'd be worried about that. I told you the Old Man was taking care of everything."

"Does that mean your father is going to deliver a quarter of a million dollars to me tomorrow?"

"Certainly not, darling. Whatever gave you that idea?"

Gideon just gaped at her for a long moment.

"Then what am I supposed to say to Thornton when he arrives at my office?" he asked when he'd found his voice again.

"You might lecture him on what a despicable human being he is for trying to blackmail a poor, innocent female," she suggested.

Plainly, he did not find that amusing. "And what should I do when I don't have the money and he says he is going to the newspapers to tell them how you cheated him out of thousands of dollars?"

"Do whatever you want, darling. Laugh if the mood takes you, although I'm sure Thornton would expect you to be angry."

"Elizabeth," he said, trying a different tack. He was being reasonable now, because he was obviously certain she was being quite unreasonable. "I need to know what is going to happen tomorrow."

She gave him a loving look. "No, you don't, darling. It's really for your own good."

"How can you say that? Do you think I need to be protected from something?"

Oh dear, now he was angry. "Gideon, my love, you know how much I hate involving you in my little endeavors."

"Little?" he scoffed.

She ignored that. "And you know how much you hate being involved in anything dishonest."

"And yes," he continued when she did not, "I

know I'm a terrible liar, so I'm not any help to you."

"Which is one of the many things I love about you," she hastened to add. "And which is also why you shouldn't know what is going to happen. You won't have to lie, and you will be genuinely surprised, just as Thornton will be."

"But he's going to expect me to give him a lot of money. Don't you even have some boodle made up to fool him?"

Elizabeth had never loved him more. "I can't believe you said 'boodle.'"

He was still not amused. "I know what it is, too. You wrap up a bunch of paper with a genuine hundred-dollar bill on the top and bottom and band them the way the bank does. Gullible people think it's all real money."

"We won't need boodle for Thornton, though, because we aren't giving him anything at all."

"Nothing?"

"Not a cent."

"And what do I say when he asks me why I don't have it?"

"I don't think Mr. Thornton will even notice. Really, Gideon, you don't need to concern yourself about any of this."

He rubbed a hand over his face, and this time when he turned to her, she saw only concern in his beautiful eyes. "You do know that none of this matters to me, don't you? I don't mean the plots and schemes. I mean the gossip and the blackmail and Thornton's threats. I know you're worried that people will shun us socially and refuse to do business with me, but even if you're right, it won't matter to me. We can just live quietly. Society isn't as much fun as you might think and my father left me some money. We won't starve."

Elizabeth thought her heart would burst. He really did love her. "And if we do become destitute, I can always run a con. I'm sure the Old Man would find something for me."

He smiled in spite of himself. "I'm sure he would."

"But don't forget my dowry. I'm afraid the Old Man will insist that we accept it, so we will actually be very comfortable, even without your job. Perhaps we can pass ourselves off as *nouveau riche*. We can create our own upstart society where reformed con artists are considered respectable citizens."

"I'm sure everyone we include in our upstart society will need help planning their estates, too. They'll have no idea how to preserve their wealth, so they will need my expertise. You see, my love, Thornton can't hurt us at all."

"No, he can't," she lied, because of course he could. Elizabeth had no intention of spending the rest of her life suffering the condescension and outright snubs of society matrons or seeing Gideon and, even worse, his mother—who had done nothing at all to deserve it—being laughed at or pitied because of her. No, she had no desire to live quietly because she had made her husband a pariah. She would do whatever must be done to take Thornton's power from him. Remembering what he had done to his wife and Thornton's warning that he knew where she lived, she might be risking her very life, but if she succeeded, she would be free once and for all.

Gideon tried to remember exactly when the course of his life, which he had once thought was immutably set, had changed so drastically. He hadn't realized until he'd actually said the words to Elizabeth last night, but he had once lived quietly. Each of his days had been much like all the others as he moved uneventfully through his life. Pinpointing the moment of change was actually easy: it was the day he'd met an auburn-haired suffragist who had been jailed with his mother for demonstrating outside the White House. One look into those startlingly blue eyes and he had been lost forever. Had he thought her just another society girl who would fit neatly into his ordinary world? Perhaps he had, at least for a moment or two. If so, he had quickly realized his mistake, however. Elizabeth Miles was not at all ordinary. He had almost lost her twice, or so he'd thought at the time, and he wasn't going to allow a villain like Oscar Thornton to ruin her.

Gideon had been sitting in his office the next morning, staring at the same documents for over an hour, and he still could not have said what any of them were about. His mind was too occupied with his upcoming encounter with Thornton. When Smith knocked on his door to announce Thornton's arrival, Gideon actually felt relief.

Thornton stepped into Gideon's office and looked around expectantly. "I thought maybe Elizabeth would be here."

"Don't you dare use her first name," Gideon warned him, fighting the urge to rise to his feet. He didn't want to show Thornton any respect, but the desire to punch him in the nose was almost overwhelming.

"Or what, Bates?" Thornton scoffed. "You'll challenge me to a duel?"

Gideon might have to punch him in the nose after all. He took a deep breath and tamped down his fury, reminding himself that Elizabeth had assured him Thornton would be suitably humbled before this day was out. "Have a seat, Thornton."

"I didn't think I'd be here that long," Thornton said, eyeing the two client chairs as if trying to judge which would be more comfortable. After another moment of consideration, he chose one and sat. "If you'll just give me my money, I'll be on my way."

"Aren't you worried about carrying a lot of

money? I was surprised to see you traveling without your two bodyguards. What were their names again? Tweedledum and Tweedledee?"

"Very funny, Bates. You should have figured out that after you and your friends cleaned me out, I had to let them go."

"Those people were not my friends," Gideon said, still angry at the memory. "David Vanderslice asked me to do the contracts, so I did. In the end, David couldn't even pay me, so if you think I had any part in that, you're sadly mistaken."

"You mean your girl didn't cut you in?" Thornton taunted him.

"She didn't have any part in that, either. You were there, so you know she doesn't owe you anything."

"She owes me all right. You notice she didn't even object when I told her how much. She already knew."

"Is that what you think?" Gideon asked, wondering how long he could keep Thornton talking.

Not long as it turned out. "Are you going to give me my money or not? Miss Miles"—he emphasized her name so Gideon could not object—"assured me you wouldn't dirty your hands with it, but I don't see anybody else here to do the honors."

Just then someone tapped on the door, and it opened before Gideon could even respond. Mr. Devoss stepped in.

"Pardon my intrusion, Mr. Bates, but I understand you are meeting with Mr. Thornton. Is that correct?"

"Yes," Gideon said in surprise. Since when did Devoss keep track of Gideon's appointments? Still, Gideon remembered his manners and introduced the two men.

Devoss was his usual, serious self, but Thornton was grinning broadly. Did he think Devoss was going to pay him? Of course he did, Gideon realized with amazement. Poor Thornton.

"Mr. Thornton, might I ask you to step into my office for a few moments?" Devoss asked. "I would like you to meet someone."

Thornton was only too happy to oblige. He was very anxious to meet this other person.

"Mr. Bates, will you join us, please?" Devoss added as he escorted Thornton from the room.

Gideon was just as eager to see what was going to happen in Devoss's office, so he followed obediently.

"Are you a native New Yorker, Mr. Thornton?" Devoss was asking as they moved down the hallway.

"I'm from Albany originally."

"And how do you like our fair city?"

"Not at all, Mr. Devoss. In fact, I can't wait to leave it."

"I'm sorry to hear that," Devoss said. "I thought you might be staying on for a while."

Devoss led Thornton and Gideon to his office, where a well-dressed man awaited them. Gideon judged him to be in his mid-thirties, his suit impeccable, his hair pomaded neatly into place. His expression was a bit sour, giving the impression of self-righteousness. Gideon realized it probably was self-righteousness when Devoss introduced him as Archibald Stevenson.

The ambitious young lawyer had gained national recognition a month ago when he testified before the Overman Committee and named a few hundred people he considered subversives. Most of those people were upstanding and loyal Americans who were outraged to have been named, but Stevenson remained unchastened. Devoss had told him the Union League Club had recently appointed Stevenson to chair a committee they had organized to investigate the Bolshevik threat to the United States. This committee was to continue the work of the League.

"Please sit down, Mr. Thornton," Devoss said, indicating one of the client chairs. Stevenson, Gideon noted, went to sit behind Devoss's desk while Devoss chose to stand just behind Stevenson's right shoulder.

Gideon stepped back, out of Thornton's line of sight but where he had a good view of everyone.

"Mr. Thornton, are you acquainted with a man named Leopold Volker?" Stevenson asked in the tone an attorney used when he already knew the answer was yes.

"What?" Thornton asked, his good humor evaporating. "What is this?"

"You heard me, Mr. Thornton. Is it true that you know a man known as Leopold Volker, who also goes by the name of Leo Vane?"

"Why are you asking me about this Volker fellow?" Thornton asked, trying for outrage.

"I should have mentioned that Mr. Stevenson is a special agent for the Military Intelligence Division," Devoss said, although Gideon knew he was no such thing. "He's very interested in the possibility that foreign governments are trying to infiltrate our country."

"Which is why I need to know if you have associated with this Leopold Volker," Stevenson said.

Thornton was still determined to bluff it out. "What does it matter if I did?"

"It matters because Mr. Volker was instrumental in smuggling a German operative into this country, Mr. Thornton."

"I don't know anything about that. I only knew Vane because he sold me some rifles back in 1917."

"Why were you buying rifles, Mr. Thornton?" Stevenson asked with renewed interest.

"I was going to sell them to the army."

"I see. And did you sell them to the army?"

Thornton glared at Stevenson for a long moment. "No, I did not."

"Why not?"

Thornton turned his glare toward Gideon, who merely stared blandly back. They had already had this conversation.

Thornton turned back to Stevenson. "I'm not exactly sure. Some soldiers came in and took possession of all the paperwork, and I never saw it or the rifles again."

"That sounds strange."

"It was very strange," Thornton agreed. "I lost a lot of money on that deal."

"You lost a lot of money on Berta Volker, too, didn't you?"

Thornton's expression was almost comical. "I don't know what you're talking about."

"I think you do, Mr. Thornton. I believe you provided over twenty thousand dollars to help smuggle Miss Volker into this country illegally. Why would you do a thing like that?"

"Who says I did?" Thornton challenged, trying for bravado this time.

"Your banker, Mr. Diller, for one."

Thornton looked thunderstruck, but he recovered quickly. "Bankers don't know what their clients use their money for after they withdraw it. It's none of their business."

"Perhaps not, but Mr. Diller had a very interesting story to tell us. He said you brought Mr.

Volker into the bank so he could cash some of Miss Berta Volker's securities. Mr. Diller was very surprised to learn that Miss Volker wasn't actually in the city, and later he was surprised to find that Miss Volker was in the city but her securities were not."

"I don't . . ." Thornton just shook his head when he couldn't come up with an explanation.

"Mr. Diller also told us that he warned you about Volker. He even warned you that Volker might be using your money to finance German spies."

"The war is over," Thornton said more confidently. "The Germans aren't spying on us anymore."

"Perhaps not, but the Bolsheviks are, and we know the Germans are financing them."

"Well, I don't know any such thing," Thornton insisted. His face had turned a dangerous shade of red.

"That is difficult to believe, Mr. Thornton, because Miss Volker confessed to everything when she was arrested."

Thornton was sweating, his gaze darting from one man to the other as he frantically considered his position. "That's not true," he tried, feigning confidence now. "Miss Volker is in New York. Diller saw her himself."

"If she is, then perhaps you would tell us where to find her."

"I . . . She's staying at the Waldorf."

"Then we'll find her there if we check?" Stevenson asked a bit skeptically.

"Uh, no, I believe she checked out."

"How do you happen to know that?"

"I . . . I tried to find her, to make sure she was all right."

"But she wasn't all right at all, Mr. Thornton," Stevenson said, "because she was in jail in Charleston, wasn't she?"

"I don't know. All I know is this woman sent me a message. She said she was Berta Volker and she had escaped and needed some funds to tide her over until her cousin arrived."

"And Mr. Diller said you gave her some funds."

"Of course I did. It was the least I could do."

"To help a German operative?" Stevenson scoffed.

"To help a woman in desperate straits." Thornton sat back in his chair and lifted his chin, as if certain he had proven himself innocent of all crimes.

"I see. So you admit that you helped Leopold Volker bring this woman into our country."

"I . . . She was going to give me half of her fortune for helping her," Thornton said.

"Half her fortune?" Stevenson plainly didn't believe that for a second. "That was extremely generous of her. How much was her fortune supposed to be worth?"

"Half a million dollars," Thornton said, obviously expecting them to be impressed.

Stevenson was frowning now. "So she was going to give you a quarter of a million dollars in exchange for . . . for what exactly?"

"For helping her," Thornton said, his confidence slipping again.

"And is Mr. Diller correct that you advanced this woman only twenty thousand dollars?"

"A . . . a bit more than that, I think."

"But only a bit," Stevenson said. "That is quite a return on your investment, Mr. Thornton. Surely, you can't expect us to believe anyone would be that grateful for your help."

"I . . . That was the arrangement we made."

"Do you have any proof of it?" Devoss asked.

Thornton's face was turning red again. "No. I burned the contracts when Vane told me Berta had been arrested."

"So you destroyed evidence," Stevenson said with great satisfaction.

"It wasn't evidence," Thornton insisted. "He told me . . . I didn't want anyone to think I was involved with them."

"And yet you were, and you obviously recognize your guilt. Tell me, Mr. Thornton, how long have you been working for the German government? Or are you in league only with the Russians?"

"I'm not in league with anybody!" Thornton

cried, jumping to his feet. "I just wanted to make some money, and Vane told me this sad story about his cousin who was rich and he was going to pay me a hundred thousand dollars if I helped get her out of Mexico and—"

"I thought you said she was going to give you two hundred and fifty thousand dollars," Stevenson said.

"That was later, when Vane got arrested."

"But Vane didn't get arrested," Stevenson said. "Miss Volker was arrested, and Vane escaped. Mr. Devoss saw the Charleston newspaper that reported the story."

"Yes, that's how we knew you were involved, Mr. Thornton," Devoss said. "According to the article, Miss Volker has named you as a conspirator. The authorities are looking for you at this very moment."

"You're lying!" Thornton shouted. "She didn't mention my name. It wasn't in the newspaper."

"Then you admit you knew all about it," Stevenson said with some satisfaction.

"Yes! I mean, no, I didn't know . . . She's not a Bolshevik, or if she is, nobody told me."

"But you knew she was entering this country illegally, didn't you?" Stevenson asked. "You are the one funding the whole plot."

"No!" Thornton shouted, pounding his fist on Devoss's desk.

Gideon had already taken a step forward, ready

to subdue Thornton if he went for Mr. Devoss or Stevenson, but the office door burst open and two rather burly men in cheap suits and derby hats rushed in and grabbed him.

"What are you doing?" Thornton demanded. "Take your hands off me."

"We are taking you to the Military Intelligence Division office for further questioning, Mr. Thornton," Stevenson said smugly.

"Let me go! I haven't done anything wrong!" he shouted. He jerked his head around to see Gideon. "He's the one! He stole my money, the money I was going to get for the rifles!"

"I thought you said the army confiscated the rifles," Stevenson said.

"But he was behind it, him and that woman."

"Miss Volker?" Stevenson said, obviously confused.

"No, the other girl. And she and her brother cheated me, too. They took the money I invested in the stock market."

"I see." Stevenson shot Gideon an apologetic look and continued in a more calming tone, "We'll get this all straightened out down at the MID office, Mr. Thornton. If you'll just come along with us . . ."

Thornton was not going to come along peacefully, but he was no match for the two men who were obviously accustomed to handling unruly prisoners. They soon had him on his way down the hallway to the front lobby, with Stevenson, Devoss and Gideon in their wake.

"There she is!" Thornton cried when he and his escorts reached the lobby. "That's the woman who cheated me, she and her brother. And she stole my rifles, too!"

Gideon had to push his way past Devoss and Stevenson to see who Thornton was talking about, and to his complete surprise—although he probably should have expected it—he found Elizabeth in the waiting area. She had jumped to her feet, and she was staring at Thornton like she thought he was a madman.

"Get her," Thornton was screaming. "She's behind all of this!"

"Who is this lady?" Stevenson asked of no one in particular.

"This is my fiancée," Gideon said, hurrying to her side and putting his arm around her protectively.

"Miss Miles," Mr. Devoss said, ducking around Thornton and his guards to join Gideon. "I'm terribly sorry about this."

"What's going on?" Elizabeth asked. She really looked as if she had no idea. Gideon was very impressed. "What is this man shouting about?"

"I have no idea," Devoss said.

"I'm telling you, she's the one you should be arresting," Thornton shouted. "She's stolen thousands of dollars from me, and she took all my rifles!"

Someone behind them started speaking rapidly in French, and a baby started to cry.

A baby?

Gideon turned to find Sergeant Kellogg with Oriel Segal who was clutching her squalling baby.

"There!" screamed Thornton, breaking free from his guards with a titanic effort. "That's Berta! She'll tell you what happened!" He lunged toward them.

Gideon pushed Elizabeth behind him and blocked Thornton's advance with a solid punch to the stomach. Thornton's grunt was gratifying. All that boxing in his youth had finally paid off.

"Very impressive, Gideon," Devoss murmured.

But Gideon was watching Thornton, ready to stop him if he tried anything. Fortunately for Thornton, the two guards had taken custody of him again, hauling him upright and pulling him a safe distance from Elizabeth and the others.

"Who are these people?" Stevenson asked Gideon.

Gideon opened his mouth to reply, but Elizabeth's fingers digging into his arm stopped him.

"This is Sergeant Kellogg and his family," she said, raising her voice to be heard above the baby's cries. "Sergeant Kellogg served in France with a good friend of Mr. Bates. Oriel here"—

she gestured to the woman who was bouncing the baby in a futile attempt to quiet him—"is a French war bride. They needed some legal advice, so I brought them to see Mr. Bates today."

"Then she's not Berta Volker, a German national?" Stevenson asked a little more rudely than Gideon felt was appropriate.

"Certainly not," Elizabeth said, with a concerned glance at Oriel. "I told you, she's French. I don't think she even speaks much English."

Oriel asked Kellogg something in rapid French, and he answered her, apparently explaining what was going on, although Gideon knew she spoke English passably well.

"Mr. Bates, what is the meaning of this?" Kellogg demanded angrily. "Who are these people and why does that man say Oriel is somebody else?"

"I honestly have no idea," Gideon said, although he felt certain Elizabeth could enlighten him if she chose to.

"She's Berta, I tell you." Thornton was croaking. He didn't quite have his breath back. "Volker tried to convince me that she was in jail, so he could get away with her fortune. I've got it all figured out now. Ask her, she'll tell you," he begged Stevenson.

Stevenson obviously did not relish doing Thornton's bidding, but he approached Oriel and Kellogg. "Excuse me, madame. I mean,

Pardonnez-moi, madame. Connaissez-vous cet homme?" He indicated Thornton, who glared at both of them.

Oriel replied in rapid French, too rapid for Stevenson, apparently. "I'm sorry, I don't . . ." he said to Kellogg who looked like he wanted to give Thornton a slug himself.

"She says she never saw this man before in her life."

"She's lying!" Thornton shouted. "She's German. She's staying at the Waldorf. Tell them, Berta!"

Stevenson eyed Kellogg and Oriel in their modest, threadbare garb. Plainly, the staff at the Waldorf would never have allowed them across the threshold. He turned back to Thornton. "So you maintain that this lady"—he gestured to Elizabeth—"cheated you somehow and stole the rifles you told me the army had confiscated?"

"Yes!" Thornton cried in triumph at finally being understood.

"And this lady"—he indicated Oriel, still bouncing her screaming baby—"is actually a German operative who sneaked into this country with a fortune in securities to fund a Bolshevik revolution."

"Exactly!" Thornton cried.

Devoss made a small sound of frustration. "Stevenson, I can vouch for—"

But Stevenson raised his hand to stop him.

"There is no need, Mr. Devoss. Clearly, Mr. Thornton has randomly chosen to accuse these innocent bystanders in order to deflect blame from himself."

"No!" Thornton cried. "It's true, all of it. Both of those women are cheats and crooks, and I'm innocent!"

"Then we'll find that out when we finish our investigation, won't we, Mr. Thornton? Meanwhile, you'll come along with us for questioning. I'm sure you are anxious to clear your name."

Thornton started swearing, shocking Stevenson and Mr. Devoss who hurried the guards along to get him away from the ladies. Gideon had no reason to follow except that the baby was still screaming, so he decided to see Stevenson and his crew out to the street, where it would be quieter. Devoss must have felt the same way, but they didn't get very far because a crowd had gathered on the sidewalk outside the office. The crowd was all men in ready-made overcoats, holding notebooks and pencils.

"What in the world?" Devoss said.

"Reporters," Stevenson said, although he didn't sound a bit dismayed. In fact, he sounded pleased.

"What are they doing here?" Gideon asked, thoroughly baffled.

"I don't know, but I suppose I should speak with them," Stevenson said, having gone from pleased to delighted. Gideon remembered that Stevenson had recently been featured on the front page of practically every newspaper in the country with his list of supposed subversives. He had obviously come to enjoy publicity.

"Mr. Stevenson," one of the reporters called. "Is it true you've arrested Oscar Thornton for financing a Bolshevik conspiracy?"

"I didn't finance anything!" Thornton shouted. He straightened in the grip of his guards and adjusted his coat because all the reporters were now looking at him. "It's those women in there. They cheated me and tricked me. They stole my money, but nobody will listen to me!"

"And what about the rifles?" Stevenson said with a slight smirk.

"Yes, yes, she stole my rifles, too! She stole my rifles and my money!"

"What rifles are those?" another reporter asked, obviously mystified.

"The ones I was selling to the army."

"Why did this woman steal them?" another reporter called.

"So I couldn't sell them to the army. She stole my money! But they won't arrest her and they won't arrest that other woman, either. She's a German spy!"

A rumble of excitement went through the crowd, but Stevenson waved his hands to calm them. "Gentlemen," he said, addressing the guards, "would you take Mr. Thornton to the MID offices? I will meet you there as soon as I finish with the good men of the press."

Thornton objected strenuously to being denied a chance to explain his grievances to the newspapermen, but the guards finally succeeded in getting him into the motorcar they had arrived in. As it drove away, the reporters turned their attention back to Stevenson.

"As you saw, Mr. Thornton has proven to be less than reliable, but we hope to discover the truth about his relationship to the Bolsheviks who are trying to undermine our government."

"Who are the women he keeps babbling about?" a reporter called.

"As I said, Mr. Thornton is not exactly reliable. It appears that he has chosen to identify two innocent women who happened to be in the waiting room as we left the building as the people he claims have wronged him in some way."

"He said one of them was a German spy," one reporter reminded him.

"Yes, he did. You see, Mr. Thornton came to my attention because he was providing funds to smuggle a German woman into this country illegally. She was carrying a fortune in securities that were to be used to fund a Bolshevik revolution. This is what I have been predicting for months, so naturally I was interested in proving I was right."

"And is the woman inside the German spy he helped smuggle into this country?" a reporter asked.

"Sadly, no. She is just a French war bride who happened to be here with her soldier husband to ask for some legal advice. And the other woman is apparently the fiancée of one of the attorneys here. She brought the couple here to see the attorney."

"So neither of them are trying to overthrow American democracy?" a reporter joked.

"I am happy to report that they are not, and I cannot explain why Mr. Thornton tried to convince us that they are. The real German operative is in jail in South Carolina at the moment, and there doesn't seem to be any explanation for Thornton's conviction that he was cheated by the army over some rifles. I'm very much afraid his mind may be disturbed, which would explain how the foreign saboteurs were able to take advantage of him and convince him to give them so much money. Apparently, he did give this German woman quite a bit, so he would be justified in thinking himself ill-used, but he also claims she was going to repay him at least tenfold, so it could also be sheer greed that is motivating him to protect her."

The reporters kept shouting questions, which Stevenson tried to answer, but eventually, the men of the press realized they had gotten as much information from him as they could. They were starting to disperse when the front door of the office opened and Elizabeth stepped out.

"Oh dear," she exclaimed when she saw the reporters had not left. Kellogg and Oriel had come out behind her and were blocking any possible retreat, so she just stood there, gazing at the crowd in dismay.

"Are these the women Thornton accused?" one of the reporters shouted.

The baby started screaming again, and Kellogg tried to create a path for them to escape, pushing between Stevenson and Devoss. Oriel began to berate the reporters in French, and the more she objected, the more closely they crowded her, calling out question after question until she burst into tears and they finally allowed Kellogg to lead her and the baby away.

"And who are you?" a reporter called to Elizabeth, having just remembered she was still there.

"No one," Gideon announced, taking her arm to lead her back inside, but she stopped him.

"Perhaps I should answer their questions, darling," she said with a beatific smile. "Once they understand that I was just escorting Sergeant Kellogg and his family and that I never saw Thornton before in my life, they'll know that everything he says about me is a lie."

CHAPTER FIFTEEN

S o we thought we should come immediately and tell you what happened, Percy," Elizabeth said after she and Gideon had explained to him, Rosemary, and Rosemary's parents about Thornton's arrest. They had gone straight to the Westerly house as soon as Elizabeth finished with the reporters, hoping to catch them during the ladies' "at home" hours. Fortunately, Mr. Westerly happened to be home as well.

"But I don't understand how you are involved in all this, Percy," Rosemary said, obviously unimpressed by Elizabeth's tale.

"Because he's a government agent," Mr. Westerly said, obviously as delighted as his daughter was bored. "Isn't that so, son?"

Percy smiled modestly. "That is not the term I would use. You must understand, I'm here informally."

"Yes, yes, on some diplomatic mission," Mr. Westerly said. He was grinning broadly, probably thinking what a good story this would be to tell at his club.

"And when information was reported to me,

naturally, I had to share it with the authorities," Percy said. "Although I am mystified as to why this man Thornton accused you, Elizabeth."

"Me and that other poor woman," Elizabeth said, trying to look just as mystified. "She was nearly hysterical with terror by the time the reporters had finished with her."

"I suppose it's a blessing she didn't speak English very well," Gideon said with only a trace of irony. "Maybe she didn't even understand what was going on."

"I'm sure that just made it worse for her," Elizabeth said, patting his hand.

"You say she was a friend of yours, Gideon?" Percy asked.

"Sergeant Kellogg served under Lo . . . a friend of mine," Gideon clarified a bit stiffly. Elizabeth noticed he had avoided mentioning that his "friend" was Logan Carstens. He also didn't mention Oriel because he couldn't refer to her as Kellogg's wife. Elizabeth had been careful not to make that claim, either. She was trying so hard not to actually lie anymore, except in emergencies.

"And what was it that man accused you of, Elizabeth?" Rosemary asked, having recognized a chance to cause her a bit of discomfort.

"Good heavens, I hardly know," Elizabeth said, not discomfited at all. "Something about stealing rifles from him."

"What would you do with rifles?" Mrs. Westerly asked, completely confused.

"Exactly," Elizabeth said. "And then he claimed that my brother and I had stolen money from him, too."

Percy shook his head, making his curls dance. "Elizabeth, I have known you since you were twelve—"

"I was thirteen when we first met," she corrected him, ignoring Rosemary's jealous glare.

"Thirteen then. Do you have a brother of whom I am unaware?"

"Absolutely not."

"I didn't think so. This Thornton fellow is obviously insane."

"Which is why the government believes this Mr. Volker was able to take advantage of him. It's all very tragic, really," Elizabeth said with a sigh.

"We are so grateful you came to tell us all this," Rosemary said, making it plain she wasn't grateful at all. She probably thought they were just being morbid. Her next statement would most likely have been a thinly veiled invitation to leave, but Percy interrupted her.

"Yes, very grateful, because now I know what I must do next." He turned to Rosemary, who was sitting beside him on the sofa, and smiled apologetically. "I'm afraid the government will need me to testify against this man Thornton."

"Testify?" Mrs. Westerly echoed in dismay.

Apparently, people of her acquaintance did not testify.

"Yes, to the Overman Committee. They are the ones investigating these things."

"The Overman Committee," Mr. Westerly crowed. "In Washington City. That will make you famous, my boy!"

Rosemary wasn't so thrilled. "Washington City? Do you mean you have to go there?"

"Of course he does," her father said. "That's where all the important business is happening."

"You always say the important business happens in New York," Mrs. Westerly reminded him.

"Government business happens in Washington City," he clarified. "We'll be reading about you in the newspapers."

"I certainly hope not," Percy said, visibly dismayed. "But perhaps it cannot be helped. One must do one's duty, mustn't one?"

"Yes, one must," Gideon agreed. Elizabeth seemed to be the only one who noticed his sarcastic tone.

"How long will you be gone?" Rosemary whined. "I was planning a party to announce our engagement." She took the opportunity to wave her left hand in Elizabeth's direction, even though Elizabeth had already admired the ring Rosemary had held under her nose the moment she'd entered the parlor.

"Not long, I hope. Perhaps a week or even less."

"A week!"

"Don't be selfish, Rosemary," her father chided. "Lord Percy is doing important work."

"But I need to announce my engagement before Logan . . ." She caught herself, although Elizabeth had no trouble at all understanding how that sentence would have ended. Rosemary wanted to announce her engagement well before Logan Carstens returned with his new bride.

"Can't you just put it in the newspapers?" Elizabeth asked ingenuously, remembering how Rosemary had revealed Elizabeth's engagement. "I'm sure your reporter friends would be happy to publish it."

"I do not have reporter friends," Rosemary replied coldly.

"Yes, indeed," Percy said. "Why not just put it into the newspapers? No sense having a lot of fuss. People will pop over to congratulate you in person, I daresay."

Rosemary frowned. She obviously wanted as much fuss as possible.

"I'm sure we've kept you long enough," Elizabeth said. "I'm sorry to have brought the news, but when Mr. Devoss told us he had learned about all this from Percy, I thought he would want to know as soon as possible."

"Indeed I did. If you're leaving now, perhaps we can share a cab."

"A cab?" Rosemary echoed in alarm. "Where are you going?"

"To Washington City, my dear. If I hurry, I can be packed and on a train this evening. I'll need to meet with some people at the British embassy before I appear before the committee."

"But you can't just leave!" Rosemary insisted.

"I am so very sorry, my dear, but needs must. I'll write to you as soon as I know when I can return."

Mrs. Westerly murmured her distress and Mr. Westerly shook Percy's hand and slapped him on the back and Rosemary pulled out a hankie and dabbed at her dry eyes in a show of grief as Percy took his leave.

The three of them walked over to the next avenue to catch a cab.

"Will you go to Cybil's with us?" Elizabeth asked Percy.

"Sure. I'm guessing Gideon has some questions."

"You bet I do," Gideon replied with a thunderous frown.

Elizabeth took his hand and gave it a squeeze. To her relief, he squeezed back. At least he wasn't too angry.

They didn't speak during the cab ride. No sense being overheard by someone who might decide to sell the story to a newspaper. When they arrived at Cybil's, Gideon paid the driver and followed the other two into the house. Cybil came to greet them, and she frowned in confusion when she saw Percy. "Jake, are you going to a costume ball or something?"

"Don't you like my outfit?" he said with mock dismay.

"The outfit is outlandish, and what have you done to your hair?"

He reached up and pulled off the elaborate wig. "I'll be glad to see the last of this."

"Keep the beard, though," Cybil advised. "It makes you look smarter."

By the time Cybil had called Zelda to admire Jake's sartorial splendor, they had removed their coats and hats and retired to the parlor. Jake sprawled in the most comfortable chair, massaging his head and making his own hair stand on end, while Elizabeth asked Cybil and Zelda to give them some privacy. Cybil in particular did not enjoy hearing about this type of exploit.

Elizabeth sat down next to Gideon on the sofa. He didn't look quite as angry as he had in the cab. "What would you like to know, darling?"

Gideon gave the question a few moments' thought. "I was figuring it out on the drive down, and I think I understand most of it. The business with the Volker woman, that was the con your father was running on Thornton."

"Yes, the Spanish Prisoner."

"The same one Kellogg and the French woman were running on Logan," Gideon said.

"Yes, but the Old Man did a much better job of it. Oriel isn't very skilled, I'm afraid."

"Don't be afraid," Gideon advised. "So how did it work?"

Elizabeth explained how Vane had "accidentally" met Thornton in the hotel dining room and then dropped the letter from Berta where Thornton would find it.

"And Thornton already knew Vane?" Gideon asked.

"He was one of the men who sold Thornton extra rifles back when we conned him the last time. Thornton always believed that part of the deal was legitimate."

"I see, so he had no idea Vane was working with your father."

"None at all. Then Vane pretended to travel to Mexico and he brought back phony stock certificates, but he couldn't cash them because they weren't signed by the owner."

"And they weren't real stock certificates," Jake added. "In case you were wondering."

"But seeing them convinced Thornton that Berta really had a fortune," Elizabeth said. "So when she needed money to buy a boat to get her out of Mexico and into New York, he was only too happy to help."

"Did he really believe she would give him half of her fortune?" Gideon asked in amazement.

Elizabeth gave him a gentle smile. "Of course. That is the whole point of the con, darling."

Gideon glared at Jake when he chuckled, but he said, "What was all that business about Berta's arrest being in the newspapers though? Berta doesn't even exist, does she?"

"No, and she certainly wasn't arrested. Vane traveled down to Charleston, South Carolina, and bought a few newspapers. Then he had the front page reprinted with Berta's photograph and the story about her arrest."

"Is that legal?" Gideon asked, somehow more outraged about this than anything else in this astonishing tale.

"I can't imagine anyone would care, darling," Elizabeth said. "So Vane brought the newspaper back and showed it to Thornton. No one questions what they see in the newspapers."

"But Devoss said he'd seen the newspaper story, too," Gideon remembered.

"Yes, Vane had two versions printed. One of them without any mention of Thornton, which he showed to Thornton, and one that did mention him, which he showed to Mr. Devoss."

"Which explains why Devoss believed Percy." Gideon gave Jake a scowl. "Lord Percy, I mean. All right. I think I understand all that, but why did Thornton insist the French woman was Berta?

And by the way, what was she doing in the office in the first place, because she certainly didn't have an appointment with me?"

"I brought her there for Thornton to see her, because she really is Berta. Or at least Thornton thought so."

"Why did he think so?" Gideon asked, even though it sounded as if he really didn't want to know the answer.

"Yeah, Lizzie," Jake taunted. "Why did he think so?"

Elizabeth sighed. "You see, Sergeant Kellogg couldn't take Oriel and the baby to live with him until he found a suitable place, but he couldn't find a job and—"

"Logan told me he was going to give Kellogg a job," Gideon said.

"Yes, that was very thoughtful of him, but I didn't know that, and in the meantime Oriel was living here."

"I've heard that baby scream. I imagine you were anxious for Kellogg to claim her," Gideon said.

"You are such a wise man. Yes, I was, but she needed money before she could leave, and I didn't see any reason why Thornton shouldn't help her out. He was only too glad to help a woman he'd never even met, after all."

"So she pretended to be Berta?" Gideon asked, hardly able to believe it.

"Yes, she did. She only got twenty-five hundred from him though. She could have done much better, but as I said, she's not very experienced at this."

"Do you have any more questions?" Jake asked with amusement.

"I understand the business with Oriel pretending to be Noelle so she could get herself to America," Gideon mused, "and now I think I've got the business with Thornton figured out. But what happens when Devoss and Stevenson and the Overman Committee find out that Berta Volker doesn't exist and wasn't arrested in Charleston and all the charges against Thornton are bogus?"

" 'Bogus' is such an ugly word," Jake objected.

"Those charges won't hold up, of course," Elizabeth said, giving Jake a reproving look, "but the Old Man did some investigating and found out that Thornton managed to cheat a few people himself during the latter months of the war. They were more than willing to provide proof of it, and that evidence will arrive anonymously at the MID offices in the morning. This will mollify Mr. Devoss, who will naturally be sorely disappointed when he can't find any proof that Berta Volker was funding Bolsheviks."

"The Old Man thinks Thornton will do some serious prison time as a result of his evidence," Jake added.

"Which means that the two of you won't have to worry about him coming after you for revenge," Gideon said with obvious relief, "but when he realizes he's in trouble, he will certainly go to the newspapers and accuse Elizabeth of cheating him."

"But no one will believe him," Elizabeth said with great satisfaction, "because tomorrow the newspapers will all report how he accused two perfectly innocent women of outlandish crimes and in general behaved like a madman."

She watched as Gideon gradually put it all together and realized what she had done. The expression on his face was glorious. "So no one will ever believe anything he says again."

"Yes, my darling. Never, ever again."

He swept her into his arms and kissed her soundly. Both of them ignored Jake's outraged hoots.

When Gideon finally released her, he turned to Jake. This time he had his attorney face on, though. "And what was all this business with Lord Percy? I know you wanted Logan to break his engagement but—"

"Logan was not going to break his engagement, even if it meant he would spend the rest of his life in misery," Elizabeth said. "That would also mean that Noelle would be miserable and even poor Rosemary would, too."

"Poor Rosemary," Gideon echoed sarcastically.

"And I suppose it didn't hurt that you got a little revenge for Rosemary announcing our engagement."

"I think I deserve a little revenge, since her meddling put Thornton back on my trail again and that almost ruined my life, but then I found out Rosemary had driven some poor girl to suicide and . . . Well, revenge wasn't my intention at all at first. At first, we were just trying to give Rosemary a good reason to break the engagement herself," Elizabeth explained. "So we introduced her to a much more interesting man. A more interesting man who came out of this with more money than anyone."

"I had to make expenses," Jake said defensively. "Do you have any idea how much those fancy duds cost?"

"Did you take money from Rosemary?" Gideon asked, outraged.

"Rosemary is a woman," Elizabeth reminded him. "She doesn't have any money."

"But her father apparently has money to burn. He was happy to give me a loan to buy some horses," Jake said.

"Horses?" Gideon echoed in confusion.

"Yes, to replenish my stables at Hartwood," Jake explained in his British accent. "Mr. Westerly was quite impressed with all those broken-down racehorses we showed him."

"But why . . . ? No, wait, don't tell me. But you

said it was a loan. Surely, he made you sign a promissory note."

"Of course he did. Lord Percy Hyde-Langdon, the Earl of Hartwood, signed it," Jake said.

"And he doesn't exist," Gideon said with a sign. "I'm sorry I asked."

"Yes, dear, some things are best left unsaid," Elizabeth said.

"And what about your engagement to Rosemary?" Gideon asked.

"Sadly, she will be jilted when Lord Percy must return to England," Jake said.

"And when her father tries to collect on his loan, he'll discover there is no Earl of Hartwood," Gideon said with obvious disapproval.

"No, darling," Elizabeth said. "He will discover from the letter that poor Rosemary will receive that Percy has actually lost the family estate and been forced to retire to the Continent to escape his creditors. He will apologize for having deceived her and promise to repay her father when his fortunes improve."

"Won't Rosemary come to you to try to find him, though?"

"I can't imagine she would ever admit he had jilted her, but if she does, I will be outraged and make every attempt to help locate him."

Gideon sighed. "At least she gets to keep the engagement ring. That was a beauty."

"Oh, it's paste," Elizabeth said. "It will probably turn her finger green in another few days."

"And having me expose the plot with Thornton and Vane and Berta gave Percy a perfect reason to leave town, so everything worked out," Jake said.

"I'm not sure I would say everything worked out," Gideon said, not nearly as impressed as Jake. "Did Anna know all of this?"

"She knew some of it. She helped with Percy, of course, and I'll explain the rest to her at the proper time."

"So she didn't really help you con Thornton?" Gideon said.

"She helped me get him out of my house," Elizabeth said.

"Out of your house?" Gideon echoed in alarm.

"It's all over now, darling. We never have to worry about Thornton again. All we need to think about now is our wedding and our new life together."

By March, the weather was showing signs of warming. Elizabeth had spent the past two weeks thinking about nothing but her wedding, and the day had finally arrived.

"Are you all packed for your wedding trip?" Anna asked as she laboriously worked to close each of the two dozen satin buttons on the back of Elizabeth's tea-length satin gown. They were in Elizabeth's bedroom in Cybil's house. This was the last day she would live here.

"Yes, although we aren't leaving until tomorrow. We're staying at the Waldorf tonight, I understand."

"Hasn't Gideon given you any idea where you're going?"

"No, he wants it to be a surprise."

"How did you know what to pack?"

"He said pack for winter and summer both."

"So he's taking you to the Caribbean," Anna said with confidence.

"Or he's just trying to fool me."

"Did you hear that Rosemary Westerly is sailing for England next week?" Anna asked slyly.

"What? You're joking!"

"She's taking her mother. She's saying that she is going to inspect her new home before the wedding."

"But Percy sent her a letter revealing that he was a fraud who had lost his estate and that he was fleeing to Europe. He definitely said he was releasing her from her promise to marry him," Elizabeth said.

"But she isn't going to want people to know she was bamboozled by a phony earl," Anna said. "I think she's going just so she can tell everyone she didn't like England at all and decided not to marry him."

"I just hope she doesn't decide to take out

her anger on me," Elizabeth said with a shudder.

"I wouldn't worry too much. I'm willing to bet Rosemary will manage to find some other impoverished aristocrat who is willing to take her in exchange for a large dowry, which her filthy-rich father will provide. She'll have herself a title before summer."

"Do you think so? I do hope she ends up in a castle somewhere," Elizabeth said.

"A drafty, crumbling castle with no indoor plumbing," Anna added.

They both laughed at that image, but the sound of harp music drifting up from below sobered them instantly.

"Time for the veil," Anna said. She picked up the delicate confection from where it lay on the bed and settled the lace cap over Elizabeth's head, taking care not to muss her hair. Then she fluffed out the netting of the veil to fall across her shoulders and down her back.

To Elizabeth's amazement, tears filled Anna's eyes. "You're so beautiful."

"And so are you," Elizabeth told her, stepping back to admire the lovely blue gown Anna had chosen.

"But look at you," Anna said, turning Elizabeth so she could see herself in the mirror.

Elizabeth's breath caught. She did look beautiful. For a moment she allowed herself just to feel the unadulterated joy of knowing she was going to be married this day to a man she absolutely adored and who adored her in return, a man who didn't care about her checkered past or her unusual relationship with the truth or her less than honest relatives. She in turn would forgive him for sometimes valuing the truth too much and trusting justice when it so often failed.

A tap on the bedroom door reminded them that they would be wanted soon. Anna opened the door and admitted the Old Man. He wore what appeared to be a brand-new, tailor-made suit. From his silver hair to his mirror-glossed shoes, he looked impeccable, and he actually gasped when he saw her.

"Lizzie, I wish your mother could see you now."

Elizabeth wished that, too, but she would be happy with the family who was left to her. "Are all the guests here?"

"According to Hazel, they are." Gideon would frown to hear the Old Man calling his mother by her Christian name, but there was nothing for it now. This marriage would make them family of sorts forever. "They make a pretty respectable crowd, although the numbers from our side are pretty low."

"Maybe we should have invited Spuds or Dan the Dude," Elizabeth joked.

"Yes, I would have loved introducing someone named Spuds to Mr. Devoss," Anna said.

They all laughed at the thought, and the Old Man turned his attention to Anna. "You look awfully fetching yourself, Miss Vanderslice."

She sketched him a little curtsy. "Thank you, Mr. Miles. Did you happen to notice how my mother is doing?"

"Very well, I think. Hazel is looking after her, and everyone is being very solicitous, although she did take me aside to tell me that David would have been the best man if he had lived."

"Oh dear, I hope she's not saying that to everyone," Anna said, touching a finger to her eye to stem a tear.

"Everyone will understand," Elizabeth said. "This must be very hard for you, too."

Anna smiled bravely. "Seeing my two best friends get married isn't hard at all." She turned to the Old Man. "How do we know when it's time for us to go down?"

"They told me to bring you girls right out. As soon as the harpist hears us coming down the stairs, she will start playing the wedding march."

Anna looked to Elizabeth who said, "Then let's go, shall we?" Anna picked up Elizabeth's elaborate bouquet of lilies from the bed and made sure Elizabeth had a good grip on it before retrieving her own bouquet of white chrysanthemums.

Anna led the way, with the Old Man coming behind. Elizabeth could hear the low murmur of conversation that ceased the instant the harpist changed her tune. All heads turned to see them coming. Elizabeth knew everyone there except for one. Cybil and Zelda sat in the front row on the bride's side. They had gleefully accepted the mother-of-the-bride duties, greeting the guests and getting everyone seated. Mrs. Bates and Mrs. Vanderslice sat side by side on the groom's side, both dabbing at tears with their lace handkerchiefs. Elizabeth saw Mr. Devoss—sitting on the bride's side, bless his heart—and her cherished Smith, who took such good care of Gideon at the office. She also saw Mr. Van Aken and his wife, and the rest of the partners from the law firm with their wives, along with several of Gideon's oldest friends. She had also invited the society reporter, Carrie Decker, who was busily jotting down notes about every detail of the wedding. Carrie had happily reported in the gossip column that a certain RW had been disappointed to learn that her fiancé had sailed for England without even saying farewell. Carrie was grateful enough for the scoop to give Elizabeth's wedding much more attention than it would otherwise have deserved.

Finally, Elizabeth caught sight of Logan Carstens, who was practically beaming, and the one person whom she had not yet met: Noelle Fortier. The two of them had only arrived yesterday, their sailing delayed because of storms. But from the expression on Noelle's face, she knew exactly what role Elizabeth had played in her life.

Only then did Elizabeth allow herself to look beyond the guests to the arch of greenery and hothouse flowers under which she would be married. Had she ever worried that Gideon might suddenly come to his senses and realize that marrying the daughter of a con man was a terrible mistake? But no, there he was looking even more handsome than she remembered, his eyes filled with the love she knew he felt for her. And beside him was the replacement best man who had been so astonished to be asked that he had determined to behave with the utmost dignity and decorum. Still, Jake couldn't resist giving her one of his most mischievous grins.

When they reached the parlor doorway, everyone stood. Anna led the way down the makeshift aisle between the rows of folding chairs, taking her place on the opposite side of the arch. The Old Man looked down at her, his blue eyes shining with what looked suspiciously like tears. He patted her hand where it was tucked into the crook of his elbow. "Shall we?" he asked, and he led her down the aisle to where Gideon waited.

The Old Man sounded a little hoarse when he responded to the question, "Who gives this woman to be married to this man?" Elizabeth found she could hardly speak above a whisper when asked to repeat her vows, but Gideon had no trouble at all, taking apparent delight in making such important promises. Jake handed over the ring with great solemnity, and before Elizabeth knew it, the minister—the new minister from their church whom she had grown to like very much—pronounced them man and wife.

Gideon's kiss was chaste enough but held the promise of much more to come. Then the minister invited the guests to come forward and congratulate the newlyweds. Cybil and Zelda, who were both crying by this time, were first in line, followed by Mrs. Bates, who whispered to Elizabeth that now she finally had the daughter she'd always wanted. Mrs. Vanderslice was still weeping, and she hugged Gideon for a long time. Mr. Devoss claimed a kiss from the bride, as did Gideon's friends and the other partners, although Mr. Van Aken refrained after a glare from his wife. Smith was entirely too proper to actually kiss Elizabeth, so she kissed him on the cheek, which made him blush furiously.

The last guests to come forward were Logan and Noelle. Gideon had gone to the dock to meet them yesterday, but Elizabeth had been too busy with last-minute preparations, so this was her first opportunity to meet Noelle.

Noelle kissed her on both cheeks, in the European fashion, and thanked her profusely. She really was a lovely young woman, and she and Logan seemed deliriously happy.

"You are married now?" Elizabeth asked.

"*Oui*," Noelle said. "We are married in France, at my home, but Logan's maman and papa will have a . . ." She gestured helplessly, trying to find the right word.

"Reception," Logan said.

"*Oui*, a reception. You will come, *non*?"

"We'll wait until you're back from your honeymoon," Logan said. "It's the least we can do, since we wouldn't be married if you hadn't figured everything out."

"If you only knew," Gideon murmured for Elizabeth's ears only.

Elizabeth ignored him. "Of course we'll come. I look forward to becoming good friends."

Anna and Jake then took their turns congratulating the happy couple. Anna shed a few tears and Jake managed to tease them a bit.

Elizabeth leaned in to Jake and asked, "Did Logan seem to recognize you?"

"Not at all. He's only got eyes for that wife of his, but Devoss is sure we've met somewhere before. I told him it's possible. I get around a lot."

Cybil of course had known him even in his disguise, but then she'd known him all his life. Ordinary people could usually be fooled by a good disguise because they tended to only focus on the most obvious characteristics. Percy's hair and beard and even his British accent would have distracted most people from noticing much of anything else. The disguise had even fooled Oscar Thornton during their brief encounter at Gideon's office, which had been the most important ruse of all.

And who would ever suspect that Elizabeth's brother would be impersonating a British earl?

The guests adjourned to the dining room where a light buffet supper had been set out. Jake, still pretending to be responsible, made sure everyone had been served a glass of champagne and gave a toast to the health and happiness of the bride and groom.

White-coated waiters served the guests, and everyone enjoyed chatting while they balanced plates and glasses. The bride and groom's final task was to cut the wedding cake, which was a beautiful, three-tiered concoction decorated with wreaths of orange blossoms and topped with a plume of feathers. Inside, it was dark, rich fruitcake. Most of the guests took theirs home in little boxes the waiters provided.

Finally, it was time for Elizabeth and Gideon to leave. Elizabeth and Anna stole upstairs, where Anna helped her change into her traveling suit, a lovely ensemble of maroon wool trimmed with satin. Since she would only be traveling a few miles uptown this evening, Elizabeth found the name "traveling suit" a bit silly, but she adored it nevertheless. By the time they got downstairs,

Gideon was waiting for them. He helped Elizabeth and Anna with their coats. Elizabeth thought all the guests must have left, which was a bit disappointing, but when he opened the front door, she realized they were all outside and had formed a gauntlet.

At the sight of them, everyone began to cheer, and Elizabeth and Gideon ran down the steps and through the aisle they had created, showering them with confetti. Jake had brought his bright red motorcar, and he stood waiting, holding the back door open for them. When they were safely inside, he helped Anna into the front passenger seat and, with another whoop of cheers from their guests, they were on their way.

Gideon slipped his arm around her and pulled her close. Elizabeth looked up into his beloved face. "It's too late to change your mind now."

"What makes you think I'll ever want to change my mind?" he scoffed.

"I'll ask you that the next time she comes up with a scheme," Jake called back to them.

"But I'm not going to come up with any more schemes," Elizabeth promised. "I'm a respectable society matron now. All of that is behind me."

Gideon just gave her an adoring smile. "We'll see," was all he said.

AUTHOR'S NOTE

I had a lovely time researching this book. Engagement and marriage customs were the most fun, of course, and Mrs. Ordway really does recommend an arch made of greenery and possibly flowers for a home wedding. She also feels confetti is superior to rice for throwing at weddings.

The Spanish Prisoner is a classic con that was run for generations, and I've been wanting to use it for a while. I had decided to use it for this book, and when I started plotting, I realized I could show three different versions of it here. What fun!

One of my research books was a history of the American Protective League that was actually published in 1919. I got the book from interlibrary loan, expecting it to be a reprint, but it turned out to be an original copy. A hundred-year-old book! The pages were yellow with age and almost too fragile to turn, but the most amazing part of the book was the hatred for immigrants that was expressed in those pages. The author rails against "hyphenated Americans," questioning their loyalties and demanding that America close its borders to all immigrants for at least twenty years to protect American heritage and values. Ironically, the "hyphenated Americans" the author was deploring were German-Americans, which is not a group modern folks would consider a threat. Of course America did not close its borders and American heritage survived for the next hundred years. The lesson for us here is that every generation has been certain that some group of immigrants were going to ruin America, and none of them ever has.

One group that post–World War I Americans were particularly concerned about were the Bolsheviks, as I explained in the book. The Russian Revolution had sent a wave of fear throughout Europe, and even America. After WWI, American workers started to demand better working conditions and minorities began to demand fair treatment, and the resulting strikes and demonstrations were blamed on Bolshevik and communist influence. Archibald Stevenson was a real person, and he was convinced the German government had made a secret pact with Russia when Russia withdrew from WWI because the revolution had caused so much upheaval in the country. Stevenson believed the Germans—who were virtually bankrupt from the war—were financing the Russian Revolution, so he was able to take advantage of the country's mistrust of the Germans to convince people of his unlikely theories. Stevenson's "list" of supposed subversives is tragically similar to the McCarthy Era after WWII and also resulted in innocent people being falsely accused of disloyalty to America.

Please let me know how you enjoyed this book. You can follow me on Facebook at Victoria .Thompson.Author, on Twitter @gaslightvt or e-mail me through my website, victoriathompson .com. If you e-mail me, I'll put you on my mailing list and let you know whenever I have a new book coming out.

Center Point Large Print
600 Brooks Road / PO Box 1
Thorndike, ME 04986-0001 USA

(207) 568-3717

US & Canada:
1 800 929-9108
www.centerpointlargeprint.com